HIDDEN SEA

HIDDEN SEA

A NOVEL BY **MILES ARCENEAUX**

Hidden Sea

© 2017 Brent Douglass, John T. Davis, and James R. Dennis

Library of Congress Cataloging in Publication Data:
Arceneaux, Miles
Hidden Sea / Miles Arceneaux
1. Title. 2. Fiction. 3. Mystery. 4. Thriller. 5. Suspense.
-

First Edition: October 2017
978-0-9968797-4-3

Printed in the United States of America
Written by Brent Douglass, John T. Davis, and James R. Dennis
Designed by Rigsby Hull: Lana Rigsby, Thomas Hull; and Think Carmen: Carmen Garza

Over four successive voyages the misguided Italian explorer Christopher Columbus searched for a new sea route to Asia. When he first sighted the island landmass we know today as Cuba, he was convinced he had found it. Later, Spanish sailors would circumnavigate the coastline and discover that Cuba was, in fact, an island.

They had to wonder about the mysterious body of water to the northwest, to question its size and contours. They could not know what they would find on the other side, not unless they were willing to venture out and explore. Until then, they would simply know it as the Hidden Sea.

*The Aztecs were transfixed by the behavior of the Spaniards in the presence of gold:
"They picked it up and fingered it like monkeys. It was as if their hearts were
satisfied, brightened, calmed. For in truth they thirsted mightily for gold; they stuffed
themselves with it; they starved for it; they lusted for it like pigs." Dramatically,
Cortés himself told an emissary of Montezuma that his people were stricken by a
"disease of the heart which can only be cured by gold."*

As recorded in the Florentine Codex—an account of the Spanish conquest from
the Aztec perspective, written by Bernardino de Sahagún

* MAP NOT TO SCALE

TEXAS

● ROCKPORT

● MATAMOROS

GULF OF MEXICO

MEXICO

● TAMPICO

CUBA

● CIENFUEGOS

● TUXPAN

STATE OF TEXAS

MEXICO

CUBA

OUR STORY

● VILLA RICA
● VERACRUZ

● MONTEPÍO

N

AUTHOR'S NOTE

In our current climate of fake news, post-truths, and alternative facts, I feel I need address a few things about this book right up front. As far as I know, the use of sea-slaves on fishing boats in the Gulf of Mexico does not exist. However, it *does* exist in the South China Sea. My primary resource for this appalling practice came from an excellent six-part series published by the *New York Times* during the summer of 2015 titled, THE OUTLAW OCEAN. I would direct you particularly to Part 3: "Sea Slaves: The Human Misery That Feeds Pets and Livestock," which provided me with ideas and details for my story.

Many descriptions of the cities, villages, flora, and fauna of the Mexican Gulf Coast were inspired by a beautiful book of photographs and travel essays, *Traveling the Shore of the Spanish Sea: The Gulf Coast of Texas and Mexico,* by Geoff Winningham (Texas A&M Press). He faithfully captures the beauty and soul of this relatively pristine slice of the Gulf Coast. I know this because I've been there.

Regarding the characters in this book, any similarity to actual persons living or dead is not only probable, but almost impossible to avoid. Every time I think I've invented a unique Gulf Coast character, someone invariably comes along and says, "I *know* that guy!"

Thanks to early readers Nancy Mancini, Mark Weiss, Clint Parsley, Gillian Cook, Rosalynn Gill, and Grant Douglass. Kudos to Carmen Garza for her beautiful book layout, and hats off to Lana Rigsby (the fourth Miles Arceneaux) for yet another kick-ass book cover, and to Thomas Hull for the cool new web design. To you readers, especially those of you who have supported me over the entire series, many thanks to all y'all.

— MILES ARCENEAUX

Augustus Sweetwater slowly emerged from a deep and resistant stupor. When his brain flickered on, his first waking thought was *I'm alive*. He tried to lift his head, but the pain was so intense it felt as if he'd been snagged through the temple with a gaff. He opened his eyes and fought to remain conscious. Were his eyes truly open? In the darkness there was nothing to fix upon.

Keep it together, Augie. Don't pass out.

A deafening noise, near his head . . . an engine, diesel . . . a rumbling, clanking roar. Goddamn it was loud. Yes, definitely a diesel, maybe two, running full throttle. He could smell hot oil and feel heat radiating from the engine block. Augie wiggled his fingers and flexed the muscles in his legs. Slowly he began to orient himself and realized he was lying face down on a hard metal surface . . . diamond plate decking . . . a factory floor, maybe?

But why was it moving?

The floor pitched and rocked, and Augie felt a surge of nausea. He drew a sharp breath. *Don't get sick. Concentrate!*

He took note of his body, his breathing, his heartbeat. Everything seemed to be functioning, more or less. Stiff muscles, a splitting headache, an agonizing thirst, but he wasn't incapacitated. Now, could he move?

He steeled himself and pushed up to his hands and knees, but when he tried to stand, something around his neck jerked him back down. He reached up and tentatively fingered a metal collar. There was a ring on the back, fastened to a chain. His hands followed the chain to a stout padlock secured to the engine mount in the floor. He yanked and twisted the heavy chain, but it wouldn't yield.

After a final desperate heave, Augie let out a howl of rage and frustration that was swallowed by the sound of the engines. Temporarily defeated, he sat cross-legged and shoeless on the greasy metal floor, turning the collar to face away from the choking fumes. He tried to calm his mind, but panic kept creeping in.

"What the hell has happened to me?" he asked the darkness.

———

CHAPTER 02

Charlie Sweetwater looked up from the boat hull he'd been sanding and watched a burly man who called himself Ragnar the Younger feed Fritos to a dog. Behind them the copper sun burned through a stubborn, late-morning fog that lingered over Copano Bay. Ragnar was a frequent visitor to Charlie's shop, and, as far as Charlie could tell, had no job, no friends, and no possessions other than a beat-up bike and a supposed runestone the approximate size and color of a flounder. Ragnar claimed to be a direct descendent of fabled Norse explorers and had even gone so far as to take on the appearance of his barbaric forefathers: dreadlocks, shaggy beard, a knee-length tunic, leather boots—the whole Viking ensemble minus the chain mail and axe.

Charlie took off his respirator and brushed the sawdust out of his hair. "Ragnar, you want some Big Red to go with those Fritos? I think I got a can floating around in the cooler."

Ragnar dumped the rest of the corn chips on the ground and watched the dog scarf them up.

"How 'bout a Big Red for your dog, then?"

The yellow mutt wore no collar and once lived under the Copano Bridge, subsisting on rats and dead fish, Charlie guessed. But the previous fall, the dog and Ragnar found each other and soon became inseparable. Now the two of them lived in a storage unit near the Aransas County Airport, a couple of miles from Charlie's house.

By most standards, Ragnar was crazy as a sprayed roach, but Charlie didn't mind the old guy hanging around. He sat quietly in the corner of the shop and seemed to take a sincere interest in the boatbuilding project.

Charlie had never been choosy about his friends. It didn't matter to him how much or how little status they had, as long as they were interesting, somewhat reliable, and not full of shit. Even though his social life had fallen off a cliff these last few years, he did worry that one day he might be judged by the company he kept. He suspected he was already in danger of being lumped, along with Ragnar, into that category of peculiar and non-essential Gulf Coast characters euphemistically referred to as "local color."

Charlie generally didn't give a damn what other people thought of him—one of the prerogatives of age—but today was his birthday, and he was feeling philosophical. He'd had sixty-eight years to make his mark in the world and what, he asked himself, did he have to show for it?

Materially speaking, he couldn't point to much. His business had been a success, but several years back he'd given the whole kit and caboodle to his longtime partners: his nephew Raul Sweetwater de la Rosa, and Sammy Dang. Soon after, he began to shed most of the possessions that semi-success had afforded him, especially the stuff that required maintenance. His assortment of boats had been whittled down to just two: his brother's old Boston Whaler, (a functional but ungainly craft that had endured for more than forty years), and the half-built wooden flats boat resting on sawhorses in front of him (a project he worked on sporadically and when the mood took him).

He'd bartered his beach-front house in Isla Mujeres to a fishing guide in exchange for a forty-foot catamaran which he'd promptly sold after sailing it on a meandering, five-month voyage though the Caribbean. A year later he'd sold his canal-front house in nearby Key Allegro and moved back into the one-bedroom stilt cottage on Rattlesnake Point that once belonged to his late brother, Johnny. After Johnny had gone missing at sea almost forty years ago, Charlie had periodically occupied the house depending on his circumstances. He had done what he could to keep the property from ruination in the corrosive climate, but not much more than that.

The only visible improvements he had made were to fortify the boat dock and add to his brother's book collection. Other than that, he'd purposely kept the place exactly the same. He'd never minded living with his dead brother's ghost. Actually, he kind of liked it, and occasionally he would catch himself talking aloud to him, usually to recount some misadventure they'd shared in their youth.

Although Johnny had sired a son, namely Raul, Charlie had done nothing to perpetuate the family bloodline. He had never married, produced kids, or even attempted to burnish his family's so-called legacy. So far, not one public building had been named after him, nor after any other member of the Sweetwater clan for that matter.

Charlie watched Ragnar watch the dog munch the corn chips and debated whether to include the Viking in his existential deliberations. Nutty as he was, Ragnar was a man of some renown, having discovered the runestone over forty-five years ago near his hometown in eastern Oklahoma. The runestone had put tiny Poteau on the map (The *Tulsa World* sent a reporter), but some people had questioned how the flaxen-haired sons of Odin had made their way to the Sooner State in the first place. Sweden, perhaps in a moment of uncharacteristic whimsy, sent a certified runeologist to evaluate the discovery. After his appraisal, the Swedish expert diplomatically informed the paper and the locals that the rock carvings were "fascinating but highly implausible."

But Ragnar (back then his name was Billie Wayne Simmons) disagreed. He was absolutely certain his stone was the real deal, and he devoted himself to proving it. He became an ardent student of Norse history and mythology, eventually becoming so engrossed in the subject that he convinced himself he was a direct descendent of Viking explorers. He legally changed his name to Ragnar the Younger and began dressing the part.

At first people thought it was all in fun—something to entertain the occasional tourists who drove through Poteau on their way to Ouachita State Park. But when the good citizens realized Ragnar was serious, they ran his pseudo-Viking ass out of town; they'd thought the rune was fake all along. Before he left town, Ragnar broke into Poteau's little museum and stuffed the heavy stone into his rucksack. He and his stone drifted south, ultimately settling on the Texas Gulf Coast, which had a much higher tolerance for colorful cranks than Poteau.

Charlie occasionally lent Ragnar some of his tools, although he couldn't imagine what he did with them. He'd also loaned him almost every book from his and Johnny's eclectic library. Ragnar never failed to return what he borrowed. Sure, he was loco, but he met Charlie's friendship threshold: he was trustworthy, he wasn't dull or dimwitted, and he wasn't full of shit. Once, he'd even shown Charlie his runestone. When Charlie asked what the magical writing scratched into the surface meant, Ragnar replied that, if he had to ask, he didn't deserve to know.

Charlie stretched his back and observed his friend speculatively. "Ragnar, tell me something. Would you say a man should be judged by the content of his character or by the quantity of his possessions?"

"Possessions," Ragnar growled.

"Hmm . . . . Well, Gandhi preached that possessions only become troublesome things, a burden—"

Ragnar snorted and shook his head in disagreement.

"No? Take Thoreau, then. Didn't he say something about frittering away our lives? And that we should simplify—"

"No!" Ragnar shouted. "Thoreau was a fraud!"

Ragnar's dog raised his head, anxiously watching his companion to make sure he wasn't having an episode. Charlie did the same.

"O-kay . . . how about John Lennon? 'Imagine no possessions . . . brotherhood of man,' et cetera?"

Ragnar fixed Charlie with a fierce glare.

Charlie sighed, noting the bloodshot eyes. He wondered if his neighbor had thrown back some mead or Sterno or whatever the hell it was Viking bums from Oklahoma drank, and he decided not to provoke him further. Marauders with names like Eric Bloodaxe and Sweyn Forkbeard were Ragnar's role models, not wimpy proponents of civil disobedience or Limey pop singers.

"Okay, my friend, I know you'll disagree with me, but if possessions do make the man, like you say, I'm afraid you and I don't count for much."

Ragnar lifted his wooly head and sniffed the air. A moment later, so did the dog. This meant someone was coming, and they would be going. Both were uncomfortable around strangers, which included everyone, it seemed, but Charlie.

Ragnar the Younger mounted his bike and pedaled off without a backwards glance, his wild beard sailing back over his shoulder, the yellow dog trotting beside him.

"See you around," Charlie yelled after him.

Watching him leave, Charlie considered the Okie Norseman's position. Did it matter if a man didn't have trophies or plunder to show for himself when he reached (Charlie hated the expression) his "golden years"? Ragnar had his runestone, which apparently was all he wanted or needed. *But what about me?* Charlie asked himself.

Lately he had begun to wonder if most of his dreams and adventures lay behind him, and if the whole of his life amounted to less than the sum of its parts. He still liked to fish, of course—fishing had intrinsic value and required no justification—but every year the Texas coastline attracted more and more people, and the bays became more and more crowded. GPS coordinates for his favorite "secret" fishing spots had been captured on the electronic fishfinders of hundreds of other anglers, and he'd all but given up trying to compete with them on weekends or holidays.

He walked outside and leaned against a palm tree, taking in the little slice of heaven behind his house. A blue heron stood motionless on the dock, fixated on something in the turtle grass below. A sudden breeze fluttered the great bird's crest and then moved across the bay, ruffling the surface of the water like an invisible hand. Charlie looked skyward and saw a flock of soaring white pelicans high in the air. They circled slowly, effortlessly, lifted ever higher by the warm currents of air, searching for the one that would launch them on their annual migration north.

Charlie inhaled the salty air. It was a fine spring day that would probably end with a spectacular sunset—best enjoyed, he decided, on the back deck of his quiet house with an iced mojito and a Cuban cigar. *Who knows?* he thought. Maybe his brother's ghost would join him, and they would watch it together.

The sound of tires crunching over the oyster shell road announced Raul's SUV as it pulled around to the back. Raul got out of the car, a peeved look on his face.

"You turned off your cell phone again, didn't you, Tío?"

"*Hola*, Nephew. You rang?"

"About a dozen times."

Charlie shrugged. "Might have forgot to plug it in. Can I offer you a beer?"

"It's ten o'clock in the morning."

Rather than argue the point, Charlie walked to the cooler and twisted the cap off a Shiner Bock. *What did the time of day have to do with drinking a beer?*

"Tío, have you heard from Augie?" Charlie could hear a tinge of apprehension in his nephew's voice.

"I thought he was in Mexico."

"He was. I mean, he is. But he was supposed to be back yesterday."

"When's the last time you heard from him?"

"We didn't talk to him last week, but we were getting emails from him up until Thursday morning."

Charlie took a swig of beer and sat down in Ragnar's lawn chair to ponder. The kid had only been out of touch for a couple of days—a little diversion to break up the trip, perhaps? If so, it wouldn't be the first time his grandnephew had deviated from his business itinerary to have a little fun.

Juan Antonio Augustus Sweetwater—Augie for short—was named for one of his infamous uncles, Flavius Augustus Sweetwater. Augie was nineteen years old and had inherited many of the Sweetwater clan's freewheeling traits. As Raul and Charlie both recalled, nineteen was sort of an itchy age, especially in a family whose motto was, "Hold My Beer and Watch This." That being so, Raul and his wife, Rosie, were prone to worry about their son. Being AWOL two days would seem like two weeks to them.

"Where was he going?"

"Matamoros, Tampico, Tuxpan, Veracruz . . . the usual Gulf Coast tour. I called some customers, and they said he'd been by."

"He took his truck?"

Raul nodded.

"Maybe he's taking his time driving back. It's a long trip."

Raul looked exasperated. "Seems like he would've told us, don't you think?"

Charlie smiled. He knew that Raul checked in with Rosie several times a day, even when he *wasn't* on the road, and it bugged the hell out of both of them that their son didn't.

"Here's what I think, Nephew. I'll bet you a dollar to a donut he took his surfboard and his fishing tackle with him to Mexico and found a place to use 'em both on his way back."

Raul sat down heavily and took a deep breath.

"He's an adventurous kid," Charlie added. "He'll show up in a day or two. He's just gallivanting."

"Then why won't he answer his cell phone?"

"Battery died? Phone got stolen? Accidentally dropped it in a toilet? Who knows? We've all lost our phones before. It happens."

Raul sighed. He had never lost *his* cellphone before. Even if Augie had, why wouldn't he use a customer's phone or a hotel phone? But what was the point of mentioning that to Charlie? He was worse than Augie about staying in touch.

Raul stood up and made ready to go. "Okay, Tío. You're probably right."

"Of course I'm right. I'm always right."

"Whatever you say."

"Well, I say stay and have a beer with me."

Raul shook his head and walked away. "Turn on your dang cell phone!" he yelled as he got into his car.

Charlie waved goodbye and then went upstairs to find his dang cell phone.

——

CHAPTER 03

Raul tossed and turned all night. The little sleep he got was shot through with troubling dreams. He kept telling himself Charlie was probably right—Augie was just cutting loose and having a good time, taking advantage of Mexico's many diversions. He was out—what had his uncle called it?—gallivanting.

He'd been that way himself once, a long time ago, before he married Rosie. Raul had been in love with Rosie Archuleta since the day he met her in Mrs. Fulbright's 10th grade English class at Rockport-Fulton High School. But it took him fifteen years to convince her and her very traditional family to agree to let him marry her. And why wouldn't they be reluctant? From their perspective he was the bastard son of a border-town prostitute and a fun-loving local boy who had been killed in a turf war with a gangster. And he'd been raised by an equally infamous uncle who fraternized with ex-convicts, Vietnamese fishermen, and crazy saloon owners.

But Raul's persistence paid off, and he ultimately won over her and her family. He and Rosie had married and made a happy life for themselves in Fulton. They had also been blessed with two wonderful kids, one of whom hadn't checked in like he promised he would. As worrier-in-chief, Rosie immediately began to imagine the horrible things that might have befallen their son. She couldn't help it. She was scared and mad and frustrated all at the same time. When her husband returned from Rattlesnake Point, she took it out on him, Charlie, and any other Sweetwater man she could think of.

"An irresponsible, reckless bunch of reprobates," she ranted. "An entire family of black sheep! The worst communicators I've ever seen *in my whole life*. Your playboy uncle is probably responsible for this."

Raul stared glumly at a plate of shrimp enchiladas while she let him have it.

"I'm sure he introduced Augie to every dangerous surf spot and bawdy cantina in Mexico when he dragged him down there on his *business* trips. It doesn't matter to Charlie if he's a bad uncle. It doesn't matter to him if people are worried. With him it's all about living *la vida loca*."

Raul nodded sympathetically. It would only get worse if he tried to argue. Their daughter, Yolanda, had already retreated to her bedroom. She knew what her mom was like when she got riled up. She also knew her high-spirited brother would show up eventually. He always did. And when he *did* come home, they would go all Mom and Dad on his ass—Mom would yell, and Dad would deliver a stern lecture, and the house would be tense for about twenty-four hours. But as soon as he and Yolanda were alone together, he'd grin and say, "Sister, it was worth it." That was Augie.

"I can't believe you let him go to Mexico in the first place," Rosie continued. "The entire country is run by drug cartels. Tamaulipas, especially! Carjacking, kidnapping . . . *murder*. And we sent our son—a teenager—down there . . . in a car!"

"Augie's fine," Raul repeated for the umpteenth time, trying to convince Rosie and himself it was true. "And he's not a kid anymore. He's almost twenty now . . . plus he's done the route before. He knows how to travel in Mexico."

Rosie looked up, and Raul saw there were tears in her eyes. "Come here," he said. He took her in his arms and held her close, quietly reassuring her that everything would be okay.

"If he doesn't show up tomorrow, I'll go find him," Raul promised. He could feel her head nodding into his chest. He wouldn't let anything happen to their son.

So, during the long night, Raul worried. And he began making contingency plans.

CHAPTER 04

Charlie waited until the next morning before he showed up at Raul and Rosie's door. He'd had trouble sleeping the night before, too.

Rosie opened the door, sighed, and let him in. There were dark circles under her eyes, and she was still wearing her robe and slippers, uncharacteristic for her at that hour. She motioned for him to follow her to the kitchen.

"The coffee's still warm," she said, pointing to the pot. "Can I fix you some breakfast?"

"No thanks, Rosie. I already ate. Where's Raul?"

"He's at the office making phone calls."

Charlie nodded. He'd made some calls himself that morning. "I decided I'm going to Mexico tomorrow."

Rosie leaned against the counter and crossed her arms. "Good," she said flatly. "Raul's going, too."

"I figured as much. We'll go together."

"Whatever makes sense."

"Rosie, everything's going to be okay. Once we find him, I'm gonna give him as thorough an ass-chewing as he's ever had, and then I'll call you immediately and tell you he's fine. After that, I promise we'll come straight home." He waited a beat, then added, "Unless the fish are biting."

She threw a dish towel at Charlie's head. He ducked, but not before he caught her hiding a smile.

"Go," she said, turning him around and pushing him toward the door. "And don't come back without my son!"

At the office Charlie found Raul, Sammy, and Judy working the phones. Judy Dang was Sammy's wife. She was probably the most valuable member of the team—efficient, no-nonsense, smart as a whip. She paid the bills, managed the books, and kept things running smoothly when everyone else was on the road.

Charlie's company had come a long way since he'd started selling his patented turtle excluder devices to local shrimpers over three decades ago. Sweetwater Enterprises had moved out of the little dockside warehouse on Fulton Harbor and into a brick office building facing Rockport's Little Bay. They had gradually expanded their business and become a reputable manufacturer's representative for nautical products in the commercial fishing industry—selling everything from nets to navigation instruments.

Raul, Sammy, and Judy ran the show now. They had changed the name to Sweetwater Marine and hired associates to work for them in Asia, South America, and the Caribbean. When Augie decided to postpone college for a while, Raul hired him to handle their business in Mexico and Central America. Augie hit the ground running, and in his first full year he increased sales by thirty percent. He loved the job, and the customers loved him. It was beginning to look like his gap year might turn into a career.

Sammy and Judy looked up when Charlie entered.

"Any luck?" Charlie asked.

"Not yet," answered Judy.

"Who all did you call?"

Sammy checked his notes. "Between the three of us? Just about every account we have on the Gulf Coast between Brownsville and Coatzacoalcos. The ones we could reach on Sunday, anyway. Those we did talk to said Augie had been there alright, that they'd had good meetings, and so forth. Nothing out of the ordinary. The last appointment we could confirm was in Veracruz on Thursday morning."

"What about the consulates?"

"I called the U.S. Embassy in Mexico City and the consulate in Matamoros," Judy replied. "They said they would put Augie's name in their database, but I didn't detect much urgency in their tone."

Charlie nodded. "Have you called any hotels?"

"The main ones. The ones you guys always used in the past."

Raul hung up and swiveled around to face his uncle. "Anything?"

"*Nada.*"

He exhaled wearily. "If Augie doesn't check in before tomorrow morning, I'm going to go look for him."

"I figured," Charlie said. "I'll go with you."

Raul shook his head. "No, you should be here in case, you know, someone calls."

Charlie felt a chill, knowing that "someone" could refer to a government official calling with bad news, or it could refer to a kidnapper demanding a ransom for the return of their boy.

"Sammy and Judy can handle the phones," said Charlie.

"They don't speak Spanish. You do."

"Yeah, but I think I'll be of better use down there than here."

"You don't need to go, Tío."

Charlie narrowed his eyes. "Is there a problem?"

Raul looked out the picture window when he answered, like he was addressing the bay instead of his uncle. "This isn't going to be an easy trip. I'll be moving fast. And I don't have to tell you it could be dangerous."

"Don't you worry about me."

Raul turned to his uncle. "Are you sure you'd be up to it, Charlie? I mean, it's been a while since—"

Charlie felt the blood rush to his face. "Listen, you little *mocoso*, I may be retired, but I'm not dead. There is no way in hell you're gonna keep me from going to Mexico to look for my own goddamn nephew, *entiendes?* Am I *up* to it? Jesus Christ. I know that country a hell of a lot better than most Mexicans. Better'n you, that's for damn sure!"

Sammy and Judy stared at him wide-eyed. It'd been a long time since they'd seen Charlie lose his temper.

Raul backed off. "Okay, okay. You don't have to yell at me, Tío."

But Charlie wasn't finished. "And I'll tell you another goddamn thing . . . ."

As Raul listened to his uncle bellow and stomp around the room, he thought of his late great-uncle Rupert, who, if he remembered correctly, took down a gun-toting desperado with one punch when he was seventy-six years old. Raul was only thirteen at the time, but he remembered thinking, *Now there's an old man with cojones.* When had Charlie turned into Rupert?

Charlie stopped his tirade when he noticed Raul laughing. "What's so damn funny?"

"Nothing, Tío. Forget what I said. Of course you're going. I don't know what I was thinking. But before you go all King Lear on me again, sit down and listen to my plan."

Charlie sat down heavily and nodded. "Sorry. It's just that I'm . . . I mean, I'm not . . . ." His voice trailed off.

Raul picked up a pencil and went to a large map of Mexico tacked to the wall.

"I propose we split up and tackle this from both ends." He tapped the pencil eraser on Veracruz at the southern end of the Gulf. "How about *you* fly to Veracruz, Charlie? Even though we've already spoken to most of the customers, I think it makes sense to talk to them again, face to face. Maybe Augie mentioned something they forgot to tell us. While you're there, you might drop in on your friends in Montepío, the Alexanders, if they're around. They're well-connected and might be able to help us."

Charlie nodded. "Good idea."

"And since you'll be in the neighborhood," he said with a sigh, "you should probably stop by Roy Lee's place in Villa Rica. There's a chance Augie went there and, uh, lost track of the time."

Roy Lee Rowlett was a notorious country-rocker from Fort Worth who had produced one hit after another from the Seventies to the Nineties and then decided to retire to his luxurious private resort near Villa Rica to live out his days as an ex-pat. His place was a black hole of hedonism, debauchery, and sloth, depending on the time of day and temperament of the owner.

Raul moved his pencil to the top of the map, pointing to Brownsville. "I'll start up here and then work my way down the coast: Matamoros, Tampico, Tuxpan. I figure we can meet up in Tuxpan. One of us is bound to run into him along the way."

"Then what?" asked Judy.

Raul twirled the pencil in his fingers. "Then the three of us drive back to Texas together."

Charlie nodded. "Good plan. I'll start checking flights."

Judy had already pulled up flight schedules, "Hold on a second, and I'll give you your options." Charlie watched her squint and do her internet voodoo.

"Of course, we'll call you guys straight away if we hear something," said Sammy. "Charlie, you *will* take your cell phone won't you?"

"No, I'm gonna have Tarahumara Indians run daily updates back to Fulton. Yes, I'll take my cell phone."

"Okay, here's what we've got," Judy interrupted. "There's nothing today, it's too late, but tomorrow there's a one o'clock United flight out of Corpus that arrives in Veracruz at five, connecting through Houston."

"Nothing earlier?"

"There are several earlier flights to Houston, but you still arrive in Veracruz at five."

Charlie nodded okay, and Judy typed some more until the laser printer went *zippity-click* and produced Charlie's boarding passes.

They were all quiet for a moment, going over the trip in their heads.

"When do you want to meet up in Tuxpan?" Charlie asked Raul.

"Let's shoot for Thursday. Unless of course we hear from Augie first."

They all agreed. "Right. Of course. Because Augie could show up or call at any time. Right, at any time. He sure could. Yep. And probably will. Yeah, definitely."

Judy handed out copies of Augie's picture which she'd printed from his bio on the corporate webpage. In the photo, Augie wore a Hawaiian shirt and had a goofy grin on his face.

"Okay, said Charlie, rising from his chair. "I guess I'll see you in Tuxpan, Raul."

Raul nodded. "Be careful, Tío."

Charlie nodded back and then looked around the room. "Well, good luck, everybody."

He walked out the door feeling a little excited, a little apprehensive, and a little foolish, like he'd just been recruited to go on a quest in some kind of *Fellowship of the Ring* deal. They'd all feel pretty silly if Augie had been hanging out with friends on South Padre Island all weekend. At any rate, Charlie was glad to be doing *something*. Thinking optimistically, he looked forward to meeting up with Augie in Mexico, sharing a few beers with him, and then helping the kid think up a plausible excuse that might keep his mom from skinning him alive when he got home.

———

CHAPTER 05

It didn't take Augie long to figure out he was at sea, probably on a shrimp boat, probably somewhere on the Gulf of Mexico. He knew the sounds and smells of a fishing trawler and recognized the pitch and roll of offshore waves. He'd worked on shrimp boats before and figured this one must be pretty big with two diesels to power it.

In the darkness of the engine room, Augie couldn't see his hand in front of his face, but he suspected he might not be the only person down there. Occasionally, he thought he heard movement nearby, but when he called out and no one answered, he wondered if he was hearing things. Someone would open the hatch eventually, he told himself, and then he would find out more. Then he would find out who the sons of bitches were who had knocked him out, stolen his shoes, and chained him by the neck to the fucking floor.

Meanwhile, he'd try to distract himself by recreating the series of events that had brought him there. He had nothing else to do, and it would help keep his fear at bay. He stilled his mind and thought back. *It seemed like a girl had been involved. And a bar. Somewhere on the outskirts of Tuxpan. On a river, maybe?* But the recollections were jumbled, out-of-focus. Why would he have been at a place like that? He normally kept to the main roads, slept in the corporate hotels, ate at familiar restaurants. His dad had warned him about the dangers of straying off the beaten path in that part of Mexico. *Keep to the main roads. Travel only in daylight. Don't draw attention to yourself.*

He retraced the path in his head: He'd crossed the border into Matamoros and then made his stops along the coast: Tampico, Tuxpan, Veracruz, Alvarado. It was his third solo trip since his dad had given him responsibility for managing the territory. Augie's Spanish wasn't up to speed yet, but having Sweetwater as a last name certainly opened doors. Charlie had blazed the trail over thirty years before when he was pushing the turtle-shooter he'd invented, and then Raul took over the region as their company grew. Augie knew he had big shoes to fill.

Like his predecessors, Augie called on the marine supply businesses to drum up sales for the manufacturers Sweetwater Marine represented. Schmoozing and drinking with clients was part of the deal. The last stop on his trip had been Alvarado, south of Veracruz. To break up the long drive home, he had decided to stop and stay the night in Tuxpan. He knew he should have called the office to tell them he'd be a day late, but now he was glad he hadn't. The sooner they realized he was missing, the sooner they would start looking for him.

But what happened when I got to Tuxpan? he asked himself. *I didn't stay at the Holiday Inn like I usually did, did I? That was my first mistake.*

He tried to remember why he'd changed his routine, and then it came to him: surfing. He'd wanted to stay near the beach, somewhere close to where the Pantepec River entered the Gulf, so he could surf. A beach bum he'd met in Veracruz had given him the tip: "Tuxpan's the spot, dude. Go a quarter mile north of the jetties, and you'll see a sand bar where the waves break hollow and fast. It's classic surfing, man, and *nobody's ever there!*"

It would be a perfect way to end a successful road trip.

That was the plan, anyway. Find a small hotel near the beach, rise early, surf for a couple of hours, and then hit the road again. He figured he'd make it back to Texas just before dark.

Augie could picture the hotel—the Hotel Tres Reyes it was called—a small, two-story cinder block building near the mouth of the Tampamachoco Lagoon. It had seemed clean enough and was walking distance to the beach. Although he remembered thinking the neighborhood looked a little sketchy, the hotel *did* have a walled parking area in front of the rooms. He reckoned his commercial samples, surfboard, and fishing tackle would be safe as long as they remained locked under the truck's camper shell and inside the hotel courtyard.

Augie's mind snapped back to the present when the sound of the diesel engines changed pitch. The vessel slowed and he tensed up, waiting for something to happen. He thought he heard voices above him, but couldn't be sure. Not long after, the engines revved up to cruising speed again. When the monotonous thrum of the diesels settled back into their familiar pattern, Augie's mind returned to Tuxpan. He would think it through step-by-step, hour-by-hour, until he figured it out. It wasn't like he was going anywhere.

He remembered it was after dark when he checked into the Tres Reyes. They put him in a first-story room, and he parked his truck right outside his door. He had changed into a T-shirt, jeans, and sneakers and gone outside to eat, but the hotel kitchen was closed. The gate guard told him there were several restaurants nearby on a street called Ribera del Pescador and that the *comida* was *muy rica*.

Augie recalled walking along the Ribera and choosing a small thatch-roof riverside cafe that was full of people. The sign over the awning read "Cócteles y Mariscos." Without looking at a menu, he had asked the waiter to bring him the house specialty, whatever it was. They served him fresh calamari and an excellent fish stew. His stomach grumbled anew at the thought of it.

It had been a mild evening with a slight breeze blowing off the Gulf, so Augie decided to stay and have a drink or two. He was sipping on his third *michelada* when he noticed the girl. Seated at the end of the bar, she watched him with her dark eyes. He smiled at her. She smiled back.

That's when I should've paid my tab and walked back to the hotel. That's where it all started going south.

The girl wore high heels and a tight-fitting dress with spaghetti straps. She had on bright red lipstick and so much eyeliner she looked like an Egyptian queen. Unlike most Mexican girls, she regarded him candidly, but Augie realized most Mexican girls wouldn't be sitting alone at a bar in a fisherman's cantina on a Friday night. She knew what she was doing, and Augie knew what she was doing, too.

He'd never been with a prostitute before, but he'd certainly thought about it—quite a bit lately, as a matter of fact. Two months ago he had learned from Uncle Charlie that his own grandmother had been a working girl in the *Zona de Tolerancia* outside Nuevo Laredo. His dad was the offspring of the girl and Charlie's late brother, Johnny. He'd often asked his parents about his Mexican grandmother, but all they'd ever said was that she died when Raul was young; otherwise, they evaded the subject. But Charlie sure as hell didn't. He told him the whole story the very first time he asked about it.

"You're old enough to know," he said. "Your *abuela* was a prostitute, son, but she was a good person, and your granddad loved her in his own way. So did your dad, although he won't admit it. She did what she had to do to survive, and I don't hold that against her. Neither should you."

The revelation had been quite a shock to Augie, and he still wasn't sure how to think about it. He was pissed off that his parents had tried to hide it from him, but he was also curious. What was his grandmother like? What was her life like? What was it like making a living as a prostitute? What was it like *being* with a prostitute? Augie sure didn't know. He'd never been to any of the red light districts on the Mexican side of the border, a traditional rite of passage for generations of South Texas boys. His mom always seemed to know when a group of guys from the high school were planning a road trip to Boystown in Matamoros or Nuevo Laredo, and she always made sure her son had something else to do.

So there in that Tuxpan River restaurant, being a little bit drunk, kinda horny, and intensely curious, he thought *Ah, what the hell? No time like the present. I'll just talk to her and see what happens.*

He joined the painted lady at the bar and bought her a drink. And then he bought her another one and another. Between her broken English and his broken Spanish, it became clear the direction the night was heading. Before they left the bar, Augie made a silent toast to his dead prostitute grandmother and his dead gringo grandfather, neither of whom he'd ever met. *This one's for you, abuelos.*

After that, things got woolly. He vaguely recalled leaving the bar with the girl and walking down a narrow road that became darker and emptier as they went. The girl said she was taking him to a place where the rooms and drinks were *muy barato*—very cheap. Eventually the road petered out, and they arrived at a solitary, nondescript building on the shore of the lagoon. He remembered a yellow light beside the door, and inside, a band playing *mariachi* music. People were dancing. Someone handed him a drink.

Augie struggled to remember what happened at the club, but his recollections were a confused jumble of drunken sensations—colored lights, blaring music, the girl's sweaty embrace . . . and then, after that, nothing.

Someone had spiked his drink—*that* was a certainty. He must have gone outside at some point to get some fresh air or to get sick. Did she go with him, or did someone else? He vaguely remembered the water, some boats . . . .

I am such an idiot! I should've seen it coming.

Augie took a deep breath. Okay, that was the how—a woman lured him into a shady club and then she, or one of her accomplices, slipped him a mickey. But why this? Why had they kidnapped him and chained him up like a fucking dog? On a fucking shrimp boat? Why hadn't they just taken his cash and left him by the side of the road? Augie tried to remember how much money he'd had on him at the time. Not much, he decided. Not his passport, either. He'd left it in the room, along with his watch, cell phone, credit cards, and driver's license. He'd put it all in the little metal room safe in the closet. At least he'd had the foresight to do that. After all, he had been planning to walk only a few blocks, grab a bite, and return early to the hotel.

Suddenly a new thought occurred to him. *Maybe it was all a mistake.* The sons of bitches had snatched the wrong guy. He could see how it might happen. He wasn't tall and lanky like his dad, but short, dark, and solidly built like the men in his mom's family. Charlie always joked that he looked like a Guatemalan *indio*. Maybe the kidnappers thought he was one of the helpless *indocumentados* coming up from Central America to find work in Texas. He'd heard the gangs preyed on them like wolves on sheep. Once he talked to the captain of the vessel and explained who he was—a by-God American citizen—the captain would apologize for the epic fuck-up and take him straight back to port. Surely.

Buoyed by the prospect, Augie closed his eyes and waited for what came next. The boat would have to stop sometime. Eventually he would be able to talk to someone. Then everything would be put right.

——

CHAPTER 06

Raul drove as fast as he dared down US-77, the divided highway that bisected the kingdom-sized ranches of South Texas. He caught glimpses of mesquite-studded grasslands and salt marshes through gaps in the oleander hedges. Although he was in a hurry, he was mindful of the DPS troopers that often ticketed unwary speeders on this stretch of road; the last thing he needed was an unscheduled delay. He had three customers to visit and a border to cross before dark.

But if he *were* stopped, Raul thought ruefully, at least the DPS officer wouldn't demand a bribe. Once he crossed the river he could be pulled over for the slightest infraction or simply because the *agente de transito* wanted some quick cash for a taco and a Coke.

But Mexican traffic cops were the least of his worries. The state of Tamaulipas had never been completely safe—in fact, the entire US-Mexican border had been a haven for smugglers and outlaws for as long as it had existed—but since the onset of the drug wars in 2006, the area had become a combat zone. Because of the precipitous rise in crime and violence, the U.S. State Department was advising citizens to "defer all non-essential travel." The advisory went on to say that "state and municipal law enforcement capacity is limited to nonexistent in many parts of Tamaulipas . . . and violent conflicts between rival criminal elements and/or the Mexican military can occur in all parts of the region and at any time of the day." The State Department's message was pretty clear: Tamaulipas was a shit sandwich.

But in Raul's mind, his trip fell under the category of essential travel and could not be deferred. He inadvertently sped up as he approached the outskirts of Brownsville, struggling to rein in the malignant feeling that something terrible had happened to his son.

He turned down a road that paralleled the Brownsville Ship Channel and pulled up to a collection of tin warehouses fronting the harbor. Over the rooftops he saw a few boat masts and riggings, but he knew the harbor would be mostly empty this time of year as boats would be in the Gulf trawling for shrimp.

His first stop was Rodriguez Marine & Supply. He entered the warehouse through an open loading bay and walked through the aisles of pallet racks stocked with cable, rope, netting, and chain. A forklift rumbled by, loaded with empty pallets. Thick wooden trawl doors leaned against metal studs along the wall, and various tools of the trade—staves, shackles, mud rollers, and even Charlie's patented turtle excluders—were on display behind and adjacent to a long counter. Chuy Rodriguez, the proprietor, called out to Raul when he spotted him.

"¡Aye, que milagro! Look what the cat dragged in." He came around the counter and gave Raul a warm handshake. "Man, I was beginning to wonder if you'd forgotten about us or maybe got eaten by sea monsters or something. We haven't seen you in forever."

Chuy had thick, jet-black hair, a profound mustache, and a body that revealed his fondness for tamales and cold beer. He lived a happy and decent life, the kind of life that was increasingly difficult to live along the border.

"Hola, Chuy. I suppose it has been a while."

"A while? It's been more than that, amigo. You think we don't notice that every few years your company sends a newer, younger Sweetwater down here to call on us?"

Raul opened his hands and shrugged to concede the point. "So, how are you? You're looking . . . prosperous."

He laughed. "I am happy and well fed, my friend."

"And the family?"

"They are well. We are like you guys. Soon as the kids are old enough, we put 'em to work in the business."

"Gotta keep the dynasties going."

"Yeah, but it's not so easy these days, is it? Shrimp gettin' harder to find, expenses gettin' higher, the Feds keep strapping us with more regulations." He shook his head. "And imported shrimp is gettin' so cheap even my wife's startin' to look at that Asian crap at the grocery store."

"Yet here you are, still in business."

"What else am I gonna do? Shrimpin's all our family knows."

Chuy had five brothers who owned and operated Gulf trawlers. He was the only one who had decided to make his living on land, in his case, outfitting shrimp boats and other commercial fishing vessels.

"So what brings you down here, Raul? Augie came by not long ago—last week, I think. You here checkin' up on him?" Chuy smiled, but when he saw the worried look on Raul's face, the smile faded. "He okay?"

"I'm sure he is . . . but last week he didn't check in after his trip like he usually does, so I thought I'd, you know, retrace his steps."

"I see. Where was he going after here?"

"South. The usual route. Tampico, Tuxpan, Veracruz."

"Drove his truck?"

"Yeah. 'Fraid so. He had samples and whatnot."

Chuy looked south and sighed. "Lotta miles between here and Veracruz . . . . Look, I don't mean to meddle in your business, but it ain't safe down there these days. Especially Tamaulipas. I got family on my wife's side still lives across the river. When night comes they don't even leave the house no more."

"Augie's pretty careful. He knows his way around."

"Oh, he's a smart kid, all right." Chuy cleared his throat and forced a smile. "I'm sure he's alright. Prob'ly met a girl or somethin'."

Raul's next stop, at Alvarez Port Supply, was just as disheartening. Betina Alvarez, the owner, greeted him warmly and then went into her own diatribe about how difficult the business was becoming. Raul listened sympathetically. It was a common refrain from just about everyone in the industry. "Nobody wants to work on a shrimping crew anymore. Used to be the captains could at least hire illegals, but now they can't find *them*, either."

Before he departed, she chided him for sending Augie into Mexico. "You, of all people, should know better," she told him. "It's *loco* down there these days, Raul. Totally *loco*."

The third stop, also near the harbor, was one of Sweetwater's biggest accounts. They ordered ten times more inventory than the outfits he'd just visited, but you wouldn't know it by looking at the layout. The business was named International Supply, LLC—a nondescript name for some nondescript corrugated metal buildings and warehouses set behind a chain-link fence. According to Charlie, the owner of International Supply was none other than Alberto Alexander, Charlie's rich friend from Mexico.

When Raul drove through the gate, a pair of pit bulls trotted up. He honked his horn and waited for someone to come out of the double-wide trailer that served as an office. He didn't recognize the dark, skinny fellow who walked toward him from the docks.

Raul rolled down his window. "Raul Sweetwater, Sweetwater Marine." The guy didn't react, so Raul handed him a business card.

The man studied the card, shooed the dogs away, and motioned for Raul to follow him. He ushered him inside the air-conditioned trailer where a heavyset man Raul didn't recognize stood up to shake his hand.

"*Señor Sweetwater,*" he began. "*Es un gran placer conocerlo.*"

Raul replied that he was glad to know him as well and then took the seat offered to him. The two of them chatted in Spanish for a few minutes, and he heard, once again, that business was tough, competition was fierce, and, yes, Augie had indeed dropped by early last week, but the man hadn't heard from him since. Raul was anxious to get back on the road, but for the sake of propriety, and perhaps out of habit, he decided to talk a little business with the manager before he left.

"Augie might've mentioned this already," Raul said, switching to English, "but we can ask our manufacturers to drop-ship your Mexico-bound orders instead of transshipping everything here. You've got, what? Six sister companies on the Gulf Coast? Five on the Pacific? Some of the bulkier orders could even be shipped by sea. It would save y'all a good bit of money on freight."

The manager smiled. "Your son suggest the same thing. And you know, we think about this . . . but we decide it is better to consolidate here." When Raul looked at him skeptically, the man added, "We look at the idea very seriously, but everything is good the way it is."

Raul nodded. "Well, shipping everything here certainly makes it easy for us." He stood up and told the manager once again how much he appreciated their business and then gave him his cell phone number. "Please call me day or night if you hear from Augie."

Raul drove to the harbor and stopped his car at the water's edge. He needed a moment to collect his thoughts. The Valley had been a bust. What he had hoped to hear was that Augie had touched base with the Brownsville customers at the end of his trip as he passed through town on his way home, or perhaps on his way to South Padre Island to play. Now he would have to look for Augie in Mexico, where it was "totally loco."

He closed his eyes, murmured a prayer, and pointed his SUV toward the border.

———

CHAPTER 07

Charlie exited the customs area at the Veracruz airport and was met by a blocky, unsmiling man holding a sign that read "Swetwatter." The man, who Charlie assumed was a driver sent by the Alexanders, pulled the suitcase from his hand and began walking toward the exit.

"Hey, hold on there, Odd Job," Charlie protested and grabbed his arm, which felt like an oak post.

The man turned and faced him. *"Ya esta arreglado. Hay que ir conmigo."*

"Arranged by who? Go with you where?" Charlie pulled out his phone and dialed Alberto Alexander. *"Hola, amigo.* I'm at the airport, and there's a rather large gentleman here who took my suitcase and insists I go with him. Is this your man?"

"Welcome to Mexico, Charlie! Yes, Pablo is my driver and bodyguard. He is a Zapotec Indian from Oaxaca. He does not talk much, but he is as loyal as they come. He will escort you to the ranch."

"Hey, I appreciate it, Alberto, but I was planning to rent a car. There's some people I need to visit in Veracruz. I thought you and I were going to meet tomorrow."

"Yes, I understand, but my people have already contacted the customers on your behalf," said Alberto. "In Veracruz and in Alvarado, too. Remember, I own most of these companies. I will give you the full report when you get here."

Even after their long acquaintance, Alberto Alexander (the grandson of Russian émigrés, hence the Anglicized surname) still spoke to Charlie in a slightly formal manner.

"Have you heard from Augustus?" Alberto asked.

"No, not yet." He could hear Alberto sigh on the other end of the line.

"We will find him, Charlie. I promise. Petra and I are committed to it. Go with Pablo. We will see you very soon."

Charlie slipped the phone into his pocket. "Okay, Pablo. I guess I'm with you." The Zapotec tilted his head for him to follow. "By the way," Charlie said to Pablo's retreating back, "it's *Sweet*water, not Swetwatter."

To Charlie's surprise, the bodyguard walked him to a general aviation terminal connected to the main airport and then outside to a six-seat Beechcraft Premier that awaited them on the tarmac. A smiling, uniformed pilot stood beside the jet's open door.

Charlie stuck his head inside and admired the plush interior. "Nice ride," he said to the pilot. "I've got two just like it."

On the short flight to the Alexanders' hacienda, Charlie gazed down at the verdant coastal plain south of Veracruz. It was only a hundred miles to Alberto's six thousand hectare "ranch" near Montepío, but it would have taken at least three hours by car. The road was narrow, rough, and went through more than a dozen little villages. Plus, he would have been slowed by buses, donkey carts, vendors, stray dogs, and myriad *topes,* the suspension-destroying speed bumps that arose in the unlikeliest of places. Under other circumstances, he would have looked forward to the drive.

From the window, Charlie could make out the small colonial town of Tlacotalpan, beautiful even from ten thousand feet up. One festival day in February, many years before, he and Alberto had fled for their lives down those same streets during the annual *corrida de toros*—the running of the bulls. Unlike the famous event in Pamplona, the bulls in the Tlacotalpan festival had free rein throughout the city and stampeded helter-skelter through markets, restaurants, and even homes if the beasts happened by an open door. Charlie figured Hemingway would have shit himself.

He and Alberto sure had some crazy times in those days. Back then, Alberto was just a wealthy and eccentric playboy, the third-generation heir to a silver fortune from Taxco, a colonial mountain town southwest of Mexico City. The first time they met was 1971 on the Pacific coast near Puerto Angel when Charlie had saved Alberto's life.

The two men happened to be spearfishing near a secluded reef when Charlie saw, or rather didn't see, the other hunter's snorkel on the surface. When he swam over to investigate, he found the man underwater, already unconscious from lack of oxygen. It was only after Charlie pulled him ashore and resuscitated him that he realized the man had been stung on the torso by a stingray. Charlie lifted him onto his back in a fireman's carry and lugged him to the village, almost a mile away, and then found someone to rush them to the nearest medical center. By the time they arrived, Alberto was having convulsions. Yet somehow he survived, and for the rest of his life he had an impressive scar across his chest to remind him of his brush with death. He and Charlie had been friends ever since.

Alberto calmed down considerably after he married Petra. Now he mostly focused on keeping his very social and very expensive wife happy. Charlie was always a welcome guest in their Montepío hacienda, or in any other residence they owned (and there were many, including a quaint little eight-bedroom cottage in Key Allegro in Rockport), but their friendship had subtly changed over the years, acclimating either to age or changed circumstances. Charlie noticed that, even now, with both men in their late sixties, Petra seemed jealous whenever he managed to talk Alberto into joining him on a Patagonia fly-fishing trip or some other far-flung adventure.

Soon the green cone of *Volcán* San Martín Tuxtla became visible, and the pilot began his descent toward Hacienda Alexander. The plane banked around the tree-covered volcano and the verdant checkerboard of fields and pastures that spread at its base. The private runway stood out like a strip of white tape against the lush vegetation. As they landed, Charlie spotted Alberto parked at the end of the airstrip, smiling and waving at him from an open-top jeep.

Alberto Alexander had never been a small man, but with age, wealth, and a few extra pounds he had become broad-chested and burly, with longish white hair and a full beard to match. The fashionable, thick-framed eyeglasses he wore provided a cosmopolitan look that his wife no doubt encouraged him to adopt, even though Charlie knew his eyesight was excellent.

He hustled to the aircraft and embraced Charlie in an affectionate *abrazo*.

"Charlie, Charlie! So good to see you, my friend!"

"Good to see you, too, Alberto. Thanks for the lift from the airport."

"What are toys for? Besides, Petra could not wait to see you. Jump in. I will take you to the house."

In the jeep, Alberto asked again about Augie, listening carefully to the particulars and then describing his exchanges with the owners and managers of the marine supply businesses he'd contacted earlier that day. "They said your nephew made his visits, talked some business, and then went on his way. There was nothing out of the ordinary and no mention of his plans after he left."

"Got any suggestions about what to do next?" asked Charlie.

"As a matter of fact, I do," Alberto replied, raising a finger for emphasis. "Although strictly speaking, it was Petra's idea. There is a man we are going to introduce you to. He is at the house now. He is from the PGR and may be able to help."

Charlie reflected on this. The *Procuraduría General de la República*, or PGR, was the equivalent of the federal office of the Attorney General, responsible for, among other things, investigating and prosecuting cartel-related crimes, including kidnapping. Recently, they had come under fire for dragging their feet in the disappearance of forty-three student protestors in the state of Guerrero. Anyone with any sense suspected a government cover-up. As a rule, and from experience, Charlie intensely distrusted Mexican politicians (all politicians, really) but he also knew that favors granted to well-connected people often produced results. And Alberto and Petra were nothing if not well-connected people.

As if he were reading Charlie's mind, Alberto said, "Sometimes *politicos* can be useful, *verdad?*"

The jeep crested a ridge, and the land opened up to a wide basin, colored by a thousand shades of green—a broad valley of grass, ferns, and tropical scrub, with thick stands of trees shading the high and low places. This area of Mexico was one of Charlie's favorites. The nearby Tuxtla Biosphere group had worked hard to halt the wholesale deforestation that had already occurred in much of the area, and each time Charlie visited, he was happy to see that developer and agribusiness money still hadn't moved in and ruined what remained.

"Your place looks good, Alberto."

He smiled broadly. "It does, doesn't it? I would stay here twelve months a year if Petra would let me. But alas, there is always another ocean view she feels we must possess. Did I tell you she has become a real estate broker in the U.S.? She is like the kid in the candy store."

"The struggles of the rich and famous," said Charlie. "I really feel for you."

Alberto braked to avoid some cows standing in the road under a shade tree. "Ha! You see my cows? I have finally become a real rancher, no?"

"How many head?"

"One hundred and twenty," he answered proudly. "Some of Petra's relatives live on the property and take care of them. If you ever want to give up shrimping, you can come here and be a cowboy, eh?" Alberto laughed his big booming laugh and slapped Charlie on the back.

"I might consider it."

Alberto looked at him, the smile still on his face. "In truth, it sounds like something you *would* consider. But Petra would never allow it. When you come here, you come as our guest."

"I don't want to be a freeloader, Alberto."

"Bah! I could *give* you my ranch, and I would still be in your debt." He pulled open his shirt and displayed the whip-like scar across his chest. "*Ves?* You see?"

The jeep entered a natural shade tunnel of trees and vines that arched over the road and shut out most of the afternoon light. It was as dark and cool as a cave inside and thousands of tiny white butterflies fluttered in the enigmatic air. Alberto shifted into a lower gear, and they began climbing a stone-paved road that led up the mountain. When they rounded a final bend, Alberto and Petra's magnificent home appeared before them. Somehow they had managed to blend the region's diverse architectural styles into a cohesive design. The thick stone walls and steep steps were reminiscent of an ancient Olmec temple, while the Spanish arches, columns, balustrades, and barrel roof tile clearly had been borrowed from the Colonial era.

They had built the residence on the foundations of an old hotel from the late 1800s, one that likely used stones from nearby Mesoamerican temples to construct its walls. Charlie was there when one of the local *campesinos* first led Alberto to the jungle-covered ruins. The men stood on the broken steps of the old structure and marveled at the breathtaking Gulf-side view. Then and there, Alberto announced his intention to build a house on the site as a wedding present for Petra, his beautiful fiancée.

Alberto wheeled the jeep to a stop. "Welcome to our home, Charlie," he said, slapping him on the back. *"Mi casa es tu casa,* and all that jazz."

Charlie climbed the steps to the entrance and noticed how the jungle was already creeping in. Lichens, molds, and moss stained the home's exterior, and vines seized onto its stones wherever they could gain purchase—the rainforest slowly reclaiming its turf.

A housekeeper opened the massive wooden front door and ushered them in. Charlie greeted the old woman, recognizing her from his last visit there fifteen years before. Footsteps echoed from a tile hallway and Petra entered the foyer with a flourish.

"¡Querido Carlito! Bienvenidos. I am so happy to see you." She embraced him and then kissed him on both cheeks. "When I heard that your nephew was missing, I was so . . . disconsolate, but then I heard you were coming here to visit us, and, *oh my God,* my heart was animated."

"Thank you, Petra. You are still as lovely on the inside as you are on the outside."

Petra's English was an interesting mix of popular American expressions and literal translation of Spanish words, but Charlie had always found it completely charming. And there was no denying her physical beauty. Her lovely black hair was pulled up, drawing attention to her delicate neck, her piercing brown eyes flecked with gold, and her red carpet runway smile. She was a popular *telenovela* actress when Alberto met her, and later she even appeared in a few Hollywood movies. At one time she had been considered the most beautiful woman in Mexico, and even now, at forty-six years of age (twenty-three years Alberto's junior), her beauty had not faded.

She grabbed him by the arm. "Come. I want to introduce you to someone." She looked at her husband. *"Querido,* would you have Elena prepare us some cocktails?"

Petra led him through a large, high-ceiling living room decorated with modern and Mesoamerican art and then out to the patio. The view over the balustrade was spectacular. Over the top of a thick canopy of trees, the Gulf of Mexico stretched out to meet the cloudless sky. Charlie reckoned he could see fifty miles in either direction. The late afternoon light deepened the blue-green hues of the sea and sky, and one side of the horizon was as beautiful as the other.

"Charlie, *quiero presentarle al Diputado Marcos Abrigo, del PGR. Marcos, el es Charlie Sweetwater,"* said Petra, making the introduction.

Charlie turned to face a middle-aged man with a thick black mustache and deep-set eyes shadowed by heavy brows. He wore brown slacks and a white guayabera shirt. "Hi, Sweetwater," he said, offering his hand.

Charlie noticed the man had a firm handshake and a direct, almost brusque manner, as though he was used to being the most powerful guy in the room. Charlie disliked him on sight.

Charlie countered the diputado's rather informal greeting with a more formal one, telling him in Spanish that any friend of Alberto and Petra's was a friend of his.

The politician presented him with a thin smile. "Where do you come from?" he asked in heavily-accented English.

Charlie continued in Spanish, telling him he was from Fulton, Texas, a small town close to the Gulf, famous for fishing and birds ("por la pesca y los pájaros").

"How about you talk in English, eh, Sweetwater?"

As a rule, Charlie always led off with Spanish when he spoke with Mexicans in Mexico, and then switched to the language that was most comfortable for all parties later on. Evidently this guy wanted to show off his English. Charlie shrugged. "Sure."

"Petra tells me you have a relative or something who has not returned to, where did you say you are from? Somewhere in Texas?"

"Fulton, Texas. Yes, he's my nephew, and he was supposed to return last Friday."

"But today is only Monday."

Charlie cleared his throat. "That's true, but he was in the habit of checking in regularly with the office."

"He is a salesman of some kind?"

"Yes. Marine equipment."

The diputado went to an end table next to the chair he had been sitting in and shook a Dunhill cigarette from a package, not offering one to Charlie. A half-full brandy snifter sat on the table, too. "Did your nephew come to Mexico to work . . . or to play?" he asked.

"Work," Charlie answered, not liking the insinuation.

The diputado grunted and leaned over the rail, smoking his cigarette and presenting his back to Charlie.

"We are preoccupied that something might have happened to him," Petra said hastily, sensing the tension. "As you well know, it can be so dangerous in the frontier states."

"Which side of the border do you mean, señora?" asked the diputado. "Hundreds of Mexicans die on the north side of the Rio Bravo every year, yet Americans only want to criticize the dangers south of the river . . . even though there are ten times more crimes in the U.S. than in Mexico." He had addressed Petra, but he was looking directly at Charlie. "American newspapers and American politicians do tremendous damage to our reputation when they inflate the facts."

Charlie listened politely. He'd seen the statistics. The "facts" were that murder rates were twice as high in Mexico, and the kidnapping numbers were higher than anywhere else in the world. *What a pompous ass*—thought Charlie, but he decided it was best not to argue. As Alberto had said, "Sometime politicos can be useful."

"Well," said Charlie. "We certainly don't want to do anything to damage Mexico's reputation. I'm just trying to find my nephew."

Alberto walked out onto the veranda followed by a girl carrying a tray of drinks. "Let's have cocktails," he said. "Scotch on the rocks for you, eh, Charlie?"

"Right you are, Alberto. Thanks." Charlie took the drink and waited until everyone else had theirs in hand. "A toast to old friends and to new friends," said Charlie, raising his glass. He touched glasses with Alberto and Petra, and when he leaned over to toast with his "new friend" the diputado, the politico's cellphone rang.

"*Diga*," he barked into the receiver. The diputado listened for a moment and then he walked into the living room to speak in private, leaving Charlie with his glass still extended.

Charlie shrugged. "Business first, I guess."

"He is very high in the PGR," said Petra, slightly embarrassed. "He will help us find Augie."

Charlie nodded. "I hope so, Petra. How do you know Marcos, by the way?"

Alberto laughed. "She knows many politicians from Mexico City. It seems like they are all fans of her *telenovelas*. Even the President himself admits he sometimes watches them."

"You exaggerate, Alberto," she said blushing. "To answer your question, Charlie, Mexico City is twenty-five million habitants, but at the top the social circles are very small. It is easier than you think to meet powerful people. I met my husband there, after all."

Alberto laughed. "I was hardly a member of any top social circle, and was certainly not powerful. I was simply lucky Petra decided to attend my lecture that night at the Bellas Artes."

"On the history of the silver industry in Mexico," she said. "How could I miss it? You were so dashing, *mi amor.*"

Charlie laughed and raised his glass. "To the rich, the famous, the powerful, and the blind-ass lucky."

Charlie wondered what it must be like living in Alberto and Petra's world, how different it would be from his. For some reason, out of the blue, he thought of Ragnar and wondered what he and his mangy dog were up to back in Fulton. As he swallowed the scotch, he decided he'd rather hang out with a costumed lunatic like Ragnar the Younger than frequent Mexico's top social circles and pretend to be friends with assholes like Diputado Marcos Abrigo.

———

CHAPTER 08

Augie shielded his eyes when the hatch opened and light flooded the engine room. *Finally, I'll get out of this shit hole,* he thought. Then he reminded himself that the hatch had opened the day before, too, when someone threw down two plastic bottles of water and then quickly slammed it shut again. He had finished his water hours ago, even though he'd tried to ration it as long as he could. The second bottle he'd tossed in the general direction of the other prisoner, hoping the guy could find it in the dark.

But this time the hatch remained open, and Augie saw a head appear in the bright square of light above him. The engines had been quiet for some time, and the boat rolled gently in the Gulf swells. The head moved away and then a second one appeared, silhouetted like the first. Someone barked a command, and a man climbed down and stood over Augie, studying him. He took a key from his pocket and unlocked the steel collar. After the lock clicked open, Augie rubbed his neck where the metal had chafed him raw. He glared up at the man.

"*Súbete,*" he said to Augie, pointing up to the hatch.

Climb? Augie struggled to his feet. As he reestablished his balance, he watched the man check on the other prisoner. Sticking out from behind the second diesel engine, he saw a man's bare ankles wrapped tightly with a length of rough hemp rope.

Augie staggered to the ladder, weakened by hunger and thirst, his muscles stiff and sore. When he finally pulled himself up, he had to shield his eyes from the blinding sunlight, but, God, did the fresh air feel good. A short, shirtless man wearing a tattered baseball cap handed him a plastic cup of water, and Augie drained it greedily. "More," he said hoarsely.

The man shook his head. *"Mas tarde."* Later.

Augie grabbed his arm before he could walk away. "Where the hell am I?"

The man blinked and acted like he didn't understand. Augie released him and looked around, shading his eyes with his hand. He was on a large commercial shrimp boat, just as he'd suspected, and the water around them was a deep cobalt blue, meaning they were a long way from land—much too far to jump ship and swim for it.

The crewman who had unlocked him shouted something up from the engine room, and the guy with the baseball cap answered and then climbed down the ladder to join him. A moment later he reappeared and rushed to the wheelhouse. When he returned, he was followed by a wiry man, older than the others, who shoved Augie out of the way and looked down the hatch. He had a rapid-fire exchange with the crewmen in colloquial Spanish, a conversation that Augie didn't understand, and then he unleashed an angry string of Spanish profanities that Augie *did* understand. The older man—the captain, Augie surmised—turned and yelled at Augie and his shirtless benefactor, wanting them to go back down into the engine room.

Augie shook his head no, which infuriated the captain. He shoved Augie toward the hatch and yelled again for him to go below and help the others. *"Ayúdales, cabrón."*

"Help them do what?" Augie asked. He felt a tingle of dread.

Reluctantly, he did as he was told. He joined the two crewmen and the three of them gaped at the body curled up on the engine room floor. The boy's hands and ankles had been bound with rope. He appeared to be in his teens and had straight, jet-black hair and strong *indio* features. His bare feet were rough and calloused—the feet of a *campesino*—and his pants and T-shirt were covered with grease and vomit. *Is he dead?* Augie wondered. *He looks dead.* None of it seemed real.

Watching the two crewmen cover their noses with bandanas, Augie realized he'd grown used to the stench after being down there so long. The men turned and stared at him. He wasn't sure what they wanted until one of them pointed at the kid and then at the open hatch above them.

"No way," Augie said. But after a moment, he complied. What choice did he have? Whoever the poor kid was, he deserved some respect. After all, the two of them had shared a terrible experience together, except that he had survived and the kid had not. Augie figured that removing his body from this squalid tomb was the least he could do.

The men handed him a knife and then crossed themselves and moved back so Augie could do his morbid work. He held his breath as long as he could while he sawed through the ropes and tugged the body to the middle of the engine room. At the foot of the ladder he wrestled with the dead weight, trying to pick it up, and realized with a shock that the kid was still breathing, if only barely.

"He's still alive," he told them. "*Él está . . .*" Augie searched for the word, "*está vivo.*"

The men relayed this information up to the captain and returned with the same command—carry him up the ladder now.

One of the men took off his belt and helped Augie fashion a kind of sling to carry the near-dead boy up the ladder. Even with the sling Augie could barely manage. He was weak and hadn't eaten anything since Friday evening. When he finally made it to the top, the captain yelled for Augie to drag the boy to the back deck. The other crewmen stood ankle-deep in fish and shrimp and assorted bycatch and stared at Augie with dismay.

"*¡Tíralo al agua, cabrón!*" yelled the captain, shoving him toward the rail. "*¡Tíralo!*"

"I'm not going to throw him in the water," Augie yelled back. "He's still fucking alive."

"*¡Tíralo!*"

"No! He needs a doctor."

The captain unsnapped the holster on his hip and pulled out a rusty revolver. He put the barrel against Augie's forehead and cocked the hammer. "*Tíralo,*" he repeated in a low, menacing voice.

Augie turned to the water, choked back a sob and then heaved the boy over the rail. The body torpedoed below the surface, and Augie saw the kid's eyes open in surprise. He drew himself into a ball in what seemed to be a half-hearted attempt to protect himself, but then he closed his eyes and his body relaxed, his long black hair gently undulating around his head. Augie watched in horror as the current carried the sinking body away from the boat.

He quietly muttered a Hail Mary even as the captain poked him in the back and yelled at him in Spanish. Augie finished the prayer, crossed himself, and then spun around and slugged the captain in the jaw.

The captain scrambled up off the deck, his face contorted with rage and disbelief. This time he didn't draw his pistol but instead pulled a two-foot length of winch cable from his belt and proceeded to whip the living shit out of Augie. Augie fell to the ground and got up several times only to be knocked down again. The beating stopped when Augie simply gave up, so exhausted that he was afraid he'd lose consciousness and be thrown overboard like his cellmate. He suffered the final blows prostrate on the slimy deck. The captain glared at the crew, his chest heaving. *You see?* He shouted in Spanish. *This is what happens if orders are disobeyed.*

The captain returned to the wheelhouse, and then a beefy, tattooed man, the foreman, Augie supposed, grabbed him under the arms and raised him to a sitting position. He slid a couple of heavy wire baskets in front of him. Augie slumped forward, his head on his chest. Next to the pile of fish in front of him were two feet wearing Nike shoes—*his* Nike shoes.

The big *capataz* pulled Augie's chin up and looked at him, grinning. "If you don't work, the captain will kill you."

———

CHAPTER 09

As Raul idled in line, waiting to cross the International Bridge into Mexico, he reflected on Matamoros. On the surface, everything seemed normal—or at least as normal as any Mexican border city ever seemed, and he knew that the vast majority of the city's million-plus citizens went about their daily lives without incident. But still, he worried. While many Americans proclaimed that "Mat" had become a bloody, lawless battleground—ground zero for the drug wars—the locals usually defended their city by saying it wasn't *that* dangerous.

But Raul knew that people could get used to almost anything, and after a while, without even being aware of it, the city's beleaguered citizens adopted a cautious, vigilant way of life that became second nature to them. They avoided the parks, restaurants, and theaters they once frequented; they stepped into doorways when unfamiliar cars or trucks sped down their street; they looked away when they saw a bullet-ridden body lying in the gutter; they kept their children close. *Don't make waves*, they told themselves. *Keep a low profile. Pay the mordidas without complaint, and never seek out the police.* You live like that every day and it becomes routine, so familiar that you forget how ravaged the city has really become. The new normal.

In the previous decade Raul had seen it happen in Juarez and Tijuana, too. No wonder most of the prominent border-town families moved themselves and their businesses across the river where they were safe. Everyone else would just have to keep their heads down and wait out the storm. Like all bad storms, the drug wars—and the death and destruction they spun off—hurt the poor and the powerless the most. They were collateral damage.

Raul's SUV crept across the bridge until he finally came to the Mexican *Aduana* kiosk. An unkempt border guard waved him through after Raul pushed the pass/don't pass button and received the green light. As he sped up to merge into city traffic, his hands tightened around the steering wheel, and he braced himself for what was to come.

Nothing prepares one for the shock of crossing the Rio Grande into a busy Mexican border town. Nowhere in the world is the transition so palpable, abrupt, or extreme. On one side of the river you're idling in your lane, waiting for the light to change, daydreaming about nothing in particular, and then, a quarter mile later, you're careening down a potholed avenue jockeying for space with smoke-belching trucks, cars, taxis, and buses. Lanes don't matter, traffic lights are discretionary, and aggressive, balls-out driving is the norm.

Raul stopped at a red light between a battered *pesera* microbus and a motorcycle carrying three passengers. During the thirty seconds before the light changed, a ragged young *tragafuego* walked out and began spewing diesel-fueled flames from his mouth into the air. A wave of child and adult vendors appeared, hawking their candied fruit, *Chiclets,* electrical power strips, balloons, and lottery tickets as they weaved in and out of the line of idling cars. Pedestrians, including a man holding a live chicken, hustled across the intersection to beat the light. Raul reached into his pocket and gave some pesos to two kids who, without asking, had hopped onto the hood of his car and washed his windshield.

The light changed, and the mad dash began again. A mile past the river, Raul turned onto the highway that led to the coast. Matamoros had no port, harbor, or commercial fishing industry, so there were no customers for Augie to see, but there was a popular beach right outside the city that Augie had mentioned visiting before (at his uncle Charlie's urging, of course). Raul figured the short side trip was worth a shot. Maybe someone there had seen his son.

Playa Bagdad was a sleepy, white-sand beach used mainly by the locals, although once it had been a popular destination for Texas bathers, too. During the Civil War, it became a makeshift shipping port used by Confederates to avoid Union blockades and to export cotton to England. A rowdy boomtown grew up, and scores of schooners and steamers crowded the Gulf waiting to be loaded with cotton. After the war ended and multiple hurricanes scrubbed the area clean, the beach returned to its previous sleepy state. Charlie said it reminded him of Port A before the condo invasion. Thatch-roof *palapas* and open-air restaurants lined the beach, interspersed with guest cottages and a few small hotels.

Raul was accosted by seashell and curio vendors the moment he got out of his car, but he waved them off and headed toward the restaurants and hotels. He pulled out Augie's picture in each locale and asked the proprietors, waiters, and bartenders if they'd seen the boy. Their reactions were furtive and evasive, and Raul wondered why.

A friendly bartender behind the counter of one particular beachside bar asked Raul if he might like a cold beer *"para la buena salud,"* for good health. Raul took note of the man's welcoming smile and sat down on a stool. He pushed a twenty-peso note across the counter and the barkeep served him the beer. After some small talk, Raul showed him his son's picture. He took it and studied it carefully. He looked up and shook his head, his eyes flat and unreadable. No, he hadn't seen him. Raul thanked him for taking the time to examine the picture and then asked him why everyone else on Playa Bagdad barely glanced at it when he pulled it out.

"They think maybe the person in this picture has trouble with the narcos," the bartender answered quietly, switching to English.

Raul looked around to see who might be eavesdropping, but the place was vacant except for a boy sweeping the wooden floor with a twig broom. "My son doesn't have anything to do with drugs," said Raul.

"In Playa Bagdad . . . is not the drugs . . . is the fish."

"The fish?"

"Yes," he thrust his chin seaward and said in a low voice, *"los pescadores furtivos."*

Illegal fishermen. Raul nodded. A Texas Parks and Wildlife game warden had told him about them. Almost every night, small motorized *lanchas* snuck into Texas waters to poach fish: sharks, mackerel, snapper, grouper, reds—all highly regulated species in Texas, and plentiful, too. Mexico had no such regulations, and as a result, their waters had been mostly fished out. So, unsurprisingly, the local fishermen moved north to richer, albeit illegal, hunting grounds. Before long, the cartels moved in and monopolized the racket.

Raul swiveled around on his bar stool and surveyed the colorful wooden and fiberglass boats beached on the shore. They seemed harmless enough in the late afternoon sun, quaint even. The tourist guidebooks called them "artisanal" fishing boats, but come nightfall, packs of them would cross over to Texas waters and wreak havoc on the fish stock. They used gill nets five miles long, electro-shock devices, and deadly longlines hung with hundreds of baited hooks that killed all species of fish indiscriminately—sea turtles, dolphins, and birds, too.

Their lines were difficult, but not impossible, to find in the open water. Game wardens looked for telltale plastic location buoys, but one officer said that poachers had recently started replacing the buoys with live pelicans which they lashed by their feet to the longlines. These illegal fishermen could haul in tons of fish worth tens of thousands of dollars in a single night. Whenever they sighted a U.S. patrol boat, it was a short run back to Mexican territorial waters where the *yanquis* couldn't follow. Raul didn't doubt the *lanchas* were handy to transport drugs, guns, and people, too. No wonder the narcos had decided to get involved.

And no wonder nobody wanted to talk to him. The mestizo-looking kid in Raul's photo might be in trouble with the cartel somehow. He might be a person on a hit list, an informer, a rival *capo*, a poor fisherman who had tried to cheat the narcos. Whoever the kid was, the locals wanted nothing to do with him, whether they'd seen him or not.

Raul drained his beer and thanked the barkeep.

The man shook his hand with a firm grip but didn't release it immediately. "He is your son?"

"Yes."

"*Mexicano o Americano?*"

"*Americano.*"

"How long is he . . . not calling?"

"Four days."

The man released Raul's hand and nodded knowingly, unable to hide the pity in his eyes. He might as well have told him to forget about ever seeing Augie again.

"You know," the man said after a pause. "If a person . . . . If your son . . . is disappeared . . . ." He chose his words carefully, but there was no way to sugarcoat the message. "Well, there is a man, a *sacerdote*, who maybe help you. He help others before. Others who have disappeared."

He handed Raul a business card. *Padre Redención Canul* the card read. *Diocese of Matamoros.* There was a Matamoros address and a phone number.

"This priest, he is a good man," the bartender said in conclusion. "You should go to see him."

Raul took the card, muttered his thanks, and hurried to the car as fast as he could. He couldn't wait to leave Bagdad Beach.

As he drove back towards Matamoros in the evening gloom, guilt began to mix with the dread he was feeling. He never should have let Augie travel to Mexico, and he was ashamed at how relieved he'd been when he turned management of the territory over to his son. Through the years, Raul had come to dislike Mexico more and more, and then almost to hate it, even though it was his birthplace and technically he was half-Mexican. He hated the disorder, the poverty, the corruption, the violence, the total waste of talent and resources he saw when he traveled there. He'd had enough of it. Why Charlie still loved the country so much was a mystery to him.

Raul silently made a vow that neither he nor his son would set foot in Mexico again once this was over. They would hire Mexican nationals to work the territory. Business would be handled strictly by phone.

The Holiday Inn where Raul had made his reservation was on the south side of Matamoros, right off the highway that would take him to Tampico the next day. He noted the sun on the horizon and pushed the accelerator, wanting to reach the hotel before it got dark, before the monsters came out.

—

CHAPTER 10

Dinner at the Alexanders was a formal affair with handcrafted sterling silver goblets for water and fine crystal for wine. Elena, the cook, was an expert in the local cuisine and made some of the best soups, moles, and desserts Charlie had ever tasted.

Tonight she served a selection of local *antojitos* with unpronounceable names, followed by a soup of wild greens *(sopa xoneci)* and red snapper *a la Veracruzana* with *arroz tumbada*—all of it delicious. Not that Diputado Abrigo enjoyed it much. He talked on his phone most of the time, pacing back and forth on the patio and smoking his Dunhills. But he did return to the table in time for dessert—mashed bananas and vanilla, topped with a mixture of milk, shaved ice, Grenadine, and cinnamon. Petra said the dish originated in her hometown of Catemaco, a nearby village famous for sorcery and witchcraft.

Charlie finished his dessert and looked at his hostess. "Well, I have to say that your dessert was bewitching."

Petra laughed. "Thank you, Charlie. I like your choice of words."

"Years ago," Charlie continued, "I received a *limpia* in Catemaco. It was during the annual *Congreso de Brujos* convention. It did wonders for some macular degeneration in my third eye, but it didn't do a damn thing for my hangover."

Alberto and Petra laughed and nodded. Diputado Abrigo smacked his lips and set down the empty dessert glass. "You know, we investigated the *Congreso de Brujos* a few years ago for the practice of human sacrifice . . . to *Nuestra Señora de la Santa Muerte* . . . Our Lady of the Holy Death."

"Oh, that is nonsense, Marcos," said Petra. "That accusation came from a rival political party to discredit the mayor. You should know that."

The diputado held up his hand. "I simply said we *investigated* the activity. The cult of Santa Muerte continues to grow, propagated mainly by drug traffickers and other criminals. Both the President and the Church would like to see it stamped out. What is ironic is that while I send my ministerial police and the army to eradicate the idol's public shrines and images," he cocked his thumb at Charlie, "American tourists come here and buy the Santa Muerte folk art as fast as the artisans can make it."

"What is also ironic," Charlie added, "is that Santa Muerte is also the patron saint of policeman and soldiers." After he said it, he held Abrigo's cold-eyed stare.

Charlie had enjoyed about as much as he could stand of Deputy Marcos Abrigo. He knew how he must perceive him: a tall, weathered gringo—worse, a Texan—in faded jeans and Lucchese cowboy boots. To the diputado, he must have looked incurably small time.

"Who wants coffee?" Alberto asked, a little too loudly.

No one responded, and the staring contest continued until the diputado's phone rang again. He stood up and marched back out to the patio.

Charlie glanced at Petra, who was looking at him with exasperation. "I know, I know," he said. "He is very high in the PGR. I'm sorry."

"I just want to help you find your nephew," she replied. She scooted back her chair and Alberto rose to help her. Charlie stood, too. "I am going to get a brandy," she said. "Anyone else?"

Alberto and Charlie both raised their hands. When they were alone in the dining room, Alberto chuckled. "You just can't help yourself, can you, Charlie?"

Charlie shrugged. "The man's a dick. What can I say?"

Abrigo reentered the room. In Spanish, he told Alberto that he had an important meeting in Tijuana the following day and asked if he wouldn't mind having his pilot fly him there in the jet; unfortunately, the PGR aircraft was currently in use. After Alberto reluctantly agreed, the diputado looked at his watch and said he had better get some sleep because he wanted to leave before daybreak. He thanked his host for the dinner and left the room to go say goodnight to Petra. He didn't even glance at Charlie on his way out.

Alberto gave Charlie a weak smile. "Would it be a problem if Pablo drives you to Veracruz tomorrow? I apologize for—"

"That would be great, Alberto. Thank you for the offer."

When Petra returned with the brandies, the three of them moved to the living room and visited quietly. Alberto and Petra didn't have kids, but they asked about Charlie's family and listened with interest when he brought them up to date. A fat white Persian cat wandered into the room and jumped onto Petra's lap, almost spilling her drink in an effort to get her to stroke its head. Charlie noticed a diamond collar on the feline's neck.

"You are *our* little baby aren't you, Consuela?" said Petra, grabbing a paw and waving it at Charlie. "Say hello to Uncle Charlie." She looked up at Charlie and smiled. "I think she likes you."

Charlie doubted it, but he waved at the cat anyway.

After they finished their nightcap and before they went to bed, Petra asked for a photo of Augie so she could leave it for Diputado Abrigo to take with him. He had promised her he would pick it up on his way out.

When Charlie gave her the picture, she looked at it and sighed. "He looks like a sweet boy." She put her arms around Charlie and hugged him. "Don't worry, Carlito. I know we will find him. And about tonight, I'm sorry—"

But Charlie interrupted her. "Your heart was in the right place, Petra. I am grateful for what you've done—for everything both you and Alberto have done."

———

CHAPTER 11

Sitting at a table in an unremarkable Holiday Inn restaurant, Raul rotated Father Canul's calling card between his fingers, debating whether or not he should pay the priest a visit. Although he wasn't ready to believe his son had been kidnapped—"disappeared" was the word the bartender had used—it just made good sense to see him now, before he made the six-hour drive from Matamoros to Tampico. If nothing else, he could give the priest one of Augie's pictures on the off chance their paths might intersect.

Father Canul's church faced the river in a run-down industrial zone on Avenida Tamaulipas, not too far from the International Bridge. Except for the simple cross over the arched entrance, one would hardly recognize it as a church. The white plaster building's only architectural flourish was a thin stripe of blue paint outlining the arched door and windows. A single bell tower rose from the structure as though appended to the façade as an afterthought.

A group of people congregated in the church's small courtyard, soaking up the morning sun. Raul opened the gate and walked through, greeting them with a friendly *buenos días* as he went, but they looked away or regarded him suspiciously. Inside the sanctuary, a dozen or more people occupied the rustic pews, many of them on their knees praying to a carved Christ on the cross or to the glass-framed image of Our Lady of Guadalupe. Raul knelt and crossed himself at the altar steps and then began looking for a vestibule door.

"May I help you, sir?" came a voice from behind him.

Raul turned and saw a tall, gaunt man with a sad face and a chiseled nose, reminiscent of a figure from an El Greco painting. Raul removed Father Canul's calling card from his pocket and held it out. "Father Canul?" he asked, noting the clerical collar. He wore no vestments, just a black short-sleeved shirt, battered khaki pants, and scuffed Red Wing work boots. Clearly, this was a clergyman who got his hands dirty.

The priest glanced at the card. "You have come from the U.S.?" he asked in English.

Raul nodded. "Your name was given to me by a friend."

"Where are you from?"

"Fulton."

"Fulton . . . Fulton," he repeated. "Of the San Angelo Diocese?"

"No, it's a town near Corpus Christi."

The priest seemed confused. "You have brought supplies for us?"

Raul was confused as well. "Supplies? No, I'm looking for my son. They told me you might be able to help, but I'm beginning to wonder if I'm at the wrong church." He glanced again at the address on the card and then in Spanish gave a short explanation of his reason for being there.

The priest listened and then laughed so loudly that many of the parishioners looked up from their prayers. "I am very sorry. I was expecting a person from a church outreach program in San Angelo, Texas. He was scheduled to bring a truckload of supplies today, but it has become abundantly clear to me that you are not him." He held out his hand. "I am Father Redención Canul. Welcome to the *Templo de la Familia Sagrada*."

Raul shook the hand and introduced himself, adding, "Your English is very good, Father."

"Thank you. I spent a few years teaching at the Incarnate Word Academy in Brownsville, but I was born in Motozintla, Chiapas." When he noticed the skepticism on Raul's face, he laughed again. "I know . . . I don't look very Mayan, do I? My mother was a Catholic missionary from Chicago who moved to Chiapas to continue the work of the Church. Ultimately, she met my father in Tapachula, where they decided to stay and raise a family. You speak very good Spanish, Mr. Sweetwater. Are you originally from Mexico?"

"I was born in Mexico, but I've spent most of my life in the United States." He decided not to go into his own family history. He kept that part of his life locked away.

Raul followed the priest to a small office off the vestibule. After examining Raul's photo of Augie, Father Canul replied that, although he hadn't seen his son personally, he would post the picture where others would see it.

"Be sure to write your contact information on the back of the picture. Many refugees pass through here, and you would be surprised how often someone recognizes a face in a picture. It has led to many happy reunions and sometimes, simply to closure."

Raul didn't like the sound of that last word, but he understood what the priest meant. He looked around the church. "Everyone here is a refugee?"

Father Canul smiled. "Most, yes. Perhaps you have a little time? I will give you a short tour."

He led Raul through a side door to the sacristy and then through another door into a busy room of long tables where volunteers separated piles of clothing, shoes, personal hygiene items, and cans and packages of food. They placed the items into labeled plastic tubs and stacked them onto shelves.

"This is for the migrants trying to cross the border?" asked Raul.

"Yes, and it is not nearly enough. The conditions to the south—in Guatemala, El Salvador, Honduras—have gone from desperate to deadly. People are not just migrating, they are running for their lives." Father Canul inclined his head toward another door. "Come, I will show you."

Raul followed him through another door that led to a long, high-ceiling, industrial-sized warehouse. The space was lined front to back with cots, most of them occupied. Raul estimated there must have been four hundred people in there: single men, single women, mothers and daughters, entire families, and in a separate section, unaccompanied kids. The smell was a puree of hot, frightened, and mostly unwashed humanity.

He had read about the "crisis" at the border, as tens of thousands of Mexican and Central American migrants journeyed to the Rio Bravo to try and make it to the United States, but when the problem became increasingly politicized, he had eventually tuned it out. Depending on which ideological bubble you lived in, it was either a national security crisis or a humanitarian catastrophe.

"All these people are waiting to get across?"

"Most have been stranded here. They either arrived with no money to cross, were abandoned by their *coyotes*, or have been victimized by criminals."

"What do you mean, victimized?" asked Raul, hurrying to follow the priest through the mass of people milling about in the shelter.

"Robbed, beaten, raped, kidnapped, these people have endured the unimaginable. So they come here . . . to this refuge of last resort."

"I suppose they can always try to get across on their own, without a *coyote*," said Raul, thinking that when he snuck over the border thirty-seven years ago, he simply waded across a shallow stretch of the river and started walking.

The priest shook his head. "Not anymore. The cartels have lookouts along the river at most crossing points. They won't let you pass unless you pay them money. And even if you do, the security on the U.S. side is ten times denser now. The difficulty has increased considerably. Only the most desperate attempt it . . . which is to say, many still do."

Father Canul entered another, quieter room, and he lowered his voice accordingly. "These are the victims who break my heart. These young girls have either lost their mothers to gangs or violence, or else they have attempted the journey on their own."

Several nuns and female volunteers cared for the dozen or so girls in the room, some of them as young as six or seven—holding them, reading to them, feeding them—doing what they could to comfort the traumatized kids. Some of the children were responsive, but others slept or simply stared blankly into space. One girl was huddled in a corner, weeping silently.

Canul sighed. "We have fallen a very long way from God's dreams for these children."

Raul studied the priest's face. There are several kinds of grief. A sudden loss or trauma leaves a certain mark on a person's face. But Father Canul's eyes bore a different kind of imprint: the eyes of a man struck by wave after wave of sorrow, loss, and uncertainty. Constant exposure to tragedy left a different kind of scar.

Raul picked up a small stuffed teddy bear he found at his feet and handed it to a prepubescent girl who was watching him from her cot. The girl took the bear passively and then looked away. Father Canul didn't say what had happened to some of the girls, but Raul was afraid he could guess.

"The stuffed bears were a donation from the San Antonio Sheriff's Department," Canul explained as they exited the sad little room. "The deputies give them to distressed kids caught up in violent domestic situations. Anyway, they work wonders. For many of these kids a stuffed animal is the only thing they believe they can trust, especially when they first come to us."

Returning to the front of the warehouse, Father Canul stopped at a wall with four large cork bulletin boards. Each board was covered with photographs of people: studio portrait pictures, small black and white Polaroids, photos that had been folded into a wallet for years, family pictures with one or two heads circled. Hundreds of photos.

Raul gulped. "Are all of these people—"

"Missing? Yes, I am afraid so. In a few cases, the families have been contacted by kidnappers demanding a ransom. Some families are able to pay, but others simply have nothing of value to trade for their loved one. But most of these poor souls . . . nobody knows. May I have the picture of your son?"

Raul reached into his back pocket, took out one of Augie's photos, and scribbled his information on the back. He handed it to Father Canul, who looked at it carefully and smiled. "I can tell that this one is a free spirit. I think I like him already." He found a tack and pinned the photocopied picture to one of the bulletin boards.

"Yes, I suppose he is," Raul replied distractedly. His eyes were glued to the board. Augie looked out at him from a sea of individual faces, each face cherished by someone, each "soul" part of a family, a past, and, if he or she were lucky, a future without pain and suffering. Many of the families of these missing might be waiting forever. Raul sucked in a breath when he realized that his family might be one of them.

The priest could tell Raul was overwhelmed—he'd seen it too many times when relatives finally understood that their beloved was only one of thousands who were kidnapped or went missing each year. He took Raul to his office and offered him a Topo Chico from a small fridge.

As Raul drank, Father Canul popped up from his chair. "I just thought of something," he said cheerfully. "I'll be right back."

A few minutes later he returned with two short *indígenas* wearing peasant pants and ragged work shirts. They appeared to be brothers.

To Raul's surprise, Father Canul began conversing with the two men in a Mayan dialect. The priest listened carefully to their story and then asked them some follow-up questions. Afterwards, he asked Raul for another picture of Augie, which he showed to the brothers. They studied the photo for a long time, talking quietly to each other as they did. They handed it back to Father Canul with their comments and soon after left the room.

"These two Guatemalan fellows were working on a fishing boat in the Gulf of Mexico before they came here," said Father Canul. "That was why I wanted to talk to them and show them your son's picture."

Raul shook his head to show he didn't understand. "So you thought they might have seen Augie at one of the ports or something? Or at one of the marine supply warehouses at the docks?"

"No, they never saw a marine supply house, and they hadn't intended to crew a fishing vessel. They were lured onto a boat with promises that it would take them to the U.S., but instead they were delivered to a bigger boat—a fishing boat—and forced to work for no pay and very little food."

"But obviously they were released."

"Oh, no. They said that after two months on the boat, they escaped by jumping overboard and swimming for a Louisiana shrimp trawler that was passing nearby. The captain of the American boat wouldn't take them back to his home port—he was afraid he would be accused of smuggling—but he did drop them off in El Mezquital, a little fishing village south of here."

"They were being held *captive* on the fishing boat?" Outside of the pages of Robert Louis Stevenson, Raul had never heard of such a thing.

The priest nodded. "They were slaves, basically. They said there were others like them on the boat and that there were many, that was the word they used, *many* of these slave ships out in the Gulf."

Raul scratched his head. "That's terrible, Padre, but . . . I can't imagine how in the world my son could end up on a fishing boat. He was working around the ports, sure, but that's about as far as it goes."

Father Canul nodded. "You're probably right. I just thought that since those two had a story that involved your industry, it might be worth a shot. At any rate, I will continue to make inquiries."

"Thank you, Padre. I appreciate it."

"And who knows if their story is accurate? It could easily be a fanciful tale." The priest chuckled to himself. "They even talked of a villainous one-eyed pirate terrorizing the Gulf . . . a pirate who serves a Santería deity and practices human sacrifice. They reported that the boat captains were more frightened of this pirate than they were of the Mexican navy."

"Sounds like a Johnny Depp movie," said Raul. The Padre's easy, jovial nature had put him at ease and lessened his anxiety, at least for the moment.

"Ha! I *love* those movies! You know, I actually saw the first *Pirates of the Caribbean* film while I was on a mission in Tapachula a dozen or so years ago. It had been dubbed into Mayan! Can you imagine Johnny Depp speaking *Quiche?*" The priest clapped his hands together and laughed.

Raul smiled. "I actually can, to be honest."

Father Canul nodded his head vigorously and laughed even harder. "Yes! You are right! With him, the dubbed dialogue seemed very authentic." He wiped tears from his eyes as his laughter trailed off. "Except according to my two Mayan friends, this pirate's name is not Jack Sparrow. It is Mal de Ojo."

"Evil Eye?"

The priest shrugged. "That is what the men said. Listen, I love those two refugees—I love all of them—but they are a superstitious people. Whatever faith they may have is deeply mixed with their indigenous beliefs. They see omens and signs in just about everything."

The priest escorted Raul out to the front gate and gave him a warm embrace. "I have enjoyed talking to you today, Mr. Sweetwater," he said, his eyes smiling. "Remain hopeful. I will light a candle for your son and pray for his safe return."

"Thank you, Padre. Thank you for your kindness. When I get home, if I can help you I will."

As he drove away from Father Canul's refugee center of last resort, he wondered how the priest managed to stay so upbeat in such a depressing place. *Remain hopeful,* he had said. Raul repeated the words like an incantation. *Remain hopeful. Remain hopeful.*

CHAPTER 12

Pablo was mildly annoyed when the man named "Swetwatter" jumped into the front seat of his armored Suburban SUV before they set out for Veracruz. The privacy window between the front and back seat was there for a reason. It signified a clear separation between him and the principal he was charged to protect. Pablo considered himself a skilled professional: a highly-trained driver and bodyguard, proficient in threat assessment and evasive driving techniques, always on the lookout for potentially dangerous situations. Not that he'd ever had to use the skills on the quiet country road from Montepío to Veracruz—the only dangers he had to watch out for were stray cattle, potholes, and dogs. But to have his client riding shotgun? It was not proper protocol.

To make matters worse, the voluble American rolled down the car window and started talking non-stop about how beautiful the morning was. It was almost too much for the stoic Zapotec to bear. For some reason, his passenger felt the need to comment on every tree, flower, and bird he recognized along the road. Or maybe he just liked hearing the sound of his own voice. Whatever the reason, he certainly seemed to be enjoying himself. When they finally reached a stretch of road that didn't merit comment, Charlie directed his attention to Pablo.

"¿De donde eres, Pablo?" asked Charlie. "Where are you from?"

Pablo sighed. "Yalalag."

"Yalalag!? I know Yalalag. *¡Muy bonito!*"

To Pablo's surprise, the American began speaking in fluent Spanish, describing the little mountain village where he grew up with remarkable accuracy. He then recounted a funny story about a long drive he and Señor Alexander had made through the Sierras one night from Yalalag to Tlacotalpan in a white Volkswagen Beetle with no headlights.

"We had to wave flashlights out the side windows to see where we were going and also to warn people we were coming," he laughed. "With the crazy light show I guess we looked like some sort of *fantasma*, because pedestrians along the way either ran away into the jungle or else dropped to their knees and prayed. Oncoming cars pulled as far off the road as they could get."

One story led to another, and by the time Pablo reached the outskirts of Veracruz, he couldn't help but like the guy. He even deviated from standard procedure and stopped at a roadside vendor's stand in La Union so they could drink a coffee and eat a couple of steamed *poc chuc* tamales.

As they approached the rental car lot in downtown Veracruz, Charlie turned to his new friend. "Tell me something, Pablo," he asked him in Spanish. "The politicians you drive back and forth to the Alexanders' house . . . are all of them *pendejos* like Diputado Abrigo?"

Pablo stared ahead stone-faced. *What kind of question was that?*

"Okay," Charlie continued. "Too direct. Let me ask it this way: if all of them are not *pendejos,* then say something, say whatever. You can even just blink your eyes if you want to. But . . . if all of them are *pendejos . . .* well, then don't do anything."

Charlie watched Pablo's expression solidify, his profile becoming as somber and still as a carved Olmec head, except that one corner of the Zapotec's mouth involuntarily raised just a fraction, suggesting a hint of a smile. That was good enough for Charlie. Earlier that morning when Charlie had left the Alexanders' house, he had seen Augie's picture still sitting on the entry hall table where Petra had left it for the diputado. The sonofabitch hadn't even touched it. He was pretty sure Diputado Abrigo hadn't come to their ranch to help Charlie find his nephew. He'd been there for different reasons. And apparently other politicos had as well.

Before Pablo left, he gripped Charlie's hand and shook it. *"Que tengas mucho cuidado, señor,"* he said solemnly.

"Don't worry, amigo. I'm always careful," Charlie replied.

Charlie picked up his rental, a beat-up Chevy Aveo, and drove to the port to visit the half-dozen marine supply companies that would have been on Augie's circuit. The managers repeated what Alberto had already told him: there was nothing unusual about Augie's visits, and he didn't mention what his plans were afterwards.

While he was there, Charlie poked around the seafood processing plants, too. Many of the marine supply houses had processing facilities near or attached to their stores. While some of the plants were struggling or had gone out of business, Charlie saw that Alberto's businesses had grown substantially. They were bigger, cleaner, more mechanized, and much busier than the others, particularly the newly-built plant at the end of the *Malecón*. The supervisor told him that his crews often worked overtime to process all the catch their boats brought in.

Charlie noticed that the plants were receiving as much or more forage fish—the innumerable mass of bait fish at the base of the ocean food chain—as they were shrimp. He pointed to one of the storage containers being loaded onto a refrigerated trailer. "Where is the container going?" he asked the foreman.

The foreman shrugged and said he didn't know, but he had heard the shipments mostly went to a pet food manufacturer.

Charlie figured that whoever was buying the product was buying a shitload of it, because reefer rigs were lined up at the dock waiting to be loaded. At any rate, he was happy to see that Alberto's investments had done so well. Twenty years ago, when NAFTA slashed U.S. tariff barriers on seafood, Alberto decided to invest in the industry. He did so partly because he wanted to diversify (the money from his family estate was large but not inexhaustible), and partly because he knew that many of Petra's relatives were fishermen, which gave Alberto an opportunity to extend his patronage to her family—something he was more than happy to do.

Of course, none of it would have happened if Charlie hadn't suggested the idea in the first place. He even introduced Alberto to companies he thought they might consider acquiring. After they'd bought the businesses, Petra and her family pretty much took over from there. Her husband had many talents, but business was not one of them. He had neither the interest nor the aptitude. In macho Mexico, Alberto might be *El Jefe* to everyone else, but Charlie knew Petra called the shots behind the scenes.

After Charlie wrapped up his visits, he debated whether to stay the night in Veracruz before driving to Roy Lee's place in Villa Rica. Veracruz was perhaps his favorite city in Mexico and certainly one of the most interesting. On the surface, the decaying buildings, overgrown gardens, and cracked sidewalks suggested a dying port town with a Graham Greene-esque tropical decadence, but the place pulsed with life. Outdoor cafes and restaurants were always busy, and energetic street vendors never seemed to lack for customers. You could stand still in any section of the city and hear marimba or *jarocho* music percolating through the humid air.

As much as he wanted to linger in the city or at least drop by the Gran Café del Portal off the *zócalo* and enjoy a couple of coffee and milk *lecheros*, Charlie knew he needed to hit the road again. There was a chance Augie might have stopped at Roy Lee's Villa Rica compound and fallen in with the lotus-eaters who dwelt there. If there was one place on Earth where you could completely lose track of time—or simply not give a shit about it—it was Roy Lee's place. It had happened to Charlie more than once there, and he could easily imagine it happening to Augie, too.

Halfway to Villa Rica, all traffic on Hwy. 180 stopped due to a horrific accident, closing the highway and backing up cars for miles. A curious motorist who had left his car to investigate told Charlie the crack-up involved a gasoline tanker, a local taxi, and a truckload of chickens. Rather than wait for the god-awful mess to clear, Charlie decided to find a nearby hotel and spend the night. He wasn't picky and figured he should probably rest up before he saw Roy Lee, anyway. Keeping up with Roy Lee required stamina.

——

CHAPTER 13

"Everyone cries at first."

Augie wiped his eyes with the back of his hand and looked over at the short *mestizo* working beside him. "You speak English?" he asked him.

The man looked around to make sure the foreman wasn't nearby. "My name is Victor."

Augie learned that Victor had lived in Atlanta for six years, working in a kitchen. The restaurant was called The Cracker Barrel; had he ever heard of it?

Augie nodded. "Where are you from?"

"El Salvador."

Augie tossed a handful of pogies into a container and Victor shook his head. "No, those don't go there; they go over there." He pointed to one of a dozen metal buckets scattered around the deck. "If Gordo—he is the big one, the *capataz*—if he sees you putting fish in the wrong bucket, he will beat you."

Augie grimaced as he rose from the wooden Coke case he'd been sitting on. The welts, cuts, and bruises on his body were still raw from the beating the captain had given him the day before, not to mention that he was unbearably thirsty and hungry. He relocated the finfish he'd just thrown into the crab bucket.

The work seemed pointless to him—and endless. He had been allowed to sleep only once, in a cramped space near the storage holds and only for a short time. The rest of the time he'd been forced to sort one load of fish after another. As soon as he and the other laborers finished icing down one catch—each category of fish went into its own fifty-gallon plastic barrel—they'd winch in the trawl nets and fill the deck again.

As a boy, he had worked on one of Uncle Charlie's shrimp boats, and they had always tried to keep the by-catch to a minimum since it had no commercial value. What they did catch they simply raked back into the sea. For that reason, they only trawled at night, when they were less likely to fill their nets with "trash fish." But on this god-forsaken boat, Augie realized they trawled around the clock, catching and keeping almost everything they pulled up.

"What do they *do* with this shit?" Augie asked.

Victor shrugged. "I don't know. But someone must buy it. A big boat comes around every week or so and picks up what we have caught. We give them our barrels of fish; they give us ice, fuel, and food."

At the mention of food, Augie looked up. "When do we eat again?"

Victor grinned. "The cup of fish soup you ate eight hours ago? That was it for the day. Sometimes they give us a tortilla, too."

Augie blinked back the tears. "I don't think I can make it, Victor."

Victor shook his head. "You will be surprised how hard it is to die . . . unless, of course, the captain decides to kill you." He used his culling stick to rake another pile of forage fish toward him. "I thought I would die many times, but here I am, still alive. It will get better." He gave Augie a sad smile. "But not much."

Augie studied his new friend. Victor appeared older than he, but it was difficult to tell how much older. He had long, unkempt hair, and his skin was baked coffee brown, striped here and there by lighter-colored scars, probably put there by the captain's cable whip. One of his fingers was missing, and Augie noticed a large boil or lesion on one of his knees. "How long have you been here?" he asked him.

"On this boat? Six months. At sea?" Victor thought for a moment, calculating. "Two years, three months, twenty-eight days."

"Without ever seeing land?" Augie couldn't believe it.

"Without ever seeing land. I've been traded three different times to three different boats . . . and had three different captains. This one is not the worst."

At that moment, it was all Augie could do to keep from throwing himself overboard. Two days on this boat was unbearable, much less two years. In his nearly hallucinatory state of fatigue, he felt as though he'd shed his old life like a snake's skin. There had only ever been the ocean, the blistering sun, the pain, and the thirst.

——

Sometime late in the night—he had no idea of the time—Augie and a few of the laborers were sent below deck to a cramped, fetid storage hold strung with hammocks. Augie rolled into the first empty hammock he found and fell immediately asleep. In what seemed like only moments later, he bolted upright to the sound of an air horn blasting down into the hatch.

He looked at Victor with alarm.

"More fish," said Victor.

Topside, he watched as they winched the bulging trawl nets onto the boat and dumped the contents. Shrimp, squid, crabs, and all types of fish, large and small, spread out over the deck, shimmering under the bright floodlights—all of it to be sorted, iced, and stored. How had Victor endured this for two years, three months, and twenty-eight days? Augie couldn't get the numbers out of his head.

Victor's story was different from Augie's, but it was just as awful. He had left Atlanta and returned to El Salvador to attend his father's funeral. On his way back, while riding on top of *La Bestia*, one of the long freight trains that carried so many migrants and refugees through Mexico, he was set upon by gangs and delivered to a broker in Tampico. The next thing he knew, he belonged to the pitiless master of a filthy fishing boat in the Gulf of Mexico.

But somehow, he hadn't given up.

"One day I will escape from all this," he told Augie. "And I expect God will punish the men who put me here."

Augie learned that some of the laborers had signed on for the job willingly. They had been promised safe passage to *El Norte*—as soon as they worked off the "fee" the captain charged to take them there. But once they boarded, they found themselves trapped in his world with his rules. The captain docked their pay if they were sick or injured. Their account was charged for cigarettes, food, and soda pop. Their debt increased if they dropped a tool into the Gulf or wanted to buy rubber boots or a windbreaker for the cold. Pretty soon they owed more than they could ever hope to repay. They effectively became indentured servants for as long as they lived.

Other unlucky bastards were shanghaied like Augie—lured into a bar or a dark alley and drugged or beaten unconscious before they were put onto the boat. Augie had noticed scars across their backs, too, and also on their faces.

He wondered if those men had tried to reason with the captain, too, a mistake he would think about twice before repeating. Earlier that morning, Augie had waited until Gordo turned his back, and then he had gone straight to the wheelhouse, where, in English and broken Spanish, he explained to the captain that there had been a terrible mistake. He was an American citizen. Powerful, influential people were undoubtedly searching for him even as he spoke. Return him to port right away and he'd tell the authorities it had just been a misunderstanding—a case of mistaken identity.

The captain unsnapped his pistol, but he didn't pull it out, and he listened to the story with what Augie mistakenly thought was interest but was really a kind of cold-blooded amusement. *Should he shoot the kid in the head and toss him overboard as a warning to the rest of the crew?* he wondered idly. He'd already flogged him. Maybe he should do it again, but this time rub salt in the wounds?

But before Augie could finish his plea, Gordo came up from behind and hit him so hard that he collapsed like an empty oyster sack.

The captain yawned. "Put him back to work as soon as he comes to," he ordered.

——

CHAPTER 14

Raul reached Tampico too late to meet with Guillermo Ramirez, the Port of Tampico harbormaster, so he spent the night at a Best Western on the outskirts of the city. Pouring himself a vodka from the minibar, he sat on the edge of the bed and made his nightly call to Rosie. He dreaded these conversations, the equivalent of an oilman's dry hole. *No, they hadn't found Augie. Yes, he was sure their son would turn up. He didn't know if Augie was okay, but he hoped so. No, that didn't mean he wasn't okay. He would see Guillermo tomorrow. Yes, maybe he could help.*

Outside the hotel window, sirens wailed as ambulances shuttled in and out of the hospital across the street. It would be a long, noisy night, but at least the hotel was safe. As far as he was concerned, the further he stayed from the city center, the better.

There was a time when he would have enjoyed staying in the *zona historica*, preferably at a hotel near the plaza. In better days, Raul, and sometimes even Rosie, would meet Guillermo and his wife, Clara, for drinks and dinner at a downtown restaurant. They'd stroll around the Plaza de la Libertad, and Clara would point out the French-inspired buildings with their intricate wrought-iron balconies and art nouveau flourishes. Back then the city seemed both easygoing and energetic at the same time, and the locals liked to say Tampico was the New Orleans of Mexico.

The drug trade ruined all that. The cartels grew more and more powerful until, ultimately, they were able to flaunt their power whenever and wherever they wanted. Kidnappings and extortion became commonplace. Shootings and killings increased. And in 2007, when rival cartels went to war with each other for control of Tamaulipas, the soul of the city died. Many of the distinctive buildings near the plaza were now abandoned, with graffiti disfiguring the once bright-colored walls, and trees and vines growing through the caved-in roofs and broken windows.

Tampiqueños wryly observed that their city did indeed bear a resemblance to New Orleans—right after Katrina. The local economy all but collapsed, and anybody with means to relocate to safer environs did. With Raul's help, Guillermo and Clara Ramirez purchased a second home in Corpus Christi. Guillermo called the purchase "an insurance policy."

Raul met Guillermo in 1995, the year that Tampico and Corpus paired up as International Sister-Cities and their respective mayors proclaimed a "new era of cultural, commercial, and technical exchange." Raul and Rosie had been part of an inaugural city-sponsored commercial junket that flew them to Tampico to mingle with local businessmen and politicians. At a banquet held in the historic Customs House on the docks, they happened to share a table with the Ramirezes, and the two couples really hit it off. They had kept up with each other ever since, even staying in each other's homes on occasion. Their kids were similar in age—Augie had taken Guillermo's son, Eduardo, fishing in Aransas Bay the last time they'd visited.

The visits had become less frequent the last few years, but Raul still considered Guillermo a close friend, and he looked forward to seeing him again, even under the circumstances. He was one of the few Mexicans on the Gulf Coast he felt he could trust.

CHAPTER 15

Charlie woke to the sound of waves breaking on the Playa de Chachalacas. He threw off the damp sheet and inhaled the pungent smell of the tropics: salt water, rotting seaweed, mildew, and something sweet. Frangipani maybe? He'd read that the Aztecs made potions from the flower to protect their warriors against lethargy, but Charlie never felt the need to try it. He believed a little lethargy was good for a man, even for a warrior.

He put his hands behind his head and watched the ceiling fan spin lazily from the ceiling, pondering whether or not to take a run on the beach before he showered. Maybe another time, he decided. He swung his feet onto the tile floor and went to the bathroom to run the shower. The hot water worked, but not the cold, and soon the entire room was filled with steam. His little beachfront motel might not have air conditioning or a television, but it was damn sure proud of its hot water. Hand-painted across the building façade in four-foot letters was *Hotel Yoli—¡Con Agua Caliente!*

Charlie checked his cell phone—still no coverage—and then dressed and walked outside in search of breakfast. He chose an open-air restaurant with a nice view of the beach. While he sipped the strong black coffee and waited for the bowl of fresh ceviche he had ordered (the waiter said the fish had been caught that very hour), the little town slowly came to life. A few delivery trucks rolled down the stone-paved streets, creaking under their loads. Roosters crowed, and a solitary bell clanged away in the church tower. A *lechero* and his donkey clopped by with cans of fresh milk, followed by a knife-sharpener who announced his approach with a high-pitched whistle.

Beachside, a man planted umbrellas in the sand and put out lounge chairs for tourists who might or might not show up that day. A vendor pedaled by on a covered three-wheeled cart piled high with sunhats, plastic buckets, floats, and cheap sunglasses. At the Río Actopan delta, local fishermen cast their throw nets into the river current.

Chachalacas was like a hundred other villages along the Mexican Gulf Coast—peaceful, humble, relatively unspoiled, but also dirt poor and somewhat shabby. So far, the area hadn't been overrun with planned communities and all-inclusive resorts. Charlie hoped it never would be.

Although it pissed Raul off to no end, Charlie had done his best to acquaint Augie with the region and its distinctive funkiness. He still harbored the faint hope that Augie might be holed up in some tiny off-the-grid beach town like Chachalacas with a beautiful woman— eating, drinking, fucking . . . completely oblivious to time and the outside world. Charlie had gone down that carnal rabbit hole before, but he hadn't had parents to fret over him back home like Augie did. Even if the kid had been cavorting with a pack of Mexican TV weather girls, he would've found a way to call home by now.

The thought roused Charlie to finish his breakfast as quickly as he could so he could hit the road. He still had a job to do, and he promised himself not to forget it as he drove his car to Roy Lee Rowlett's wanton pleasure palace in Villa Rica.

Jobs, responsibility, and best-laid plans had a way of falling by the wayside where Roy Lee was concerned. So did sobriety, good judgment, girlfriends and/or wives, and all manner of good intentions.

Before Roy Lee hit it big, Charlie had guided him on multiple fishing expeditions up and down the Coastal Bend. The two men became good friends, united in their fondness for fishing, good bourbon, country music, and a life outlook largely dictated by whimsy.

In the beginning, Roy Lee Rowlett and His Cowboy Outfit played in dive bars and bingo halls, struggling to pay expenses and hoping to move up the record charts with their rowdy Texas-centric anthems that made most of what was coming out of Nashville sound like chamber music. Roy Lee finally made it big with "Dusty's Last Ride," a tear-jerking ballad about an aging rodeo cowboy who is run over by a semi-truck full of cows en route to a packing plant. It went triple platinum. "Damn thing would have made John Wayne cry," wrote one critic.

The hit would make Roy Lee rich, and when his first big royalty check arrived, two ex-wives showed up on the doorstep fifteen minutes after the mailman, hands out. "You ain't never seen a tarpon hit a lure as fast," Roy Lee told Charlie.

Before "Dusty," Roy Lee and his band had never had the disposable income to indulge most of their vices, but once the hits started coming, they let it rip. A typical backstage deli tray at a Roy Lee show consisted of cocaine, Lone Star Beer, eight-thousand-dollar-an-ounce polio weed, tequila, and assorted pharmaceuticals that Roy Lee lumped under the catchall category of "go-fast." Gonzo journalist Hunter S. Thompson once spent two weeks on the road with Roy Lee and His Cowboy Outfit working on a story for *Rolling Stone*. He came away drained and shaken, muttering about six months' sleep and all the charitable works he meant to undertake once the trembles stopped.

"You know how you know you've gone too far?" Roy Lee once said to Charlie. "It's when you look over your shoulder and go, 'Yeah . . . that was prob'ly it back there.'"

Royalties from "Dusty's Last Ride" and a mess of other hits paid for Roy Lee's forty-two-foot Hatteras yacht and his Mexican getaway compound near the small seaside town of Villa Rica, fifty miles north of Veracruz. Roy Lee said he chose the spot because he liked the fishing, but Charlie suspected it was because Villa Rica was a great place to hide from the record label scumbags, outraged girlfriends, and process servers who often pursued him.

Not that Roy Lee had much of a clue or even cared, but the area had a rich and fabled history. It bordered an ancient Totonac Indian temple and burial ground. It was also a stone's throw from the spot where Hernán Cortes and his Spanish conquistadors first landed on the American continent in 1519 and went on to irrevocably fuck over an entire civilization.

As Charlie turned off Highway 180 and began grinding his rental car up the narrow road that led to the compound, he marveled at the fact that he and Roy were still friends at all, given their short and inglorious business history.

Many years ago, Roy Lee talked Charlie into investing a good chunk of his money in a musical show that Roy Lee planned to take all the way to Broadway. *Send in the Rodeo Clowns* was conceived as "a cowboy singer's life, loves, and journey to semi-wisdom in three acts." Charlie, as co-co-producer, wrote the checks and hung around backstage through blocking, rehearsals, re-writes, screaming hissy-fit hysterics, meltdown auditions, and all the other karmic mayhem that attends any theater production from grade school plays in the cafeteria to The Old Vic.

But this play went above and beyond. Way beyond. Leading ladies came and went, often in the course of the same day. One incident regarding a musical difference of opinion led to members of Roy Lee's own band beating the shit out of their boss on stage. Ubiquitous stockpiles of booze and dope added their own chemical dementia to the scene. Charlie watched in horror as his investment of many dollars grew little snow-white dove wings and fluttered away.

On the night of the play's premiere at the stately Grand Opera House in Galveston, Roy Lee got drunk before the curtain rose, whereupon he forgot the words to the opening musical number and fell backwards into the drum kit. Shortly after, he announced to his patrons, fans, and colleagues that he, Roy Lee Rowlett, no longer felt moved by the theatrical Muse and was off to seek new inspiration in Mexico.

And that's where Charlie found him now, sitting in the kitchen of the main house drinking black coffee and asking Charlie again what month it was.

"March . . . unless you're using the Aztec calendar."

Roy Lee's eyes widened. "March? Really?"

"Yep."

Charlie waited patiently for his friend to emerge from his dormant state. He'd learned you couldn't rush the process. At the moment, things were quiet at Roy Lee's little Shangri-La. Through the window, Charlie saw a handful of other, smaller bungalows tucked back into green areas to ensure maximum privacy. Roy Lee was no fool. He made the cottages freely available to politicos, high-ranking police officials, and other well-connected mexicanos as a hideaway for them and their mistresses. The arrangement insulated Roy Lee from the inevitable bureaucracy and petty hassles that came with being an ex-pat in Mexico. But if anyone was in residence at the moment, they were lying low.

Over Roy Lee's shoulder, Charlie admired the infinity pool that gave a sweeping view down the hillside to the ocean. He noticed a television half-submerged in the water.

"What's up with the TV, Roy Lee?"

Roy Lee looked up at the television floating placidly in the blue chlorinated water as though seeing it for the first time. *"Downton Abbey,"* he said, shaking his head. "I couldn't stop watching it, man. And then last night, *right in the middle of season six,* the TV stopped workin'. Just up and quit. It pissed me off, I guess."

Charlie was trying to process that little tidbit when a girl in a string bikini strolled into the kitchen. "Hidy," she said, offering her hand. "I'm Claudette."

"Morning," said Charlie. She blew a kiss in Roy Lee's direction and sauntered to the counter to pour herself a glass of fresh-squeezed orange juice.

Charlie cocked an eyebrow. Roy Lee shrugged his shoulders.

"It ain't what you think, Charlie. She's got a master's in archeology. She's down here poking around some of the ruins we got in the jungle out back. I gave her a place to stay, and that's it. Believe me, I got all the ex-wives I can stand. But I got to admit, for a Ph.D. candidate, that girl's ass is a thing of beauty."

Claudette turned around. "Why, thank you, Roy Lee . . . . And for a washed-up country singer, you've got some fine-looking Mesoamerican ruins." She drained her orange juice and exited through the sliding glass doors towards the pool.

Charlie laughed. "Ouch."

Roy Lee shrugged. "Obviously, she's too quick for me."

There was a splash and then a shout. "Roy Lee! How am I supposed to do my laps with a TV in the pool?"

Roy Lee put down his coffee mug. "Be right back." He reached into a drawer beside the oven and yanked out a pistol approximately the size of a loaf of Wonder Bread. He stalked outside and Charlie heard two loud bangs and one female scream followed by any number of colorful expletives. The TV set, thoroughly perforated, sank to the bottom.

Roy Lee came back in, smelling of cordite. "So can *you* fill me in on what happened on *Downton Abbey?*" he asked.

CHAPTER 16

Guillermo and Raul had exchanged emails earlier that morning. Unfortunately, Guillermo had meetings all day and asked if Raul could come by late that afternoon, so Raul spent most of the day methodically visiting Sweetwater Marine customers along the river.

He learned nothing new. Yes, Augie had called on them last week. No, he didn't say where he was going next. And oh, by the way, the kid was doing a really great job taking care of them. Any other time, Raul would have been beaming with pride at the comments he heard, but he was so worried about his son that he rushed through one meeting and moved onto the next one as quickly as he could.

Raul felt no emotional connection to the city itself and never had, even though he had actually lived in Tampico once. When he was a boy, his mother would leave him with relatives for months at a time while she did her morally ambiguous work on the border, until one day she didn't return—killed in a car wreck they told him—and Raul took it upon himself to emigrate to Texas, specifically Fulton, where he was told his father lived. So at thirteen years of age, he set off for the Lone Star State the only way he knew how—he walked.

Once settled, he never tried to contact his grandparents again, or any other member of the de la Rosa family for that matter. As far as he knew, they'd never tried to find him, either. After his dad disappeared at sea, Charlie became his legal guardian, and Raul rarely mentioned that he had been born in Mexico.

The Port Administration Building was located on the banks of the Pánuco River in the old part of town. Raul always thought that the art-deco building looked out of place next to the turn-of-the-century red brick Customs House. Someone told him it was supposed to resemble the prow of an ocean liner, but for the life of him, Raul couldn't see it.

After sitting in the waiting room for half an hour, Raul watched Guillermo Ramirez emerge from his office. He was tall for a Mexican and bore a striking resemblance to ex-presidente Vicente Fox.

"¡Raulito!" He gripped Raul's hand, released it, and then gave him the traditional *abrazo:* a big hug, two firm slaps on the back, repeat the handshake.

"*Hola, Memo,* how have you been?" said Raul in greeting.

"It is so good to see you! Come into my office. Can I get you something to drink?"

"Sure, Memo. Some water would be good." Raul knew that Guillermo liked to use English when he visited him in his office, both to show off his fluency and to acknowledge his American friend's special status.

Guillermo had a few words with his secretary and then invited Raul into his spacious office. "Sit down, sit down," he said, pointing to a leather chair across from his big desk. Raul took a seat, and Guillermo sat casually on the edge of the desk. "So you are down here pushing your marine products again? I thought Augie was working Mexico for you now."

Raul suddenly realized he hadn't told Guillermo that Augie was missing. "I should've mentioned it in the emails I sent you, Memo, but I'm down here looking for him. He never checked in after his business trip last week."

Guillermo's cheerful expression vanished. "He was in Tampico?"

Raul nodded and described what he knew and what he didn't know about Augie's trip. Guillermo listened closely and grew increasingly agitated as Raul talked.

"This concerns me, Charlie," he said as he paced around the office. "Your son, he has never done this before? He has never forgotten to call you?"

"For a day or two, sure—you know how teenagers are—but never five days."

Guillermo nodded. "Yes, Eduardo is the same. It drives Clara crazy when he forgets. But other than that, they are sensible boys. Have you checked the hospitals? Could he have been in a traffic accident?"

Raul felt his stomach tighten. That possibility had occurred to him. "Check *which* hospital, Memo? There are hundreds of hospitals and emergency clinics between Matamoros and Veracruz. If he were in one, he still would have contacted us. Or someone would have." *Even if he had been killed,* he thought grimly.

"But no one has called?"

"No."

"Not the U.S. embassy, not the consulate?"

"No, neither. Besides, the Mexican authorities handle missing persons in their districts. And we don't have any idea where he is or what district to contact."

"You are checking in regularly with your office and your home?"

"Yes, of course. Several times a day."

Raul knew what calls Guillermo was really asking about. If kidnappers had abducted Augie, it followed that they would contact his relatives to demand a ransom. If the families couldn't pay (or even if they could), the kidnappers would then contact the victim's business office. American corporations were often willing to pay good money for valuable employees. For the kidnappers, it was strictly business, and the sooner they extorted their money, the sooner they could move on to their next target.

"No one has called, Memo," Raul added.

Guillermo turned and stood at the window with his hands clasped behind his back, looking out at the Pánuco River and the busy port. Neither man spoke for some time, and it seemed to Raul that his friend was deep in thought.

"Let me make some calls," Guillermo said without turning around.

Raul waited for him to say something else and, when he didn't, he cleared his throat to break the silence. "Okay, Guillermo. That would be helpful. I appreciate it."

The harbormaster came around the table and opened the office door. At first Raul thought he was going to ask his secretary something, but when he saw his friend looking at him expectantly, he realized he was showing him out. Raul stood up slowly, wondering why their meeting had ended so unceremoniously.

"Do you have another meeting to go to, Guillermo?"

"No, no . . . well, yes I do have something . . . a conference call with the *Director de Aduanas*. I had forgotten that he was going to call me at," Guillermo glanced at his watch, "at seven-thirty."

"What about the phone calls *you* were going to make? I could wait outside until your conference call is over?" If Guillermo knew people who might help him locate Augie, Raul wanted to follow up on those leads right away.

"I will make the calls. It will take a little time, but I promise you I will make them." He put his hand on Raul's shoulder and looked him in the eye. "Don't worry. We will find Augie. Give me a day or two."

"A day or two?"

"Yes, like I said, I will need a little time. Some of the contacts are in other port offices, which are closed now, and there are people in . . . in law enforcement who are not so easy to reach."

Raul sighed. What the hell had gotten into his friend? "Okay, Memo. While you're doing that, I guess I'll head down to Tuxpan. I'm supposed to meet my uncle there tomorrow. But if I need to come back here, I'll do it right away."

"You are going there tonight?"

Raul noticed the troubled look on his friend's face. Guillermo's anxiety was worrisome, but Raul had passed the point of caution and was willing to take chances—like making the three-and-a half-hour drive to Tuxpan at night. "Don't worry, Memo. I'll be careful."

Before Raul stepped onto the elevator, Guillermo Ramirez, *Capitán de Puerto*, pressed one of his calling cards into his hand. It was embossed on heavy cardstock and had the Tampico Port Authority seal on it.

"Keep this with you in case you . . . in case you need it."

"Sure, Guillermo," said Raul, taking the card. "Thanks."

———

Lights illuminated the long cable-stayed bridge that carried Raul over the Pánuco River and away from Tampico. On the dark road to Tuxpan, he puzzled over his friend's reaction to Augie's disappearance. Either Guillermo assumed the worse (Raul had been guilty of the same), or he knew something he didn't want to share. And what kind of people, exactly, was he going to call?

Two hours outside of Tuxpan, Raul had to slow to a stop at a police roadblock set up on an unmarked, three-way intersection near a village named Tamiahua. A feeble streetlight revealed a pair of patrol vehicles parked at angles across the mouth of the intersection. Raul squinted to read the official logos on the side of their blue-painted pickup trucks and then he studied the uniforms of the two men approaching him. Both of them had their flashlights out, and one of them carried an AR-15. The two policemen looked legitimate, but he knew that that didn't necessarily mean they were the good guys. And why didn't they have their emergency lights on?

As he rolled down his window to speak to them, he took note of the narrow ditches bordering both sides of the road and also the fenced grass pastures beyond—not enough space for him to turn his car around if circumstances required him to bolt.

"*Buenas noches, señor,*" said one of the policemen. He shined his flashlight though the window, and Raul had to cover his eyes with his hand.

He wondered whether he should speak to the cop in Spanish or English. "What is the problem, officer?" he asked in English. Sometimes it was better to play the dumb American.

While one policeman kept his light on Raul, the other flashed the interior of the car.

"Has there been an accident?" Bad wrecks happened all the time on Mexico's rundown country roads, especially at night, and if a crash had blocked the motorway ahead, then this intersection would be the logical place to redirect traffic.

The policeman nodded. "Yes, an accident."

Raul saw highlights in his rearview mirror as another car pulled up behind him. Neither policeman so much as glanced at it.

"Can I pass through . . . to Tuxpan?"

The policeman looked over at one of the *patrullas* and gave whoever was inside a brief nod. "Yes, we give you an escort around."

One of the patrol vehicles maneuvered around in front of Raul's car with its wheels turned onto the dark road that led to Tamiahua and the Gulf, while the other vehicles in front and back of him continued to block his escape routes.

"*Siga la patrulla,*" said the cop at Raul's window. "You follow."

Raul's hands gripped the steering wheel. If he followed the cop car down that empty side road, he would be at their mercy. He was pretty sure they were going to rob him or worse. He could ram the truck blocking the road in front of him and try and make a run for it, but then there would be three armed, extremely pissed off state cops out to get him.

"*Siga la patrulla,*" the cop repeated more forcefully. He waved his flashlight forward.

"I don't understand," said Raul, stalling for time. He stared straight ahead, fighting to control his fear while he considered his options. Then he noticed something odd about the decals on the side of the police truck.

POLICÍA TAMAULIPAS, DIVICION FUERZA RURAL it read.

The fake cops had misspelled the fake names on their fake cop cars. *División* should be spelled with an "s" not a "c," and they'd completely forgotten the accent mark over the "o." *Ignorant bastards,* thought Raul.

"I have an idea," he said to the man in the cop uniform.

His "idea" was to give the thieves all the money in his wallet and hope that the bribe—the *donation* to their police fund—would satisfy them, and they would let him go. He reached slowly into his pocket, making sure they could follow his hands, and then made a show of pulling out his billfold. When he opened it up to get the cash, Guillermo Ramirez's business card fell out. Acting on instinct, he handed the card to the man at his window.

The man read the card carefully and then looked over at the other truck. "*Espera,*" he said. "Wait." He walked over to the bogus police truck and handed the card through the window, standing nearby while his accomplice studied the card and talked on his radio.

Raul watched and waited. *What the hell was going on?*

Minutes passed and finally the cop returned with Guillermo's card and handed it back to him. "The accident has cleared," he said. "You can go now."

Raul's pulse quickened as the pickup truck blocking the road to Tuxpan backed up and sped away toward Tamiahua, soon followed by the other two vehicles. He sat alone for a moment in the quiet, deserted intersection, watching their taillights disappear into the night.

Raul rolled up his window, glanced around, and then drove away, slowly at first, and then as fast as his car would go. An hour later, he was holed up in a room at the Tuxpan Holiday Inn with the curtains closed and the door locked and bolted, still shaken from his close call with the highwaymen. He really wanted a drink, but that would require that he leave the sanctuary of his hotel room. He sat up long into the night thinking about what had happened, what it might mean, and what he would do next.

CHAPTER 17

After six days on the shrimp trawler, Augie saw another fishing boat heading their way, and his hopes were momentarily lifted. He made up his mind that he would jump ship and swim for the vessel if it came close enough and if he got half a chance.

His anticipation was short-lived.

"I know that boat," said Victor. "Our captain has done business with them before."

"What do you mean, 'done business with them'?" asked Augie, catching his friend's dark tone.

Victor continued mending the trawl net that was spread across his lap. "Do you know how to swim?" he asked.

"Yes."

"Don't let them know that you do."

"What? Why?"

They stopped talking when Gordo, the big foreman, looked back at them and glared. The other boat approached and Augie studied it carefully. It was larger than the trawler he was on, and instead of outriggers on each side, it had one long boom projecting from the mast. The *El Dorado*—the name was hand-painted across the bow—slowed and stopped about sixty or seventy yards away.

"Sardine boat," said Victor. They use the *redes de cerco* to catch the fish. I think you call them bag nets, or something like that.

"Purse seines?"

"Yeah, that's it.

Augie knew that a small fleet of sardine boats worked out of the East Texas and Louisiana ports. Up until now, he had only paid attention to them as a blip on Charlie's shrimp boat radar, something to be avoided when they were night trawling. Augie had learned that the Mexicans used the word *sardina* or *sardinita* for any and all bait fish: for pogies or menhaden, for glass minnows, herring, anchovies, pilchards, scad, and for any juvenile fish.

"Do you know the captain of that boat, Victor? Can he be reasoned with, or is he. . . ?" Augie wasn't sure what word to use.

Victor supplied the word for him. "Is he a criminal?"

"Yes, is he a criminal?"

"If he is a friend of our captain, then, yes, I think he probably is."

The two boats held their positions, and Augie heard but did not understand snatches of conversation on the radios as the captains communicated.

"What are they talking about?"

Victor shook his head. "I can't tell. I think they are negotiating."

Augie had difficulty following the informal, profanity-laced Spanish used by the captains and the crew. His parents never spoke Spanish at the house, and the Spanish he heard on the boat was definitely not what he'd been taught in high school or even what he heard when he talked to his Mexican customers. Moreover, his exhaustion had put him on the edge of delirium. Since he'd left the engine room, he'd either been hunched over a never-ending pile of live fish—sorting them into baskets and icing them down in barrels—or cleaning the boat before the next load arrived. Gordo always seemed to be watching, yelling at him, or beating him whenever he made a mistake.

The captain took sadistic pleasure in assigning Augie the worst tasks on the vessel—including swabbing the backside of the boat, which served as the latrine for everyone except the captain. When Augie removed the copious deposits of shit oozing down the transom, he discovered the boat's name, *Mañana*, stenciled across the back.

There was a pause in the crackling chatter on the radio while the captain yelled something to his foreman. Gordo motioned to Augie, calling him to the port-side gunwale.

"Me?" ask Augie.

"*¡Ven acá, cabrón!*" he yelled.

Augie rose and walked hesitantly toward Gordo, who slapped the rail to indicate he wanted him to stand on top of it.

"*¡Súbete! Súbete aquí,*" he yelled.

Augie climbed onto the rail, holding the outrigger for balance. Across the water he could see the other captain looking at him through a pair of binoculars, and he could hear the sardine boat's diesel engines laboring to hold position in the strong Gulf current. A dozen crew-members stood at the rail of *El Dorado,* all of them watching Augie.

The captains kept on jabbering while Augie waited. He felt like he was being evaluated by buyers at a livestock auction. The radio chatter ceased, and the captain stuck his head out of the wheelhouse window, barking an order at Gordo.

When Augie turned around, the big Mexican was wearing the same malevolent grin he'd worn after Augie's first beating. "You know how to swim?"

"Swim?" asked Augie.

"Bye-bye *pendejo,*" said Gordo, and shoved him overboard.

Augie plunged into the Gulf and then surfaced, choking on salt water. The current moved him quickly, and he briefly looked back at the *Mañana.* Most of the crew watched him without emotion—a conditioned response to the cruelty they witnessed on the boat every day—but Victor thrust an emphatic, open-fingered palm toward him, a gesture Augie chose to remember as both a defiant farewell and a kind of salute.

The captain of the *Mañana* watched the kid swim like crazy for the *El Dorado.* He hoped the little fuck made it. If he didn't, the deal was off, and he wouldn't get the fifteen thousand pesos they'd agreed upon. The skipper on the *El Dorado* had insisted on testing the boy's swimming skills before he paid one *centavo,* and now the bastard was backing up against the current to make it harder for the swimmer to reach his boat. *What an asshole,* thought the captain.

When the kid finally did reach the *El Dorado,* the crew helped him up the ladder and the sardine boat captain grinned, giving his counterpart a thumbs-up signal. Augie collapsed on the deck, gasping for breath.

The captain of the *Mañana* rubbed his fingers with his thumb, indicating that it was time to pay up. A package was tied to the end of a rope and tossed toward the *Mañana.* As the line floated by, a crewman grabbed it with a boat hook and ran the package up to the wheelhouse so the money could be counted. When the captain was satisfied, he picked up the radio, said *adiós* to the *El Dorado* skipper, and yelled for Gordo to crank up the diesels. It was time to get back to work.

The captain was glad to be rid of the troublesome kid with the too-intelligent eyes. Besides, he had begun to wonder if his crazy story about being an American citizen was true—he certainly didn't talk or act like the ignorant peasants who usually wound up in his service. If he was an Americano, thought the captain, he didn't want anything to do with him. The kid had brought a good price, and he could buy two more workers with the money he'd made on him. He made a mental note to radio his supplier in Tuxpan to place the order.

━━━━

CHAPTER 18

First things first, thought Charlie. *No sudden moves.* He made his way slowly, carefully into the kitchen, past the bodies sprawled on couches, chairs and, needless to say, the floor. The big living room looked like the aftermath of a zombie massacre.

The sun had just begun to rise, but Charlie did not dare gaze in its direction. He was fairly certain that if he did, his eyeballs would explode, or he would burst into flames like a vampire who had stayed up past his bedtime.

What time had he gone to bed? *Had* he gone to bed? It scarcely mattered.

A chef's knife protruded from a wooden cabinet door beside the refrigerator. Three paring knives, a meat cleaver, a pair of scissors, a switchblade, and even some garden shears were stuck in the door, as well. Charlie vaguely remembered a knife-throwing contest, just one more festive sideshow in Roy Lee's chronically batshit-crazy life.

Searching through the food-and-drink detritus that covered the granite kitchen island, Charlie miraculously uncovered an intact watermelon (several less fortunate fruits had been sacrificed to target practice out by the pool). He pulled the chef's knife out of the door and sliced the melon in half, scooping out the juicy innards and cutting them into ragged chunks, and then chopped up a guava, a mango, and a papaya. Prying a half-full bottle of Havana Club rum from Roy Lee's inert fist, he poured a double shot into the melon hull, added some fistfuls of fruit, a bottle of Topo Chico, and a tray of ice cubes. He gave it all a stir with the knife blade and then stuck his head inside and began slurping.

Many years ago back in Fulton, Charlie and Johnny had called this particular homeopathic hangover treatment a *casuela*. Rum—or tequila or vodka or gin—was the actual curative. The fruit was merely a bow toward nutritional virtue. Mostly it was to keep Charlie and Johnny from feeling like total sacks of shit after a long night of drinking. Sometimes it even worked.

Blowing rum and soda bubbles, Charlie came up for air.

Hanging with Roy Lee had been hard enough when Charlie was in his prime, hanging out-wise. Now, as a bona fide senior citizen, he was supposed to know better. Wasn't he? The lyrics to an old Guy Clark song came to mind: *You'd of thought there's less fools in this world.*

Still, the night hadn't been a total waste of brain cells. Roy Lee had told him that some folks were due in who might be able to shed light on a missing gringo. "Charlie, I promise you, if your liver can stand it, it'll be worth your while to stay another night."

Charlie wondered who these "folks" might be. Villa Rica was the Casablanca of this part of the Mexican coast; a wild assortment came and went under a sort of mutually-agreed ceasefire. Politicos and narcos, smugglers and cops, could and did mingle with film actors, ballplayers, models, and musicians.

When Charlie mentioned to Roy Lee that he was supposed to meet Raul in Tuxpan, Roy Lee had insisted otherwise.

"Naw, man, you gotta stick around. Besides, we're gonna celebrate Texas Independence Day tomorrow. Party on the beach, drink a toast to ol' Travis and Crockett and Bowie and them . . . remember the Alamo."

"Texas Independence Day was over a week ago, Roy Lee."

"Well, don't tell the Mexicans."

Claudette, or, as Charlie thought of her, the half-naked archeologist, came tip-toeing through the wreckage, wearing a pair of cut-offs and a T-shirt that said, "Throw me the idol, I'll throw you the whip."

She whispered "Good morning" to Charlie and looked around. "Four billion years of evolution, and this is what it's come to?"

Charlie grabbed a beer out of a cooler, both to tamp down his hangover and to keep the buzz going, and followed her outside.

While he lazed in the shade of the portal, Claudette stripped off her clothes, slipped into the pool, and commenced swimming her laps, placid and unhurried. She looked sleek as an otter, happy as a clam, and naked as a jaybird.

He heard the shuffle of bare feet behind him and turned and beheld Roy Lee, who fumbled to light a fresh cigarette.

"How you doing, Roy Lee?"

"Depends on who you ask," he muttered blearily.

He sank into a leather *equipale* chair and pinched his nose. "I feel like one of them Mayan ballplayers who wound up on the losing side. The winners shot goals with their heads."

"I told you to go to bed."

"You ain't earned the right to tell me when to go to bed." Roy Lee looked up and his hangdog expression brightened marginally. "Hey, there's ol' Claudette." Claudette paused in her Australian crawl, or whatever it was, long enough to wave. "She used to be an ex-ballet dancer," he said.

"Ramblin' Jack Elliott," Charlie replied. He and Roy Lee had spent many an idle hour waiting for the fish to bite and trying to stump each other with songwriters and lyrics.

"There's only two things in life, but I forget what they are," said Charlie.

"Aw, man, that's too easy—John Hiatt."

Charlie went inside and returned with a couple of beers. Various groans and moans began to resound as the night's survivors started the laborious task of greeting the day.

"You're gonna find your groove if it kills you, aren't you, Roy Lee? Y'all still planning to celebrate Texas Independence Day tonight?"

"Hell, yeah, we are. And I was serious about you sticking around. Like I said, there's a big shot or two coming who might have enough stroke to help us find your nephew. And there's someone else you'll wanna see, too. She was doing some business in Veracruz and asked if she could stop by."

"She?"

"Yep. When I told her you were coming here, she sounded so happy you'd have thought I bought her a new pickup truck. I guess that Sweetwater charm's lost on me."

"Thank God," said Charlie.

Raul called an hour later and told Charlie he was returning to Tampico to speak once again with his buddy at the harbormaster's office. "Things aren't adding up, Tío," he said. "I thought of some more questions to ask him. It would be better if I ask them face to face. I'll see you in Tuxpan tomorrow."

So Charlie decided to stay another night. Now the only decision he had to make was whether to go back to bed or keep drinking.

———

CHAPTER 19

Raul had his identification ready when he pulled up to the Port of Tampico security gate, but the guard waved him through without hesitation. Raul had tried calling Guillermo Ramirez several times that day to tell him they needed to talk, but his friend couldn't or wouldn't answer his cell phone. And each time he called the Port Authority landline, the secretary insisted her boss was in a meeting. Raul was plenty pissed when he finally got in to see the *Capitán de Puerto*.

Raul entered the lobby and found Guillermo standing by the door waiting for him.

"Come with me," he said.

No greeting, no apology. His friend's tone was so solemn, that Raul instantly feared the worst. "What has happened, Memo? Have they found Augie?"

Guillermo inclined his head toward the street. "Let's talk over lunch."

Raul followed as Guillermo walked briskly away from the Port Authority and onto a busy street that paralleled the river. Two blocks later they turned into a crowded market filled with food and produce stands, clothing kiosks, and stalls selling CDs and household items. The marketplace spanned an entire city block, and as they wound through a jumbled maze of interconnected tarp-covered passage-ways, Raul struggled to keep up.

At a small *torta* stand squeezed between a sugar cane vendor and a peddler who specialized in dried fish, Guillermo sat on a stool and directed Raul to do the same.

"What do you want to eat?" Guillermo asked.

"What the hell, Memo? I tried to contact you all day and—"

"Dos Cocas y un par de tortas de barda," Guillermo said to the old lady behind the counter. He turned to Raul. "If that's okay with you."

Raul took a deep breath. "Memo, what the hell is going on?"

"I'm sorry. It is not safe for us to talk at the office." He turned on his stool and began scanning the market. "Not about this, anyway."

Raul thought about asking Guillermo why the cloak-and-dagger shit, but he supposed he knew already. He'd thought about it a lot since he was held up on the road outside of Tamiahua the night before. The criminals who had intended to rob him had the wherewithal to procure phony cop cars, phony uniforms, real AR-15s, and a communication network sophisticated enough to contact leadership on a walkie-talkie from a remote location. Guillermo Ramirez had given him what amounted to a get-out-of-jail-free card, which meant the criminals either worked for him, or more likely, they both worked for the same organization. The fact that one of the cartels was powerful enough to monitor "private" Port Authority communications in one of Mexico's largest ports indicated just how far Tampico had fallen.

"How long have they had their hooks in you, Guillermo?"

The two men locked eyes. "It's not as simple as you think, Raul."

"No? Seems pretty simple to me. You either choose to collaborate or you choose not to. But you know what, *amigo?* I don't really care. I just want to know one thing: do you know where my son is?"

Guillermo's face sagged. "No. But I think I know what happened to him."

"What happened, Guillermo? Is he still alive?" When he hesitated, Raul grabbed his arm. "Talk, goddammit! Is . . .my. . . son . . . alive?"

"I don't know!"

The old woman glanced up from the *tortas* she was making and then quickly went back to work. Whatever quarrel the two English-speaking men had, she was sure she didn't want to know about it.

"You said you would make some calls. Who did you call?" When Guillermo didn't answer, Raul asked more forcefully. "Who?"

"People who might know," he answered.

"The kidnappers?"

"I don't know who they are. They are . . . contacts I have. I don't know their real names or what they do."

"They are in the cartel?"

Guillermo nodded hesitantly.

"And what did your *contacts* say?"

"They said they didn't have your son."

Raul closed his eyes and took a deep breath, not sure if that was good news or bad news. If they had him, he could pay the ransom and probably get him back. And at least he would know the score. But now he was back where he started. Augie was simply missing.

"But they did say," Guillermo continued, "that he might have been . . . taken."

Raul's head snapped around. "What do you mean, taken?"

"There is another thing the narcos do . . . that is not kidnapping for ransom, but is still kidnapping."

"Go on."

"Commercial fishing boats," Guillermo began, "have trouble finding laborers. Nobody wants to work on them anymore. The pay is too low, the work is too dangerous. There is better work in the cities or in the U.S. So the syndicate supplies men for the boats."

"How do they *supply* these men, Memo?"

The old woman put the sandwiches and the Cokes on the counter, but neither of the men took notice.

"Often they trick them with promises of money or passage to the U.S., but usually they simply drug them and put them on the boat."

"You think this is what happened to Augie?"

"I don't know for sure. But one of my contacts said he might have heard something about an American being taken . . . unintentionally."

"Where, Guillermo? Where did this happen? Was it here in Tampico?"

Guillermo shook his head. "No. I would've known about it. He says he thinks it was in Tuxpan."

Raul didn't miss the implication that Guillermo "would have known about it" if it had happened in Tampico. It meant that his friend knew it went on there and that he permitted it to happen. But as the information about his son's predicament sank in, he felt a tiny spark of hope. At least this was something he could understand.

"They can't keep someone on a boat forever," said Raul. "If Augie was forced to work on a trawler, the boat will have to return to port. And when it does, Charlie and I will be waiting. He's been out there what, six days?" Raul thought for a few seconds, "They will probably return next week, maybe as soon as this weekend. The boat will need fuel, ice, they will need to offload their catch."

Guillermo shook his head. "That's not how it works. These boats link up with supply boats out in the Gulf. They offload their catch to these vessels and get food and fuel in return. The fishing boats can stay offshore for months. Years even. And the unpaid crewmen effectively become forced labor. Slaves."

Slaves? Years at sea? Raul couldn't believe what he was hearing. "Your contact . . . he said the American was taken in Tuxpan?"

"That is what he said."

"Who do I talk to in Tuxpan? And how do I get in touch with him?" Guillermo didn't answer and Raul pressed harder. "Who, Memo? Tell me who."

"I don't know *who*, exactly. It would be a lieutenant in the organization."

"In the cartel?"

Guillermo nodded.

"And I can find this lieutenant in Tuxpan?"

"Yes."

"Tell me how. Tell me how to find him."

"I don't know . . . . You would look around the port first, since that is where he operates."

"What if you contact the harbormaster in Tuxpan? You must know him. Could he lead me to this guy?"

"I doubt it. And even if he could, he wouldn't dare. It would be a death sentence for him. These are the Zetas, Raul. You have no idea how dangerous these men are. They will kill you for looking at them wrong."

"What choice do I have, Memo? I have to go after my son."

Guillermo sighed deeply. "I know."

Raul watched his friend's face contort in shame and sadness. He suddenly realized what was at stake for him. As soon as Raul and Charlie began asking around Tuxpan for the kidnapped American, the Zetas would know where the information came from. Guillermo's calls to his contacts and Raul's visits to the Tampico Port Authority would be enough to connect the dots.

"What about your family, Memo?" Raul asked.

"I put them on a plane to Texas this morning. They will be safe in Corpus Christi. I will join them when I can."

"Why not now?"

"I have an important position here, Raul. I can't just walk away from it. Besides, we reap what we sow, is that the saying?"

"Maybe the cartel won't come after you."

Guillermo looked at him and shook his head.

"Maybe they won't find out. Maybe they won't know it was you." Even as Raul said it, he knew it wasn't possible.

Guillermo waved his hand in resignation. "They seem to know everything. They know we are friends. They have seen us together. And I have asked them too many questions already. I even offered to pay your son's ransom . . . . They will know."

Raul looked at his friend. He had offered his own money to get Augie back. It was a principled gesture, but it didn't absolve him of his corruption or of his complicity in the entire region's slide into lawlessness. What happened to Augie was not Augie's fault. He was in the wrong place at the wrong time—it was bad luck. But Guillermo?

"Memo? How could you let this happen to you?"

Guillermo smiled weakly. "Like I said, it is not as simple as you think. A man comes to your office and tells you you have a choice. We will pay you good money, he says, and all you have to do is look the other way when an unregistered ship goes in or out of your port. He tells you that you will ignore certain activities that might occur on your docks. It will be so easy you will hardly be aware of it. You can say no, of course—that is your choice. And then he says, oh, by the way, we know where you live and that you have a wife, a son, and a daughter, and here is where they go to school." Guillermo looked at Raul. *"Plata o plomo,* as they say. Silver or lead. So I chose the *plata,* and I took their money and used it to buy a house in Corpus Christi."

"Because you knew this day would come."

"Yes. And I am so terribly *sorry* it involved Augie."

Raul noticed that Guillermo's eyes had teared up. "Me too, Memo."

Raul stood up to leave, but before he walked away, his friend placed his hand on Raul's shoulder. "My family knows nothing of this problem I have with the cartel. When you and Augie return to Texas, will you look in on Clara and the kids if I am not there? Will you make sure they are okay?"

Raul covered Guillermo's hand with his own. "If that's the way it turns out, Memo, then of course, you can count on it."

"Thank you, my friend."

Raul took a couple of steps and then turned around. "Maybe you can reason with them."

Guillermo nodded and presented Raul with a brave smile. "Yeah, maybe I can reason with them."

But Raul could tell by the look in his eyes that he knew his days were numbered.

———

CHAPTER 20

Augie had hoped the sardine boat would be different from the floating sweatshop he'd been on before, and so far, it had proven to be so. When he finally reached the *El Dorado,* swimming almost to exhaustion against the strong current, the crew cheered and helped pull him over the rail. The Captain walked back to look him over and then ordered a young crewman to take him to the galley for food—a full plate of eggs, potatoes, and beans. Augie shoveled the food into his mouth as fast as he could, washing it down with a cold soda.

After he ate he was given a change of clothing and taken to his berth, one of a dozen hammocks strung across a low-ceilinged compartment below deck. A couple of men were stretched out in their hanging beds, snoring away. The young crewman grinned, pointed to a hammock, and mimed going to sleep. Augie gratefully accepted the offer, rolled into the mesh sling, and almost immediately fell into a deep, relatively untroubled sleep for the first time in over a week.

Around dusk he was shaken awake by the same kid who had shown him his bunk eight hours before. Augie observed him more carefully. He seemed friendly enough, smiling at him with a mouth full of crooked teeth. He was small, dark-skinned, and younger than Augie by five or six years at least. "Do you speak English?" Augie asked the kid. "¿Hablas Inglés?"

The boy didn't respond but continued grinning.

"What's your name? ¿Como te llamas?"

"Chango," he answered.

Monkey? After a few minutes of trying to engage him in conversation, Augie began to understand that Chango had some sort of mental impairment, and he wondered if the kid had joined the crew willingly or had been forced, or more likely, tricked onto the boat.

Augie asked Chango how long he had been on the sardine boat.

He shrugged and turned to leave. Augie shrugged, too, and followed the boy topside and into the galley.

"*Café caliente,*" said the boy, pointing to a pot on the burner, "*y un sándwich.*" Chango grabbed the cheese and jalapeño-filled *bolillo* (the last one on the plate) and handed it to Augie. "*Muy bueno.*"

While Augie ate his sandwich, Chango showed him around. He took pride in the job, but the tour was mostly a string of arbitrary one-word observations focused on whatever seemed to catch the boy's eye as he walked around. *Motores* (motors), *escalera* (ladder), *¡peligroso!* (dangerous!), *el baño* (the head), *el esquife* (the skiff). He pointed to the wheelhouse. "*Capitán,*" he whispered and then held up his index finger and wagged it. "*No entrar.*"

The *El Dorado* looked to be about a hundred and twenty feet long with three levels: below deck the engine room, sleeping quarters, and fish storage wells; at deck level the galley and mess; and on top, the wheelhouse and captain's quarters *(¡No entrar!)*. An old-fashioned crow's nest was perched atop the main mast.

From the galley rooftop, Augie watched the crew winch in the long nets and then maneuver them into piles on the back deck. He figured they had just finished sorting and storing the last haul of fish and were stacking the seine nets for the next one. None of the crew paid him much attention, and he wondered what his role would be on the boat. Would he be a crewman? A cook? A guest? No, strike that last one. He reminded himself that he'd been bought and paid for. He was just another piece of the ship's inventory.

The captain stuck his head out of the wheelhouse window and hollered something at Chango, who grinned at Augie and said "*Adiós.*" Then with astonishing speed and agility the kid scurried up the mast to the crow's nest, where he immediately began scanning the surrounding sea with a pair of binoculars.

"*Oye*," said the captain, to get Augie's attention. "*Tu nadas bien.*"

"I'm sorry, what?" said Augie, shaking his head that he didn't understand.

The captain stared at him a moment. "I say you swim good."

"Oh, right."

"You no speak Spanish?"

Augie rotated his hand, palm down, to indicate that his Spanish was so-so.

"Where you from?"

"Near Corpus Christi, Texas," Augie answered. "I am an American citizen."

The captain laughed and shook his head. "*¡Coño!* And I am from London." His laughter trailed off. "*Váyase, pendejo. Martín, el Martillo, te enseñará tu trabajo.*" Martín, "The Hammer," would show Augie what his work would be.

A dark, compact man with a square jaw and a full beard climbed up and spoke briefly with the captain. After the captain disappeared, Martín turned to Augie and looked him over. "*Vamanos*," he said.

Augie followed the Hammer down to the afterdeck to receive his first lessons in purse seining. Even though Martín spoke quickly, Augie understood most of it. Sweetwater Marine carried many of the items he talked about, and Augie had learned the lingo so he could sell the products in his new territory.

A seine-fishing "set" was fairly simple. When a large group of schooling *sardinas* was spotted, either by the sonar in the bridge or by Chango in the crow's nest, the *esquife* would run one end of a long rectangular net away from the mother ship and slowly encircle the fish. The net's cork line kept the top of the net floating on the water's surface, while the weighted chain line pulled the bottom of the net down to its maximum depth of about a hundred and twenty feet, creating a nylon mesh wall that circled the fish. Two cables were looped through steel rings, one through rings at the bottom of the net and one through the rings of the top net. When the schooling fish were completely surrounded, the winch pulled in the purse cable, much like an old-fashioned drawstring purse, closing the bottom of the net first, and then the top. Martín used a small try-net to demonstrate how the purse net closed.

"*¿Entiendes?*" he kept asking.

Augie nodded that he understood.

There were various booms, pulleys, and winches that Augie knew he'd have to familiarize himself with, but he figured he could handle it. He was glad he would have a job that required something more than just culling fish and crustaceans from giant piles and throwing them into buckets. And at least he wouldn't be washing crap off the back of the boat.

Additionally, the food was pretty good, and they served two meals a day instead of one. The skipper might not believe he was an American citizen (not yet, anyway), but he wasn't a sadistic prick like the previous captain. Yet Augie knew that none of that changed the fact that he was essentially still a prisoner—property of the *El Dorado* until the captain said otherwise.

Around dusk the crew ate their evening meal and then either slept, mended nets, or tidied the boat. Mostly, everyone just waited. Chango had been up on the masthead for hours, searching the Gulf for schooling fish. When Augie asked what he looked for, one of the crewmen said he looked for agitated patches of water where forage fish would be gorging on plankton, which in turn attracted larger predator fish that gorged on the forage fish. Flocks of seagulls usually swooped in soon after to pick up the scraps. In other words, he looked for feeding frenzies on the water.

It was an uneventful night, which was fine with Augie. As he began to regain some of his strength and equilibrium, he began to think about a strategy to free himself. He wondered who would be searching for him. His dad for sure, and probably his uncle Charlie, too. Both of them knew their way around Mexico, and eventually they would figure out a way to track him down, unless he could find his way to them first. The only problem was that Mexico lay at least a hundred miles beyond the blue-green horizon, maybe more. He might as well have been in outer space.

The absence of fish didn't seem to bother the crew much, but it put the captain in a foul mood, and Augie noticed that everyone avoided talking to him or even making eye contact whenever he walked by. Hardly any of the crew spoke to Augie, either, but gradually he learned that about half the men had hired onto the boat voluntarily, while the other half were either stuck there because they owed the captain money or because they had been forcibly recruited to work on the boat without pay, like himself. One laborer said that the *El Dorado* hadn't been to port in over a year and that only the skipper, first mate, and a few of the crew had taken any shore leave during that time. This worried Augie. Another man warned him never to cross the captain. "*Es un hombre brutal,*" he had told him.

No one seemed curious about Augie. They didn't ask where he came from, what it was like working on the *Mañana*, or even his name. It was as if they actively avoided getting to know him. *Well, so what,* thought Augie. He didn't plan on being around much longer anyway.

———

CHAPTER 21

Charlie finally got tired of waiting for Diputado Abrigo to pass out. Roy Lee had spiked the politico's Cuba Libra over an hour ago, after everyone had grown tired of his insults. From what Charlie could tell, the PGR official had a stick up his butt about the United States and everything about it: from the *yanqui* assholes at the DEA who presumed to tell him how to do his job, to the rich *gabacho* kids who consumed Mexican drugs and made his job harder. He even blamed American tourists for ruining his favorite beach resorts. He especially hated Texas. "Fuck the Dallas Cowboys," he had sneered, and several guests had to restrain Roy Lee from shoving the windbag into the fire pit.

His latest tirade was against snobby *apretada* American women, comments which Charlie suspected had to do with Claudette the archeologist's emphatic rejection of his sexual advances earlier that night. (She had thrown a drink in his face). When Abrigo began slurring his words, Charlie thought he might be fading, but then another hour passed and the blowhard somehow managed to find a second wind. Charlie's mood soured. *Of all the Texas Independence parties in all the world, this pendejo has to walk into mine.*

The party had seemed promising at first. Roy Lee's cooks had built a big beach fire and were spit-roasting a couple of young goats over the flames and steaming banana leaf-wrapped redfish under the coals. The crowd was eclectic, as always. In addition to the household guests, Roy Lee's fishing guide was there, as was his boat captain. A Mexican Formula One driver and his beautiful girlfriend had come, along with a wanna-be bad boy actor from Los Angeles and a photography professor from Rice University who was working on a coffee table book about Mesoamerican ruins. Roy Lee was holding forth in typical fashion, a bottle of Pappy Van Winkle bourbon in one hand and a six-inch long Austin Torpedo of *primo mota* in the other. He wore a Texas flag wrapped around his head like a turban.

The party began going downhill when Diputado Abrigo arrived with some of his PGR cronies. Roy Lee had promised Charlie that a powerful politico would visit the compound that night—someone who would surely be able to help him find Augie. But when Charlie saw that it was Marcos Abrigo, his spirits fell. Roy Lee was apologetic.

"Sorry, man. I didn't know you'd already met him. To be honest, he kind of invited himself. Said somebody loaned him a jet and a pilot, so he figured he'd take it on a little joy ride."

Charlie had no doubt the jet was the Beechcraft that belonged to Alberto and Petra. The diputado evidently felt entitled to abuse their generosity.

"I figured, hey, he's a big shot at the PGR, and those are the guys who investigate kidnappings." When Charlie jerked his head around Roy Lee held up his hands. "Of course, I'm not saying Augie was kidnapped."

Charlie sighed. "It's okay, Roy. I've considered that possibility, too. I just hadn't wanted to admit it."

Laughter erupted around the campfire as Abrigo told another offensive joke. Roy Lee shook his head. "I mean, I knew the guy was an asshole, but I didn't know he was a total asshole."

Charlie left the bonfire behind, jumped into one of the golf carts from Roy Lee's golf cart stable, and rode it up the winding road to Quiahuiztlan. The site was an official *zona arqueológica* and theoretically closed to the public after hours, but like many of Mexico's historic ruins, it was about as well-guarded as a kid's lemonade stand. In the dark, Charlie had to walk carefully up the short trail to get to his favorite look-out—an east-facing burial site that overlooked Roy Lee's rancho, the tiny village of Villa Rica, and the Gulf of Mexico.

The pre-Colombian site included remnants of wall fortifications, residences, pyramids, and a ball court. What stood out, though, were the little tombs, almost a hundred of them grouped around the site, each one shaped like a miniature temple. A massive basalt peak, El Cerro de Metates, loomed above the former Totonac stronghold, its sheer cliffs carving out a sharp silhouette against the stars. The official sign at the road entrance said that Mesoamericans had occupied the site for almost a thousand years and that the hilltop city once sheltered sixteen thousand souls. But it was deserted now except for Charlie, the tombs, and the bones of the dead.

He sat on the ledge of one of the tiny temples and listened to the silence. Below he could see the lamplights of Roy Lee's main house and the porch lights to the cabañas that were scattered around his property. In Villa Rica some of the houses were still awake, but most were dark. Fishing villages generally turned in early on this stretch of the Mexican coast. The men would be out on the water before dawn, ready for work. At the end of the pueblo, where the beach edged up against a small inland bay, Charlie spotted the bonfire and wondered if, by now, Abrigo was lying face down in the sand. If so, he sincerely hoped the high tide would carry him out to sea.

Charlie sat quietly and tried clear his head so he could focus on Augie. The sum total of his five days of searching had yielded precisely *nada*. He hoped Raul was having better luck. Tomorrow they would meet in Tuxpan, and he would have to tell his nephew that his investigative trip to Camp Roy Lee Rowlett had been a complete waste of time.

Charlie sat up straight when he saw headlights climbing the hill. A security guard, maybe? When he realized the lights belonged to another golf cart, he supposed others might've decided to break away from Roy Lee's party like he had and were heading up for some peace and quiet or possibly a piece of something else. More than a few amorous couples had snuck up there to make love among the ruins.

Charlie waited and soon heard voices and footsteps in the dark.

"Charlie? You up here?"

"Over here, Roy Lee."

A beam of a light sliced through the darkness, and Charlie could hear Roy Lee cursing as he tripped over the sacred sticks and stones of Quiahuiztlan.

"I swear to God, Charlie, if I break my neck I'm gonna dedicate my entire afterlife to fucking with you."

"I'm over here."

Roy Lee walked around to the front of the tomb and shined his flashlight directly into Charlie's eyes, blinding him temporarily. "Jesus, Roy, the light."

"You ran away, you bastard, but I figured I'd find you up here."

"I see you got tired of listening to the diputado, too."

"God, that sumbitch would not shut up. I think it's only him and a few of his buddies left at the campfire now. Everyone else fled."

Charlie noticed Roy Lee was slurring his words a little; he'd noticed it more and more over the last few years.

"No," Roy Lee continued, "the only reason I came up here was because she asked me to."

"What are you talking about, Roy?"

Roy Lee chuckled and then Charlie smelled a familiar perfume. Someone sat down beside him on the stone ledge.

"Hello, Carlito."

Charlie's eyes still hadn't adjusted to the dark, but there was no mistaking who sat next to him. "Hello, Sasha." He tried to sound cool and composed, as though it were nothing to have a ghost from his past suddenly materialize in an ancient Totonac ruin at midnight. But his heart was racing.

"Are you up here contemplating your afterlife, too?"

"Something like that." He felt around for her hand in the dark. She leaned over and kissed him on the cheek.

"I've missed you, Charlie Sweetwater."

Sasha Vasiliki's voice was low, soft, and self-assured. It thrilled Charlie to hear it again. He had known her for twenty-five years, initially because of his friendship with her parents, and afterwards as something more. The daughter of a spirited Greek father and an elegant, artistic Ukrainian mother, Sasha had inherited all of her parents' best traits. Charlie met Yannis Vasiliki, Sasha's father, when he used Yannis's boat brokerage firm to acquire a new shrimp boat. Subsequently, he became good friends with both Yannis and his wife, Inga. Ten years later, they both died in a terrible car crash in Russia, leaving the business to their only daughter.

"I've missed you, too, Sasha. What have you been up to?"

"She's been kicking ass, that's what she's been up to," said Roy Lee. "She's still the baddest maritime repo-lady in the business. People call her when normal channels fail. She basically steals their boat back for them. True adventure shit. You wouldn't believe some of the schemes she's used."

But Charlie already knew. One of Yannis's side businesses had been to repossess stolen, detained, or financially defaulted boats— "Anywhere on the seven seas" was his motto. Most of the boats were seized by crooked local officials in search of bribes and kickbacks. Yannis considered himself to be working on the side of the angels. Plus, it indulged his adventurous side, and he became exceptionally good at it.

When Sasha took over, it was the part of the business she enjoyed the most. She used any ploy she could muster to slip onto a seized vessel and then haul ass for international waters.

In Haiti, she'd hired a local witch doctor to spook a port authority official. Nothing scares a corrupt bureaucrat like a voodoo zombie curse. Once, she'd posed as a Greek shipping tycoon's daughter to gain entrée to a yacht which had been impounded in Nassau. Another time, she'd hired a samba band she'd seen performing in the local Junkanoo festival to parade through the Jamaican customs house while she cut an anchor line on a seized catamaran and slipped away. It wasn't all *Mission Impossible* shit, though. Usually a combination of bribes, hookers, and booze did the trick, especially in the case of night watchmen or low-level harbor patrol grunts. But the closer to the edge the repo job came, the more she liked it.

Charlie had used her to find his Chinese junk, the *Li Shishi*, after it was stolen from Montego Bay while Charlie was on a "nature" tour in the Jamaican interior. She rescued the junk a week later in Miragoâne, a port city in Haiti notorious for pirates and smugglers. When she delivered it back to Charlie, she surprised him by accepting his invitation to sail with him to the Cayman Islands, just the two of them—an intimate ten-day trip he was sure he'd never forget. They had vowed to keep in touch, but Sasha bounced all over the Gulf and Caribbean in the course of her job, and Charlie returned to Texas to focus on his own growing business. Looking at her now in the starlight, Charlie wondered how he'd let her get away.

"So business is good, is it?" asked Charlie.

"I keep busy. Roy Lee tells me you're down to one boat these days. Please tell me that your shrimp boat and junk were stolen, so I can get them back for you."

"No, nothing so dramatic. I sold 'em. End of an era."

"Charlie's going all ascetic on us," Roy Lee interjected. "I'm surprised he hasn't shaved his head."

"Is that right, Carlito?"

"I'm not a full-on monk yet, but I have attempted to uh, simplify things a little. How about you? Is it all work, all the time?"

"Yeah, pretty much."

"Well, you're still about two-thirds pirate, just like your daddy."

"That's what I tell her," added Roy Lee. "As a matter of fact, one of her biggest clients *is* a pirate."

Sasha leaned toward Charlie and whispered. "Roy Lee embellishes."

Charlie whispered back. "I know."

"I don't embellish," Roy Lee complained. "I flat-out lie sometimes, but I don't embellish. Sasha not only *works* with actual no-shit pirates, she *cavorts* with them."

"That true, Sasha?"

She sighed. "First of all, Roy Lee is drunk. Second of all, I don't think he even knows what 'cavorts' means. He's referring to one visitor, a client from Cuba, who I brought to Villa Rica for a couple of days last year."

"His name is Mal de Ojo," said Roy Lee. "Who else but a pirate would have a name like that."

Sasha laughed. "Yep, you got me there, Roy. With a name like that, he's definitely got to be a pirate. See what I mean, Charlie?"

"So what's the deal with this Señor Ojo? Are you two . . . together?" Charlie had to admit he felt a tinge of jealousy.

"He's another maritime extraction expert, from Cienfuegos, in Cuba. We help each other out sometimes, that's all."

"Is that why you're in Mexico? You're working?"

"I was. I returned a fishing boat to a client in Veracruz yesterday. After I finished the job, I called Roy to say hello and he told me that you'd be here, so I decided to drop by and surprise you."

"Well, I'm surprised."

"I'm trying to talk her into going fishing this weekend," said Roy Lee. "I'm taking out the Hatteras."

"What about you, Charlie? Are you planning to stick around?" she asked.

"I have to meet my nephew in Tuxpan tomorrow."

"Work?"

"No."

"No? Then you should stay here and play. Although I have to say, this is a funny place for you to be if you're trying to become a monk."

Sasha noted the uneasy silence that followed. "Speak up, boys. Is something wrong?"

Roy Lee cleared his throat. "I'll think I'll leave y'all to talk. Can you two share a cart back to the house?"

"Sure, no problem," Sasha answered hesitantly, catching Roy Lee's somber tone. "So what's going on, Charlie?"

———

CHAPTER 22

Martín the Hammer ordered Augie to help mend the seine nets on the back deck of the *El Dorado*. Augie sat apart from the other crewmen, working alone and wondering why they continued to treat him like a pariah. They went about their duties quietly and seldom looked his way.

The afternoon was hot and unseasonably calm for March, and sweat ran down Augie's face as he fumbled with his net repair tool—an eight-inch plastic netting shuttle wrapped with tarred twine. Martín had given it to him earlier that morning along with a ball cap and a filthy work shirt that reeked of another man's sweat. Augie stretched his back and scanned the horizon for activity—nothing but water in all directions. He hadn't seen another boat since he'd come aboard. Nor had he or anyone else seen any fish, which seemed to have put the captain in a foul mood. Augie figured it was one of the reasons everyone was so subdued, afraid they might attract his attention.

Chango interrupted the silence when he began calling out from the crow's nest.

"¡Capitán!" he hollered, drawing out the last syllable. *"¡Capitaaan!"*

The captain came out and looked up at Chango to see where he was pointing. He reentered the wheelhouse, and soon they were speeding eastward as the crew hustled to ready the nets. Augie found himself caught up in the excitement, but each time he tried to help, the crewmen waved him off; he was only getting in their way.

He ran to the bow and searched the Gulf for signs of the fish, eventually spotting a circle of convulsed water about half as large as a football field. On such a calm day, the frothy, churning water stood in stark contrast to the placid surface of the surrounding sea. As the boat neared its target, seagulls arrived as well and began dive-bombing the shoal of fish.

The boat slowed and Augie returned to the galley roof, watching the men untie the motorized skiff at the back of the boat. In the wheelhouse the captain took note of the current, the waves, and the wind direction as he maneuvered into position, and then he stepped outside and shouted the order to drop the skiff. It slid off the stern and splashed into the water. Two men boarded the skiff, took one end of the long seine net, and then motored away at an angle. The folds of net began to tumble off the back deck of the *El Dorado*. As the seine played out, the skiff made a wide circle around the mass of forage fish, quickly surrounding them with a deep curtain of nylon mesh. When the boat rejoined the mother ship, the net was set, but the fish continued to feed, unaware that they had been surrounded.

While the skiff idled alongside the *El Dorado*, fishermen fastened the loose ends of the two purse cables to big hydraulic winches. The first winch rumbled as it reeled in the lower purse cable, slowly closing the bottom of the net. Crewmen guided the line by hand to make sure it wrapped evenly around the winch drum. It was tricky work and not all the men could still boast of ten fingers.

Augie watched as the crew worked quickly and quietly, careful not to alert the fish of their imminent capture. If spooked, the fish would begin searching for ways to escape and eventually they would realize they could swim under the trap. Some of the crew rushed portside when a large mass of fish moved to one side of the net, driven there by the tuna, mackerel, jack crevalle, and other predator fish trying to eat them. Augie could feel the mood on deck changing, the tension ratchetting up. At first he didn't understand the reason, but then he noticed that a thin silvery stream of fish had begun to appear on the other side of the net. Martín looked anxiously at the captain.

When the captain saw the leak, he reacted quickly. "Tex-as!" he screamed. "*¡Ayúdales!*"

When Augie realized he was yelling at him, he wasn't sure what to do. The captain gestured emphatically for him to climb down and join the crew on the back deck. Augie descended the ladder, and Martín rushed over, grabbed his arm, and hurried him to the lee side of the boat where the skiff was idling alongside. Some men were lowering a portable gas-powered air compressor into the skiff, as well as a large coil of plastic hose. When Augie asked what was going on, Martín handed him a scuba mask and a pair of swim flippers.

"I don't understand," said Augie. "What do I do with these?"

The Hammer grinned. "Your work, *cabrón*."

As Martín guided Augie down into the skiff, Augie wondered what "work" he was expected to perform. At the last moment, Martín called for another crewman to join them in the skiff. "Hector! *Tu hablas inglés. Explicale lo que tiene que hacer.*" You speak English. Tell him what he needs to do.

Hector nodded and turned to Augie. "Put on the flippers and mask," he said in confident if somewhat accented English. "If you have rings, take them off. Anything shiny. We are going to repair the net."

The skiff and its four-man crew sped to the area where the escaping fish had been spotted. One of the men grabbed onto the cork line to hold the skiff in place. Frightened by the boat, the shoal of fish moved away, back to the center of the circle. Augie put on his flippers and spit in his mask. *So this is why they wanted a swimmer,* he thought. He slid into the water and looked down, seeing dark shapes cruising below. The fish were too deep for him to make out what they were. *Ling? Billfish? he wondered. Sharks?*

"If the hole's too far down, I can't mend it," he said to Hector. "I can't hold my breath that long."

Hector handed him a netting shuttle. "Yes, you can."

The third crewman, a man Hector called Luis, pulled the cord on the air compressor, and it rumbled to life, and then he attached an end of the plastic hose to the compressor. Hector picked up the coil and put the loose end of the tube near Augie's face so he could feel the blowing air.

"See . . . air."

Augie looked at the hose. It was ordinary 3/4" clear vinyl tubing, the kind that could be found at any hardware store. "You can't be serious," he said.

"Clinch the end in your teeth, like this." Hector put the hose in his mouth. "Like a pipe. And whatever happens, do not lose it." He looked at Augie. "Got it?"

"Fuck, no, I don't got it! This is crazy. What if the rip in the net is a hundred feet deep?"

Martín and the captain were both yelling at them to get to it and hurry the hell up.

"You have to do it, Texas," said Hector.

"What if I don't?"

Hector's eyes widened for a brief moment. "Not good. Very bad . . . for you."

Augie pulled the mask over his face and Hector handed him the end of the tube. "Luis and I will try and keep the line untangled. Remember, do not lose the tube, or you will die."

Augie nodded, his heart racing. A large swell picked up the skiff and dropped it into the following trough. The little boat listed dangerously, increasing Augie's anxiety. If a wave engulfed the skiff, it would flood the generator and snuff out the motor, cutting off his air supply. Not to mention that the net was moving. He could hear the weights clanging together as the winch reeled in the chain line, collapsing the net.

"One other thing," said Hector. "When you come up, don't come up too fast . . . or you will get the . . . " he searched for the word, *"la enfermedad de descompresión."*

"The bends? Great." Augie took the hose and stuck it in his mouth.

"Good luck, Texas."

Augie took a deep breath before he went under, and he saw Hector do the same, as if he were the one about to submerge.

At first, Augie gagged and coughed at the constant flow of air being forced down his throat, but he quickly learned to moderate the intake, letting the excess air escape through the side of his mouth. The bright sunlight allowed him to see a long way underwater. Even so, when he looked down at the wall of net, it seemed endless—a semitransparent curtain that disappeared into the dark depths. He descended parallel to the net, swiveling his head side to side in search of the hole, trying to remember how deep Martín said the net was. *Thirty meters, was it? No, it was more. It was fifty meters deep. Shit. As deep as the Rockport water tower was tall.*

As Augie swam downward, his eyes bulged, and he had trouble equalizing the pressure in his ears. The water seemed filled with noise:

the hum of the skiff's outboard, the deep rumble of the *El Dorado's* big diesels, and the clanking of the metal purse rings as they collided with each other and against the boat's steel hull as the crew reeled in the net. The noise fed his fear and intensified his disorientation.

Augie's head jerked sideways as a barracuda flashed by in pursuit of a smaller fish. A moment later he saw a yellowfin tuna rocket past. The tuna appeared huge in the refracted light. Augie continued to descend until he finally discovered the hole—a four-foot rip almost midway down the net curtain. The loose fold of netting undulated with the current and he watched a small group of determined fish probe the area and then shoot through when the hole open up.

When Augie arrived at the tear, the bubbles from his hose spooked the fish back into the interior of the net. He had been gripping the air hose tightly with his hand, fearful that he might lose it, but then he realized he would need both hands to repair the net. He looked up at the cheap, flimsy tube that rose lazily to the surface, seventy feet up. *Some lifeline,* he thought. He found a solution by running the end of the breathing tube through the elastic strap of his mask and into his mouth, freeing his hands.

He worked steadily, wanting to finish as quickly as possible. The less time he was down there, the better. With the bottom of the seine pulling inward, the wall of the net began to incline, forcing Augie to expend more energy to hold himself in place opposite the hole. Occasionally, inside the net, he'd see a tuna or a kingfish swim by, probing the confines of the mysterious pen surrounding them. When they spotted Augie, they zipped away. He was also aware of larger fish *outside the net* passing below and behind him, and he hoped like hell no shark mistook him for prey. For reassurance, he glanced up at the skiff. It seemed so tiny, way up there.

Augie tried to focus on the task before him, but he wondered where the main school of forage fish had gone. He hadn't seen them since he'd submerged. Had they discovered that their corral had no bottom and escaped under the net? Was there another opening somewhere? God, he hoped not. Through the mesh he could see the bottom of the net now; it was almost closed. Soon there would be nowhere for the fish to go.

Augie had almost finished repairing the tear when he spotted the school—a huge shimmering mass of silvery fish that reflected the bright sunlight above. They moved through the water as one unit, with defined edges that held even as the shape shifted and changed.

Whether it was the bubbles from Augie's breathing tube or the realization that the net was collapsing, the baitfish seemed to panic all at once. The mass convulsed and briefly broke apart. Movement accelerated as the fish swam chaotically every which way. Suddenly, they re-formed into an enormous elongated sphere that resembled a bulging waterspout and then, a moment later, an overinflated football. Augie had heard about the phenomenon. It was a defensive maneuver to protect the school from predators. Tons of forage fish came together to form a dense impenetrable mass—a bait ball they called it—with tight contours that shifted and undulated slowly like a single organism.

Augie hurried to finish his task, glancing down frequently to make sure nothing was rising toward him from the dark depths. His work completed, he allowed himself to drift upward, using the side of the net to slow his ascent. He couldn't take his eyes off the bait ball. Dorado, bull sharks, thresher sharks, bluefin and skipjack tuna, even some sailfish, all made darting runs at the pulsating monolith, trying to penetrate its dense walls. As the predators nipped at the bait ball, Augie noticed the current carrying away clouds of blood and shredded flesh. He climbed faster. The torrent of chum would attract every shark in the area, and there was no telling what would happen in the ensuing feeding frenzy.

He could see the hull of the *El Dorado* now, a massive shadow looming above him. With the purse net closed, the fishermen began reeling in the cork line and soon the area inside the net was greatly reduced. Perhaps sensing this, the bait ball disintegrated, and the *sardinas* began to dart around frantically, many dying when they jammed themselves into the mesh openings trying to escape. It was a free-for-all now, every fish for himself.

When Augie surfaced, Hector was waiting for him. "Not so bad, eh, Texas?" he said from the skiff. Hector helped him in and then eyed him carefully. "How do you feel?"

"Tired."

"Any pains on your body?"

"A few."

"Show me where."

Augie pointed to his elbow and shoulder and Hector began massaging the areas vigorously. "Don't get the wrong idea, man," he said, smiling. "This is to remove the bubbles in the joints." He made Augie work the joints in his arms, legs, and shoulders and then massaged the areas where he still ached. Gradually the dull pain subsided.

"You did alright, Texas," said Hector. "Kept the captain from losing a lotta fish. Most of the crew was betting you don't survive the first dive."

"They were betting I'd die?"

Hector shrugged. "The last guy didn't make one week. That's why nobody wants to know you."

"What happened to the guy before me?"

"Don't know. Drowned, I guess. Or maybe a shark got him."

"Where are you from?" Augie asked as the skiff headed for the fishing boat.

"Mexico City. I was a waiter at the Maria Cristina Hotel. Do you know it?"

"No."

"Nice hotel. Lotta Americans stay there. I learned a lotta English." He sniffed and shook his head. "Then my cousin say, 'Come work with me in Houston. Make a whole lotta money.' So I go. Made it as far as Tampico when I go to the wrong bar with the wrong girl." Hector laughed bitterly. "So, I end up here instead."

"Have you tried to escape?"

"Once. But I don't do it again. Better to stay alive and wait."

"Wait for what?"

"I don't know. For my luck to change."

Luis manned the tiller and guided the skiff back to the *El Dorado*. When they climbed aboard the ship, the crew had already pulled in the excess net, concentrating the fish into a tight mass. Then they began the brailing process—scooping the fish out of the sea with a large mechanical bucket and dumping them into bins below. They had to work fast to refrigerate the fish before they died.

"The protein content goes down after they die," Hector explained. "Bring less money. With the captain, it is always about the money."

Afterwards, Augie helped with the cleanup, and he noticed a difference in everyone's attitude toward him. Luis shared a Coke with him. Even the men who lost money betting on his demise treated him with respect, like he was one of the crew now, like he was one of them.

Augie appreciated the recognition, but he had other plans. *The hell with waiting for my luck to change,* he told himself. *I'll make my own damn luck.*

CHAPTER 23

The lobby of the Tuxpan Holiday Inn reeked of hair spray. The local branch of the *Asociación de Cosmetólogos* was hosting its annual meeting there, and the hotel was teeming with beauticians. Raul sat on a lobby couch near the window, waiting impatiently for his uncle to arrive. He had said he'd be there by noon, but it was almost two o'clock and Charlie was still a no-show. He'd called his phone a dozen times, leaving increasingly aggravated messages. *Worse than a teenager,* thought Raul.

He thumbed distractedly through a tourist brochure about Tuxpan's *"famoso" Museo de la Amistad Mexico-Cuba.* But Raul didn't give a damn about Mexico's friendship with Cuba, or the revolutionary plot to overthrow Batista hatched fifty years ago by Fidel and Che in the house across the river, or their miserable ten-day voyage across the Gulf in their overloaded yacht. All Raul could think about was the information he'd received from Rockport. Judy Dang had called to tell him that the hotel Augie had stayed in in Tuxpan had finally run his credit card. Raul had written down the hotel's name and address, and it was burning a hole in his pocket.

A group of hairdressers sat down next to him and began chattering loudly about hair products, so Raul went outside, dialing Charlie's number as he walked. Unexpectedly, a woman picked up.

"*¿Bueno?*" she answered, with a distinct *gringa* accent.

"Who is this?" Raul demanded.

"Um, this is Claudette."

"Who?"

"Claudette, the archeologist. I think this is Charlie's phone."

"Is he there?"

Raul heard some springs squeaking and then footsteps.

"Nope," Claudette the archeologist replied. "Don't see him. Hey, if you run into him, will you tell him I've got his phone?"

Raul closed his eyes in exasperation. When he opened them, Charlie was driving his rental car through the hotel's porte-cochere, grinning at him from behind the wheel. Charlie rolled down his car window, and Raul handed him the phone without comment.

He took the phone with a perplexed look on his face. "Hello . . . ."

Raul walked away. He wasn't interested in hearing about his uncle's evident debauchery.

With the phone to his ear, Charlie turned off the car engine and ran inside, the parking valet guy chasing after him and begging for the keys so he could move the automobile, which, Raul noticed, completely blocked the entrance. Charlie returned a few minutes later, drying his face with his shirttail.

"Had to pee," he said. "Sorry I'm a little late. I kinda lost track of time. And I, uh, somehow misplaced my phone."

Raul launched straight into the news he'd received from Guillermo Ramirez the night before in Tampico and from Judy in Rockport a couple of hours ago.

Charlie jumped back into the rental car without a word, and Raul ran around to the passenger door. Soon they were speeding down Avenida Independencia toward the Laguna de Tampamachoco and the Tres Reyes Hotel.

Raul wondered if the navigation app on his phone was wrong when it instructed them to turn off the main avenue onto a narrow dirt street, but the hotel was right where the map said it would be, a whitewashed U-shaped building with a high cinderblock wall surrounding it. Shards of broken glass glittered atop the wall, a deterrent to thieves. They passed under the arched gateway and drove slowly into the courtyard.

"There's his truck," said Raul, his heartbeat accelerating. Seeing the truck gave him hope—it was the first tangible evidence he'd seen since

Augie had disappeared. But that feeling quickly gave way to dread. The truck probably hadn't moved all week. If his son was indeed on a fishing boat, he might be hundreds of miles away.

Charlie pulled up to the small office and they went inside. A plump, middle-aged woman came through a curtained door. "*Buenas tardes.*"

"*Buenas tardes,*" answered Raul. He pulled out Augie's picture and explained why they were there and why they needed to get into Augie's room, but no matter how much he explained, the woman stubbornly refused to give up the key. Raul turned to Charlie in disbelief. "I think she's waiting for a bribe."

Charlie shrugged and left the office.

When Raul pulled out a handful of twenties, the woman became more cooperative. She took the bills, counted them out, and with a sigh, retrieved the key from a desk drawer under the counter.

"*Sígame, por favor,*" she said.

Raul followed her to a first floor room directly in front of Augie's truck, but the door was already open wide. The hotel manager began complaining loudly when she saw the hinge hanging loose on the splintered door jamb. "*¡Válgame Dios!*"

"What the hell, Charlie?" said Raul. "I just paid this woman a hundred bucks to let us in."

"She can apply it to the door repair," said Charlie. He pointed to the room safe and demanded that the woman open it.

She folded her arms defiantly. While Raul pleaded with her, reminding her how urgent it was that they get into the *caja fuerte,* Charlie went into the closet and began tugging on heavy metal box, trying to rip it off the wall. Raul looked at the woman with concern and told her that his uncle was *muy loco* and there was no telling what the crazy bastard might do next.

She glanced at Charlie, thinking the old man *did* seem crazy. And she was right. Charlie hadn't received the news about Augie's kidnapping well. He was ready to take a sledge hammer to the place if she didn't act quickly.

The manager went to the *caja fuerte* and entered the default code. The door opened, and she stepped back to let the crazy Americano look inside.

Charlie scooped up the contents and dumped them on the bed. "Gracias," he said to the lady, staring at her until she left the room. "Okay," he said to Raul. "Let's see what we got: passport, truck keys, wristwatch, billfold with driver's license, and a cell phone," Charlie tried to turn on the phone, "with a dead battery."

Raul rummaged through Augie's suitcase, found the charger, and plugged in the phone. While the phone charged, he went through Augie's things, checking the pockets of his pants and shirts and then carefully, lovingly, refolding them and placing them on the bed. Charlie watched and noticed Raul's eyes tearing up. To give his nephew some privacy, he grabbed the truck keys and went outside.

"I'm gonna look around."

Charlie unlocked Augie's truck and examined the cab. He found an empty Coke can, a *Guia Roji* book of Mexican road maps, a pair of cheap sunglasses, and a Stevie Ray Vaughan CD case. Under the camper shell were the boxes of sample product he'd brought for the trip, along with two fishing rods and a surfboard. When Charlie saw those he almost lost it, and then he became angry, thinking of the revenge and mayhem he would inflict on whoever had taken his nephew.

The sun was low, pitching cool shadows across the courtyard. Clouds drifting offshore began to glow as if illuminated from within. When Augie was in high school, he often dropped by Rattlesnake Point to drink beer with Charlie and watch the sunset. It had been their little secret, a family ritual they shared together.

We have to find him, Charlie told himself. He leaned against the truck and tried to think it through. *Augie was going to spend the night at this hotel. Did they abduct him here, or somewhere else? If he left the hotel on his own, where would he go? What would he do?*

Charlie studied the courtyard. The place seemed almost vacant. A few cars, some live chickens, a dog sleeping under a jacaranda tree. The small restaurant inside the compound seemed permanently closed. In the shadow of the gate, he noticed an old man sitting in a straight back chair—the night watchman and gatekeeper, Charlie supposed. He strolled over as casually as he could manage.

"*Buenas tardes, señor,*" he said.

The man said good evening back, and they chatted a few minutes about the weather until Charlie steered the conversation around to Augie. He pulled the folded sheet of paper from his back pocket and asked the old man if he'd seen the boy in the photograph. Two minutes later Charlie burst into the hotel room.

"Let's go," he said to Raul. "I think I know where Augie went."

They locked up the truck and walked the short distance to the Ribera del Pescador, the narrow potholed lane that followed the Tampamachoco Lagoon for about a mile and then dead-ended at the water's edge. Over a dozen restaurants and bars lined the road, plus a few fish markets and grocery stands. The hotel gatekeeper told them this was where he had steered Augie, *"para la comida muy rica."*

It was nearing suppertime, and they realized Augie might have walked past these very shops and restaurants at the same hour one week ago. *Which spot would he have chosen?* Charlie asked himself. *Which would I choose?*

The street was bustling and cheerful, the cantinas and cafes beginning to fill with the evening's customers. Raul proposed they begin at the first restaurant and work their way down from there, showing Augie's picture as they went.

Charlie shook his head. "I don't know, Raul. Kidnapping is narco business. People aren't gonna want to cooperate. They'll be too scared."

Raul didn't argue, remembering how skittish the waiters and restaurant owners in Playa Bagdad had been when he searched for his son there. "What else can we do? We can't ask the police to help us."

"You're right about that. Maybe we'll get lucky. Why don't you take one side of the street, I'll take the other. Describe Augie, but play it cool, like we're supposed to meet him for dinner. Keep the photo in your pocket. If they believe we're looking for a missing person, they'll clam up."

Charlie kept his voice low and even, but inside he seethed with frustration. He could almost feel Augie's presence around him. His adventurous, happy-go-lucky nephew had strolled down this very street only seven days ago—out for a cold beer and a bite to eat, completely unaware of the danger ahead of him. Charlie gazed at the throng of people on the Ribera. Dozens of them had probably seen Augie. At least a few of them would remember him. At least one of them would know what had happened to him.

———

CHAPTER 24

The captain of the *El Dorado* must have spotted a shoal of fish on the sonar, because he instructed Martín to shout the command for the crew to mobilize and prepare for the next set. Chango happily climbed to his spot in the crow's-nest to begin searching the Gulf for visual confirmation, while another sailor manned a powerful spotlight mounted above the wheelhouse.

After the terror of the first set earlier that morning, Augie was apprehensive, but he figured at least he wouldn't be asked to dive again. Not in the dark. He'd been observing Martín and the captain most of the day, watching their patterns, taking note of when they ate their meals, when they napped, when they used the head. Several times he observed that the bridge had been left unoccupied and unlocked. Routine led to complacency.

Augie figured the marine radio on the *El Dorado* would be similar to the one on his uncle Charlie's shrimp boat—a standard VHF with a range of about sixty miles. If he could sneak into the wheelhouse without being detected, he could send out a general distress signal and hope like hell someone picked it up.

When Chango yelled down that he had spotted fish, the captain sped toward the spot. Up ahead, Augie saw a circular patch of sea that seemed to be lit from underneath. He wondered if he was the only one seeing the strange phenomena.

"*Es una bola de fuego,*" said Hector, who was standing behind him also watching the luminous circle. "They call it a ball of fire. The organisms that the fish eat, the *plancton,* they light up when they are attacked. I don't know why."

The boat slowed and Hector hustled to the afterdeck to man his station. Augie followed but was told to stand well away from the nets, especially when the skiff began dragging them off the boat.

"If you get tangled, we cannot stop them," said Hector. "They will pull you out to sea."

Augie nodded and stationed himself on the port side of the boat, well away from the cables, machinery, and nets. The spot also allowed him to watch both the back deck and the wheelhouse, and he hoped the distraction of the set might give him the chance to slip in and use the radio. The captain positioned the boat adjacent to the glowing shoal of fish and instructed Martín to release the skiff.

Before the skiff left to encircle the fish, the captain turned off all lights except for a dim deck light—just enough light for the men to work the winches and guide the nets, but not so bright that the fish would see the net as it surrounded them. Except for the *bola de fuego,* the Gulf appeared pitch-black under the moonless sky. Overhead, the radiant smear of stars that formed the Milky Way seemed to reflect the eerie, glowing mass of sea life under the water's surface.

When the skiff returned and the fish corral was set, Martín gave the order to begin tightening the purse line. Twenty minutes later, the encircling net was closed, and the captain turned on a bright flood-light that lit up the entire back half of the boat. Augie scooted into the shadows and waited. Just as he had done that morning, the captain left the pilothouse to go back and evaluate the haul. He remained portside, giving orders and directing the men. As the outer nets were pulled in, the circle tightened and the fish became more and more concentrated. Martín began working alongside the men, and it appeared to Augie that tonight the captain was taking over his first mate's responsibilities.

"It's now or never," said Augie under his breath. He hunched over as he darted to the starboard side of the boat where the door to the wheelhouse was located. As soon as he placed his hand on the door lever, he heard the captain's booming voice.

"*¡Maldición! . . . . ¡Tex-as!*"

Augie jerked his head around to see if he'd been discovered, but he saw no one. *How could the captain have known?*

He heard voices and then a moment later, Hector appeared beside him. "The captain want to see you," he said. *"Now."* But before they left, Hector gave Augie a pointed look. "If he catches you in there, he will kill you."

Augie returned to the back deck, and when the captain saw him he pulled him portside where the captured fish were churning the water below. On one side of the boiling mass of baitfish, a feeding frenzy was going on as larger fish attacked smaller fish that were escaping the net.

"Mira dónde están escapando," the captain said excitedly, pointing to the escaping fish. *"La red se enredó con la linea. Hay que repararlo."*

Augie looked at the captain and shook his head, although he understood him well enough. *Are you fucking crazy?* he thought to himself. No way he was going into that dark dangerous water to repair a fouled line.

The captain must have thought Augie didn't understand because he cursed in frustration and asked Hector to translate.

"He say the fish are escaping because the net is tangled with the float line," said Hector. "He want you to go into the water and fix the problem."

Augie glanced down at the frantic mass of fish inside the net and then at the large glistening shapes that swarmed outside the net. Predator fish—tuna, mackerel, bonito—chased and devoured escaping forage fish with a fury that roiled the sea. In and around the area illuminated by the powerful floodlights, he also saw dorsal fins flashing and knifing the water's surface—rigid triangular fins that clearly belonged to sharks.

"Tell the captain I'm not doing it." It would be like jumping into a blender.

The captain didn't need a translator for that. He shook his head in frustration and then bull-rushed Augie, sending him flying over the gunwale.

Augie hit the water and seized up, almost incapacitated from the unexpected shock. He felt himself sinking, aware of furious movement around him but unable to move himself. Something bumped his leg and then brushed the small of his back. He continued to drift downward, dimly aware of the hull to one side of him and the seine net to the other. It became dark very quickly as he sunk deeper. The rough surface of sharkskin sliding across his feet finally jolted him out of his trance.

Swim! he told himself. He looked up and began swimming for the light with powerful kicks and strokes. When he broke through the surface, the first thing he saw was Hector leaning over the side of the sardine boat with swim fins in one hand and goggles in the other.

"Work quick, Texas. The captain will not let you on the boat until the problem is resolve."

Augie reluctantly put on the mask and flippers and then stuck his head under the water to look around. Vague, shadowy shapes appeared and disappeared in the murky depths. He saw no sign of the fouled gear.

"There's sharks everywhere!" he yelled up.

"Hold on," said Hector, who reappeared a moment later with a two-foot-long length of PVC pipe. "Use this to push them." He thrust the tube like a rapier to demonstrate.

Augie almost laughed at the puny plastic pipe, but he grabbed it anyway, took a deep breath, and submerged. At first he worried so much about the sharks that he forgot to search for the fouled net. When he resurfaced for air, some of the crewmen were pointing to an area beyond the stern of the boat.

"*¡El problema está en la línea de corcho!*" they yelled. "*¡La línea de corcho!*"

"The cork line!" said Hector. "Over there."

Augie swam to the spot on the cork line and saw that part of it had tangled with seaweed, leaving large gaps between the net and the floats. The netted fish moved away from him while he jerked and pulled on the Sargassum vines. The seaweed and line were well tangled, and Augie realized the chore would take awhile. The small fish continued to stay away, but the larger fish outside the net did not. He felt a bump on his shoulder, and when he looked behind him, he saw a large dorsal fin slide by and then disappear.

The first bump was just a probing nudge to determine if the object qualified as prey. Augie put his head underwater and watched the shark swimming away—a massive mako. In the dim light it looked like a leviathan. Augie slid over the cork line and submerged again so he could see the shark coming if it returned. The net was poor protection, but it was better than nothing. The mako reappeared alright, attacking from an upward angle, swiftly, single-mindedly. When it reached him, Augie thrust the PVC pipe at its nose. The momentum of the shark propelled Augie backwards almost ten feet, the netting the only barrier between him and the animal's gaping jaws.

Temporarily repelled, the shark banked away, its white underbelly flashing in the light. Augie realized he had been screaming underwater. When he gathered his wits, he also realized that the shark attack had dislodged the seaweed from the float line and that the gaps were mostly closed. Plenty good enough for him. He knew the shark would be back, and he didn't trust the nylon netting or the ridiculous plastic baton to protect him.

He swam toward the boat, straight through the congregated mass of sardines. He could feel them all around him and all over him, a sensation like nothing he'd ever experienced. When he reached the side of the boat, a pair of crewmen helped pull him onto the deck. He crawled away from the gunwale and threw up a bellyful of seawater and then dropped to his hands and knees, gasping and shivering.

"Easy, Texas," said Hector, seeing Augie's wild eyes. "Once again, you are still alive." He began rubbing the outside of Augie's arms. "*Tranquilo. Tranquilo.*"

The crew continued working until the fish were stored below and the nets stacked and ready for the next set. While they worked, Augie sat alone in the galley, wrapped in a blanket, his mind repeating the same thing over and over: *I've got to get off this boat. I've got to get off this boat.*

The captain stuck his head in the galley and inspected Augie, making sure his property was not damaged, and then he walked away. *Away from the wheelhouse,* Augie belatedly noted.

Without thinking twice about it, he threw off the blanket, slipped into the control room, and grabbed the radio mic. He tried to remember the Mayday protocol Charlie had taught him. *Tune to the emergency channel, what the hell was it? Sixteen, yes, that was it.* He found the frequency and pressed the talk button on the mic, "Mayday, Mayday, Mayday. This is the fishing vessel *El Dorado.* We are in need of immediate assistance."

Augie released the mic button and looked around to make sure he was still alone. "Mayday, Mayday, Mayday," he repeated. "This is fishing vessel *El Dorado.* We are in need of assistance." Augie tried to read the controls to determine his coordinates, but he was too hyped up to make sense of them. "To anyone who can hear this. This is the *El Dorado.* I have been kidnapped and am being held against my will. My name is—"

The mic flew out of Augie's hand as someone slapped it away. Before he could turn around to see who it was, he felt a fist crashing into his jaw.

"*¡Hijo de la chingada!*" shouted the captain. He continued pounding Augie with his fists until Augie fell to the floor where, wedged between the helm chair and the wall, the captain kicked him repeatedly. Augie tried to ward off the kicks, but he was cornered and couldn't escape. He felt his nose break, then a rib. He wondered if the captain would ever stop, and then, finally, he was dimly aware of someone pulling the captain back.

"*¡No lo mates, capitán! ¡El es el único que sabe como nadar!*"

Hector . . . pleading with the captain not to kill him . . . because he was the only crewman who could swim. *Good ol' Hector,* Augie thought dreamily before he lost consciousness.

———

CHAPTER 25

Everyone up and down the Ribera del Pescador seemed to be enjoying their Friday night, but Charlie and Raul were not among them. When they talked to the bartenders, waiters, fish mongers, and peddlers along the Ribera, asking about Augie, they got either a blank stare or a nervous shake of the head. About a quarter way down the avenue, Charlie decided it was time to try another tack. He stopped in front of a lively thatch-roofed restaurant/bar called Frutos del Mar, situated on the banks of the Tampamachoco. Just the kind of place Augie would be attracted to, thought Charlie. Nice breeze, view of the water, lots of people, and a sign that promised Cócteles y Mariscos.

"This one looks promising, Raul. I'll go in first and sit at the bar. You wait about half an hour before you come in. Don't sit next to me. Don't act like you know me. This will work better if it appears we aren't together."

"*What* will work better?" asked Raul. "What are you going to—"

But Charlie had already stepped into the restaurant. "*Hola, amigo,*" he said loudly to one of the waiters. "Y'all serve *cerveza fría* in here?"

Raul wasn't sure what Charlie was up to, but he did as he was asked and walked around a bit before returning. He took a seat at the bar several stools down from Charlie, who had attracted quite a crowd. Probably, Raul surmised, because he was buying drinks for anybody and everybody who looked his way. He'd only been there for thirty minutes and already there were two empty beer bottles and two spent shot glasses in front of him.

Raul watched with disapproval as Charlie continued to hold court, playing the obnoxious Texan, chattering in gringo Spanish, laughing too loud, slapping patrons on the back. So much for keeping a low profile. What the hell was he doing? Raul's attention turned to the bartender who had been standing in front of him asking what he wanted to drink.

"*¿Algo de tomar?*" repeated the barkeep for the third time.

When Raul hesitated, the man leaned across the bar and told him that he might as well order whatever he wanted because the noisy American was buying. Raul ordered a beer.

"So there I was . . . ." In bad English and worse Spanish, Charlie had launched into a fish story about an injury he said he'd received near Coatzacoalcos from a twelve-foot thresher shark. "I had finally vanquished the beast," he recounted, "and had even hoisted it onto my yacht, when the big sumbitch caught me right here with its whiptail." Charlie pulled up his pant leg and threw his leg onto the bar, showing the long scar to anyone who cared to look.

It was an entertaining story, except that Raul happened to know that Charlie received the scar during Hurricane Lana thirty-seven years before, that he'd never owned a yacht, and that he'd never fished anywhere near Coatzacoalcos. Plus, he was acting a lot drunker than he really was.

Raul saw what Charlie was up to. If his uncle got the locals to let their defenses down, maybe he could get them to talk. He didn't expect, however, that one hour, two beers and three tequila shots later, Charlie would start asking the bartender where he could find a woman for the evening.

If the bartender was surprised by Charlie's request (Raul certainly was), he didn't show it. He saw that Charlie still had plenty of money to spend and he wanted to make sure he spent it there, at his cantina. He accepted the twenty bucks that Charlie slipped into his hand then made a quick phone call. About ten minutes later, a pretty girl took a seat next to Charlie. The barflies who had been flocking around him in hopes of more free booze drifted off. The show was over for now.

Charlie bought the girl a drink and the two of them talked quietly. She wore lots of makeup and a tight red dress that emphasized her sensual curves but also her wide hips and thick waist. To Raul, she looked like a country girl, probably an ethnic Mayan from the low country along the Yucatan coast, probably no more than seventeen years old.

He understood the play now; Charlie was after information. Guillermo had said the Zetas ran the kidnapping business in Tuxpan, and if they supplied men to the boats, they most certainly supplied girls to work as prostitutes. The sex trade was just another revenue stream to the cartel.

Raul watched Charlie pay the bar tab with a wad of American bills and then escort the girl out to the street. The two of them talked for a moment and then began walking in the direction of the Tres Reyes Hotel. Raul gave them enough time to reach the hotel, and then he paid his tab and followed.

When he reached the hotel room, he pushed open the busted door and saw Charlie and the girl sitting across from each other: she on the bed, he in the chair. Both were fully dressed. She looked up anxiously when Raul came in.

"This is my nephew," said Charlie in his normal Spanish. "He is the father of the boy in the picture."

Raul saw that the girl was holding Augie's picture in her hand.

Charlie looked at Raul and continued in Spanish. "Lila is from Chicxulub, a village not too far from Merida. She was on her way to *El Norte* when men pulled her off the bus and put her to work along this river. She says she remembers our boy. Lila was with him the night he was kidnapped. She thinks he was drugged and taken away on a boat."

Raul stood rigid at the door, watching the girl as Charlie spoke. She seemed sad, a bit innocent, and yet she was the one who had delivered his son to the fucking narcos.

"Why the hell should we trust her?" Raul said in English. "She works for them."

Charlie shook his head. "She doesn't have a choice. She's a victim, just like Augie."

"Everyone has a choice. Can she take us to the sonofabitch who kidnapped my son?"

"I think so, but you need to ease up on the righteous indignation, nephew. If we scare her and she clams up, then we're back where we started. You understand?"

Raul nodded and sat down in the chair next to Charlie. "I understand." And then after a pause. "Why would she help us?"

"Because I told her I'd pay her."

Charlie continued to interview the girl, gently, taking his time. It became clear to Raul that she hated the man she worked for. He beat her regularly and had threatened to hurt her family if she ever tried to run. She lived with five other girls in a small apartment close to a club on the Ribera del Pescador. The other girls were captives like she was. She said she had been in Tuxpan for seven months and twelve days. She had told her family she would call them when she arrived in the U.S., but her captors wouldn't let her use a phone, and she worried that her family might think she was dead.

When Charlie finally got around to asking the girl if she would take them to her boss, she balked.

"*El me va a matar. Es el demonio, te lo juro.*" He will kill me. He's a demon, I swear to you.

Raul was not unsympathetic to the girl's story, but at the moment he didn't care what kind of monster her pimp was or even that he'd kill her if he found out she was helping them. He just wanted the man who sold his son into slavery. And when he got ahold of him, the bastard would tell them where Augie was, no matter what it took to make him talk.

Charlie kept coaxing the girl to lead them to him, pleading with her to help save the boy's life. He took a pair of hundreds off his money clip, folded them lengthwise, and lay them on the table between them. The girl paused, seeming to weigh her options and the consequences. Then she picked up the bills and began talking.

The man was in the Zeta cartel, and he called himself Z-17, she told them. He came by every other day to collect money and to check on his businesses. His office was above a nightclub and brothel called El Farolito, located at the end of the Ribera.

"*Vamanos,*" said Raul, standing up to go.

"*Él no viene hasta mañana en la noche,*" she answered.

Raul looked at Charlie. "He won't be there until tomorrow night? Are you kidding me? What are we supposed to do until then? Lock her in this room until Z-fucking-17 shows up at the office? How do we know she's not lying? How do we know she's not setting us up just like she did Augie?"

Charlie watched Raul pace around and waited until he finished ranting.

"We don't have a choice, nephew. And we have to let her go back to work or her people will get suspicious. We have to trust her."

"If she's lying, they'll come for us."

"I'm willing to take that chance."

Raul looked at the girl and then his uncle. "Fuck it," he said in frustration. "I hope you know what you're doing, Charlie."

—

CHAPTER 26

Augie vaguely remembered being carried from the bridge and then dragged to the back of the boat. He wondered distantly if they were going to throw him overboard. Then someone, maybe El Martillo, opened a deck hatch and threw him down into a dark hole. *Shit, another dark hole,* he thought to himself. Augie knew he was alive because of the piercing pain in his ribcage and because he could hear his own breathing as air whistled through the bent nasal passages in his broken nose.

He felt around him: a coil of rope, rubber fenders, a spare anchor— *The lazarette,* he concluded, *I'm in the lazarette.* He recalled seeing its flush-fit hatch near the stern. Fetid water pooled in the center of the floor and sloshed back and forth with the movement of the boat. A couple of times Augie attempted to move to a drier, more comfortable position but found the effort too painful. Something his friend Victor from the *Mañana* had told him kept running through his head: "You will be surprised how hard it is to die."

On the metal deck above, he heard occasional footsteps and then later the boat slowed and he heard the skiff slide into the water, followed by the nets. *Chango must have spotted another school of fish,* Augie told himself. To keep his mind occupied, he visualized the events taking place above him as he listened to the crew run through the set. *Now they're winching in the purse line, now the cork line. Now they're transferring the fish from the net to the storage compartments below deck.* He could hear the voices of crewmen through the metal bulkhead next to his head.

Well, he thought, *at least I'm not a hundred feet underwater sucking on a skinny plastic tube and dodging sharks.*

Sometime later, Augie wasn't sure how long, the boat engines slowed to idle and the hatch flew open. The early afternoon sunlight hit Augie like a flash grenade. "Jesus!" he yelled, shielding his eyes. Through a space between his fingers he saw Hector standing above him.

"Sorry, man. You prob'ly got a concussion. It happen to my cousin once. He wouldn't go outside in the light for three days it hurt his head so much." Hector took off his T-shirt and handed it down. "Use this to cover the eyes."

Augie fashioned a blindfold from the shirt. "What's going on? Why did the boat stop?"

"Meeting with the mother ship, man. Fill the fuel tank, get more food, more water, unload the fish. Hand me up the fenders. We gotta hang 'em over the side of the boat."

Augie looked down at the heavy rubber fenders. "I don't think I can."

"You gotta, man. You don' work, the captain will throw you overboard."

"Hector, I don't—"

"You gotta."

Augie groaned and began pulling out the bumpers, slowly, painfully handing them up to Hector. Other crewmen began hanging them over the rail, glancing over at Augie and wincing when they saw his splattered nose and bloody shirt.

"You want me to help you outta there, Texas?"

Augie shook his head and attempted to pull himself up. He gasped and fell back.

Hector jumped down into the lazarette and helped Augie onto the deck and then steadied him when he tried to stand. "I take you to get some water." As Hector led Augie toward the galley, he whispered in his ear. "Hey, man, better you keep away from the captain for a while, okay? Don' even look at him."

The galley was cool and out of the sun, so Augie returned Hector's T-shirt. Then he took a piece of paper towel, wet it, and packed his broken nose. As he stood at the sink splashing his face and drinking water from cupped hands, he looked out the window and studied the freighter anchored nearby. The rusty utility vessel was larger by half than the sardine boat, with a line of cabins amidships to stern, and on the second deck, the wheelhouse and captain's quarters. Forward of the bridge, a sunken well deck was notched into the hull. The name *Pegaso* and some letters and numbers were barely visible on the bow.

In the far distance, beyond the supply boat, he spotted a shrimp trawler drifting in the current, its nets strung up on the back deck for cleaning and repair. Augie wondered if any of the crew were there against their will, or if some poor bastard was chained up in the engine room or the lazarette. He turned away and walked unsteadily to the mess table. "I used to like shrimp boats," he said to Hector. He sat down heavily. "Why aren't we unloading? What's the captain waiting for?"

"He is prob'ly negotiating with the other captain."

"Negotiating? For what?"

Hector looked down at Augie. "For men, mos' likely. You and me could be working on another boat tonight."

Contemplating being sold again—for the second time in a week—Augie put his head in his hands. Would that be a good thing, he wondered? Surely any boat would be better than this one. But that's what he thought the last time, and since then he'd nearly drowned, been eaten by a shark, and almost beaten to death.

"Hector, I'm not sure I can make it."

Augie sat up straight when he noticed the alarm on his friend's face. Hector's hands gripped the window ledge as he stared intently at the sea.

"Something's happenin'."

Augie joined him at the window and saw that two Zodiac inflatables had suddenly appeared in the gap between the supply ship and the *El Dorado*. They were speeding straight toward them. Suddenly, the *El Dorado* diesels throttled up and the boat lurched forward, almost throwing Hector and Augie to the ground.

"Who are they? Augie yelled.

"I think they are pirates!"

"Pirates? From the supply ship?"

Hector shook his head. "Prob'ly from that shrimp boat."

At first, Augie thought Hector was joking—there hadn't been pirates in the Gulf for almost two hundred years—but when he saw how frightened his friend was, he studied the approaching boats more closely. Three armed men sat in the front of each Zodiac, with another man in back operating the tiller. With their massive outboard motors, the inflatable boats reached the ponderous sardine boat very quickly. One of them pulled alongside the port beam, and Augie could see men climbing over the rail, boarding the boat. A third man stayed on the Zodiac and trained his automatic weapon on the pilothouse. The second Zodiac cut the wake of the *El Dorado* and circled around to starboard.

In his peripheral vision, Augie sensed movement behind him and through the galley window saw El Martillo creeping down the starboard passageway with a pistol raised to his shoulder. Hector had seen him, too, and when Augie saw his friend crouch down behind the galley stove, he did the same. The shooting commenced almost immediately, two pistol shots followed by a staccato burst of automatic fire, and then another burst, then another. Augie heard bullets hitting the galley and shattering window glass above him, and then he heard the thud of a body hitting the deck.

A shadow crossed the window, and Augie glimpsed one of the pirates hurrying past, his weapon pointed at the pilothouse. Someone climbed the steps to the bridge and there was another gunshot. The diesels shut off, and the fishing boat pitched forward as its trailing wake crashed into the transom. The boat sat down in the water and began rocking gently in the Gulf swells.

Augie rose to one knee, but Hector pushed him back down. "Not yet. They will shoot you. Wait for them to tell us what to do."

They didn't have to wait long. A man entered the cabin, aimed his gun at them and then yelled for them to move to the back deck. Augie and Hector showed their hands and did as they were told.

On the back deck, the other crewmen sat in a line while two gunmen stood guard. Augie saw El Martillo lying dead near the cable winches, his spilled blood snaking across the deck toward the scupper hole. The diesels revved up again, and the *El Dorado* made a wide circle, then expertly pulled abreast of the bigger vessel. Lines were thrown down, and the fishing boat was secured alongside the *Pegaso*.

From where Augie sat, it appeared that the pirates had taken the supply boat, too. Two more Zodiacs were tied off to cleats on the other side of the ship. Two armed men stood at the rail looking down on the fishing boat, while two others guarded the *Pegaso* crew. Like Augie and his fellow crewmen, they were lined up on the back deck.

"Now what?" asked Augie.

Hector shook his head to indicate that he didn't know.

Behind him, Augie heard one of the pirates open the lazarette and retrieve the extra anchor. He dragged it over to El Martillo and wrapped the anchor line around the dead man's feet. The pirate then instructed Hector and another crewman to throw the anchor overboard. The anchor dropped, the rope became taut, and El Martillo's ankles snapped upwards, violently flipping him overboard. A stunned silence followed the splash.

One of the pirates watched El Martillo sink until he had disappeared. "*Singao,*" he said to his comrades. They laughed, and when Chango laughed with them, they turned their attention to him.

One of the pirates began berating Chango in Spanish that Augie couldn't follow. To him it sounded like one long string of obscenities, but to Chango, it must have been amusing because he wouldn't stop laughing. It was guileless laughter from a simple-minded boy, but it irritated the armed men.

"*¿Que bola con este comemierda?*" the pirate asked his comrade.

The other shrugged. "*Tírale en la agua.*"

That Augie *did* understand. "No! Don't throw him in the water. He doesn't *comprende.*" The pirates turned and stared at him. Augie showed his empty hands. "He's slow, you know?" he twirled his finger next to his ear. "Slow in the head. *Es, uh, loco en la cabeza.*"

"Shut up, Texas," Hector whispered urgently.

A pirate began walking toward Augie, but someone shouted from the supply boat for them to quit fucking around and start transferring the fish. The storage hold was opened, and the pirates made the crewmen form an assembly line: four men were placed in the hole to secure lines around the fish-and-ice-filled barrels, four remained on deck to hoist the barrels out of the hold with block and tackle, and two guided the barrels across the rail to the supply boat. Crewmen on the other vessel used dollies to move the fish into the freighter's refrigerated hold. The process took about an hour.

Augie was one of the crewmen sent below to secure the barrels, but thankfully, the crew let him sit on a crate and watch. What good would he be anyway? They'd seen what kind of shape he was in when El Martillo threw him into the lazarette. It was cool and dim in the hold, and Augie was grateful for the reprieve, although his cracked ribs ached with every breath.

After the transfer, Augie and the *El Dorado* crewmen were sent aboard the supply ship where they were instructed to sit cross-legged on the deck with the other captives. One by one, they were escorted upstairs to the bridge, where the pirate captain questioned them individually. After each interview, the prisoner would either descend the stairs and join the others, or he wouldn't come down at all. It looked to Augie as if some kind of sorting was taking place, but he couldn't figure how or why. He wondered what they had done with the captain of the *El Dorado*.

"I don't understand their Spanish. Where are they from?" Augie asked Hector under his breath.

"The accents sound Cuban."

"Cuban pirates? What are they after? Fish?"

"Fish, boats, fuel. Whatever they can sell, I suppose. Maybe they have other reasons. I don't know."

"*Ojalá no sea el Mal de Ojo,*" said the man sitting next to Hector.

Hector agreed and they both crossed themselves.

"Who the hell is Mal de Ojo?" Augie asked.

"You don' wanna know."

The line advanced until it was finally Augie's turn to climb the stairs. The guard looked at Hector and gestured for him to follow. When they entered the bridge, it was filled with cigar smoke. Augie was startled to find an old man sitting in the captain's chair. His feet were propped up on the dashboard, and he casually puffed on a long cigar. He was dressed like a common fisherman: loose pants, sandals, and a sweat-stained work shirt. His hands were scarred and weathered, his forearms thin and wiry. He had a scraggly grey beard and wore a knotted scarf under a grimy ball cap. The cap was pulled down low on his head, shading his face. A pair of Ray Ban Wayfarer sunglasses concealed his eyes.

At first glance, there was nothing terribly imposing about him, except that he was weirdly calm, as if he were bored by the interviews. He didn't look directly at either Augie or Hector, but simply gazed out the window at the Gulf.

"*Cuéntame tu historia,*" he said, his voice deep and raspy.

Hector and Augie looked at each other. *Tell him our story?* Hector shrugged and then began. Augie knew Hector's story already and was able to follow most of it as he spoke in Spanish to the reclining pirate. When he finished, the pirate asked him about his "*amigo.*"

"*Es un Americano, señor. Fue secuestrado en Tuxpan, como yo.*" As Hector continued, Augie tried to follow, but he soon lost the thread.

"What are you telling him, Hector?"

Hector hesitated until the old pirate nodded his head slightly, indicating that it was okay to translate. "I tell him you are an American, kidnapped in Tuxpan like me, and that you were traded from the *Mañana* to the *El Dorado*. I tell him you are a good diver . . . the bes' I have ever seen." He turned and looked at Augie. "I hope that is okay."

"You said more than that. You mentioned the radio."

"He ask about the Mayday call, and I say how you use the radio on the *El Dorado* and that the captain almost kill you."

"Ask him what happens to us now."

Hector shook his head nervously. "*You* ask him."

Augie looked at the captain. "*Que pasa con nosotros?*"

The pirate swiveled around in his chair and slowly raised his hands to remove his sunglasses. Hector looked down, averting his eyes. When the pirate looked at Augie, Augie saw right away there was something not quite right about his face—it seemed to droop on one side, and one eye didn't focus like the other.

"*Ellos adentro,*" he said to the armed man standing behind them.

"Inside where?" Augie asked. He and Hector were ushered through an interior door and led down a companionway. "They're not putting me in another fucking dungeon, Hector," he yelled back.

"Texas, be *quiet . . .* please."

They were herded into a room which appeared to be used as one of the ship's sleeping quarters. Augie counted eight more prisoners inside, some of them from the *El Dorado*.

Augie looked at Hector, confounded by what had happened. "Hector, who is that old man? What is he doing with us?"

When their escort left and closed the door behind him, Hector answered. "It's him, El Mal de Ojo."

"Are you sure?"

"Yes . . . *¡Maldito! Estamos bien jodidos.* We are very fucked."

A short time later, four more men joined them, one at a time. Augie heard them talking low to each other, describing their meeting with the pirate. They, too, had been asked to tell their stories. As Augie listened to them talk, he was able to gather that all of the men in the room had been kept on the fishing boats against their will— they had all been conscripts, like himself and Hector. He also learned that most of them were Central American and had been en route to the United States when they were abducted or tricked by the boat captains and their suppliers. More than one had been drugged.

When Augie pointed this out to Hector, his friend nodded. "Yes, I notice the same."

"Do you think they plan to sell us?"

"I don' know. Most of us have been missing for so long I think they know they can do with us whatever they want. What do you think?"

Augie sat down on a bunk. "Shit, I don't know, either. Maybe that creepy sonofabitch captain will let us go. Did you see that fucker's eye?"

Augie looked up when he felt Hector staring at him. His friend seemed uneasy about something. Hector opened his mouth, but no words came out.

"What is it?" asked Augie.

"*¿Te miraba?*" one of the men finally asked.

"Did he look at me? Yeah . . . so what?"

"*¿Viste su ojo?*"

"Yes I saw his eye. Why is that such a big deal?" Augie noticed the talking had stopped, and now everyone was staring at him.

The man said something under his breath and the other men crossed themselves.

"Hector? What the fuck? What'd he say?"

"He say Mal de Ojo cast the evil eye on you."

Augie almost laughed, but he paused when he saw the look of fear on the men's faces. He turned to Hector. "You don't really believe in any of that crap, do you?"

"If you do escape," Hector said stone-faced, "you must find a *curandera* and do a *limpia* immediately."

A pirate opened the door to the cabin and waved Augie and the other prisoners to the back deck. Outside in the open, Augie glanced forlornly at the setting sun. *What next,* he wondered?

Hector nudged him in the side and tilted his head toward the *El Dorado* skiff, which floated off the starboard bow about a hundred feet out in the Gulf. Fifteen sailors or more—Augie noticed they were all hired crewmen—were crowded onto the boat. They were packed together so tightly that the men had to sit on top of each other so the oarsmen had room to row. The outboard, Augie noticed, had been removed. The overloaded skiff rocked precariously in the Gulf swells.

"Those are the other crewmen. What will happen to them?"

"I don' know. But at least they have a chance." He looked at Augie. "Do we?"

When they heard the pirates laughing, their attention turned to the sardine boat. The captains of both the *El Dorado* and the *Pegaso* had been led to the middle of the boat deck. The pirates had bound the two men together, one man's leg tightly lashed to the leg of the other, as in a potato sack race. Augie could see that the *El Dorado* captain was badly injured, his shirt soaked red with blood from his shoulder to below his waist.

The bound captives were positioned so that they faced Mal de Ojo's first mate, who delivered what Augie took to be a pronouncement of some kind. When he finished, a couple of pirates led the bound men to the rail and pushed them overboard. "*Adiós hijos de puta. Vamos a ver lo bien que trabajan juntos ahora,*" said the first mate.

The pirates roared with laughter, and some of the men standing next to Augie crossed themselves, while others smiled with a kind of dismayed satisfaction.

"What'd he say?" asked Augie.

Hector arched his eyebrows. He say, 'Le's see how well you sons-of-bitches work together now.'"

The two captains flailed away in the water, but it was clear that the injured *El Dorado* captain could not do his part to keep them afloat, leaving his companion to do most of the work. It didn't take long for the supply boat captain to tire. He called to the men in the skiff, who watched in horror but made no effort to help. When he began cursing at his bound partner in fury and desperation, the pirates cheered him on. But within minutes, both men gave up and then dipped below the water once, twice, and then a third time before they disappeared altogether.

In the ensuing silence, the pirates divided the captives who remained on the supply ship into three groups, distributing them among the three vessels: nine stayed on the *Pegaso*, three were moved to the *El Dorado*, and two were transferred to the shrimp trawler that Augie had seen earlier. Augie stayed on the *Pegaso* while Hector was ordered to board one of the Zodiacs bound for the shrimp trawler.

As the Zodiac pulled away, Augie yelled goodbye to Hector.

Hector responded with a halting, uncertain wave.

———

CHAPTER 27

Charlie and Raul spent the day laying low. To kill time, Charlie repaired the broken door at the Tres Reyes Hotel. Lila had agreed to meet them later that evening at the same bar as before and then escort them to El Farolito, the club where she had lured Augie. All she had to do, Charlie told her, was nod toward the man who called himself Z-17. Then she would be out of it.

Raul called the Rockport office and told Judy and Sammy what they had learned of Augie's probable fate and urged them to reach out again to the U.S. consul's office. He called Rosie, too, but was more circumspect. Especially with words like "kidnapped," "drugged," "enslaved," and "cartels." He certainly didn't tell her about their half-baked plan to confront a Zeta gangster on his own turf in his own nightclub. The whole deal seemed crazy, the more he thought about it. There were so many ways it could go sideways.

Raul had read about the violence wrought by the cartels. The *narcotraficantes'* penchant for barbarity was widely known and explicitly covered in Mexican newspapers. Photos of corpses and graphic descriptions of gruesome deaths often made the front page: lopped off limbs, beheadings, stories of people being thrown down wells or burned alive in barrels of oil. Bodies cut up and left in trash bags all over town. One notorious killer called *El Pozolero* boiled his victims in a grisly stew that he said reminded him of *pozole*.

It was the stuff of nightmares.

When the sun was low on the horizon, they left to go to the Frutos del Mar restaurant to meet Lila. Both of them wondered if she'd show. As they walked to Augie's truck, Raul's legs felt like they weighed a hundred pounds each.

Charlie was grimly determined, but more optimistic than his nephew. He'd been in tight spots before, and somehow he'd always found a way through them. Even though his plan was half-formed at best—an imprecise jumble of conjectures and contingencies—he mostly figured he'd just wing it like he usually did. He kind of wished he had a gun, though. The only weapon he had was a slim fillet knife he'd found buried in Augie's tackle box. It was in its leather scabbard tucked into the shaft of his cowboy boot. He could feel it every time he pushed off the ball of his right foot.

As soon as Charlie walked into the restaurant, the bartender came around and welcomed him, wiping down the bar stool where, the night before, the Texan had spent three hundred dollars on drinks. Raul waited a moment at the street corner and then walked in unnoticed, everyone's attention having turned to his uncle, the voluble one-man fiesta with the pocket full of money.

When Lila came in, Charlie bounded to his feet and greeted her with a big hug. He led her to the stool next to his and put his arm around her, making it clear to everyone in the bar that this lucky girl would be his date for another night at least. He ordered a Bohemia and a bowl of fish stew for himself. The girl asked for a *Torito*. Raul sat at a corner table and ordered a shrimp cocktail, even though he had no intention of eating it. He watched in amazement as Charlie wolfed down the soup and drank two bottles of beer. Stress stimulated his uncle's appetite. For Raul, it produced the opposite effect. His stomach felt like someone was squeezing it like a sponge.

When Charlie and Lila finally left the bar, Raul paid his tab and followed behind. The three of them climbed into the truck and sat together in the cab. They were tense and silent on the short ride to the club. Fishermen, fishmongers, families, and old and young couples crowded the road for the first few blocks. Then the road turned to crushed shell, and the people and buildings thinned out. At the end of the road sat El Farolito, a two-story cinderblock building painted baby blue. The nightclub's name was hand-painted over the door, and its namesake (a hanging lantern) hung beside it, a single yellow lightbulb glowing inside.

They paused at the entrance, and Charlie took a deep breath. "Here goes nothin'."

He pushed open the door and was met by a blast of trumpets from a mariachi band at the front of the room. Couples bounced around the dance floor in the dimly-lit interior. Charlie spied the bar across the low-ceilinged room, grabbed Lila by the hand, and plowed his way through the dancers to the other side. Raul reluctantly followed.

"*Bue-nas noches, Señor Garçon,*" Charlie bellowed to the barkeep. "How 'bout a round of tequilas for me and my friends?"

The bartender's eyes cut from Charlie to Raul to Lila. Lila grabbed Charlie's upper arm to remind the bartender that she was on the clock. Raul wasn't sure the loudmouth-Texan hustle would work in this room. The crowd was a rougher looking bunch than at the restaurant, but Charlie evidently had decided to roll the dice.

"Do you speak English Mr. *Garçon?*"

The bartender regarded them contemptuously as he poured cheap tequila into three shot glasses.

"Well, I'm gonna pretend like you do." Charlie leaned toward Raul and winked. "They all speak more English than they let on."

The barman pushed the glasses toward Charlie. "*Tres cientos pesos.*"

"Shee-it. That's more than fifteen bucks. I think the drinks are cheaper at the Crown Plaza." He picked up one of the shot glasses. "But it don't matter none. This is my nephew's bachelor party, and I'm gonna get him drunk *and* laid. And, you know what?" he tossed back the tequila and glanced lewdly at the bartender, "I might just join him."

Charlie thrust Lila into Raul's arms. "I think she wants to dance with you, nephew."

Raul shook his head. "You're kidding, right?"

"Dance with her, goddammit," said Charlie, his voice low and insistent.

While Raul and Lila shuffled around the dance floor, Charlie surveyed the room. One, no, two, bouncers were standing on the perimeter; a third was stationed at the door. The tables were occupied by groups of partiers or else single men with women who worked at the club. But one table, which rested on a slightly elevated platform in the corner of the room, sat empty. Charlie assumed it was reserved for somebody special.

Charlie saw a group get up to leave, so he grabbed the drinks and claimed the empty table. Out on the dance floor, Raul struggled to feign interest in his "date" while Lila tried her best to act like it was business as usual. Charlie looked around and noticed that many of the prostitutes were sitting on their clients' laps, so when Lila and Raul returned to the table, he patted his knee and asked Lila to sit.

He put his mouth to her ear. "You sure he is coming?" he asked in Spanish.

"He will come."

A half-hour later, he did. Two men emerged from a hallway at the back of the club. They paused by the bar and scanned the room. Charlie couldn't see any guns, but he didn't doubt that they were armed. Soon after, a short, slightly stocky man walked by the bodyguards and went to his table. Lila nudged Charlie with her elbow.

"Z-17?" he asked in a low voice.

She nodded yes.

The Zeta lieutenant didn't look much older than Augie. His hair was buzz cut and the black silk shirt he wore was unbuttoned far enough down to reveal a tangle of gold chains hanging around his neck.

So he's the motherfucker who kidnaps boys and girls and sells them into slavery, thought Charlie. *The leader and gran chingón of the Gulf Coast kidnapping and extortion business.* He didn't look much like a leader to Charlie, but he knew that to rise in the *narcotraficante* world, men like Z-17 didn't have to be leaders necessarily, or even very smart. They only had to be killers, and the crueler and crazier they were, the higher they rose in the ranks. They didn't live very long, of course—hardly any of them made it to thirty—but while they were on top, they could get away with almost anything, virtual warlords on their own turf.

Charlie and Raul had thought Lila could slip out unobtrusively once she had fingered the narco boss, but now, in the moment, Charlie saw the folly of that part of the plan. The bouncers and bartenders kept a close eye on the girls and their customers. For Lila to leave without completing any sort of carnal transaction would be highly conspicuous and possibly dangerous for her. The only thing Charlie could see to do was keep up the act. He whispered as much to Raul.

"Vamos al dormitorio," Charlie told Lila. Then to Raul. "You ready to close this deal?"

"Can both of us go back to the room with her?" Raul asked, fuzzy about the logistics and the rules. He'd never once set foot in a whorehouse.

"Bachelor party, remember? They'll just charge us extra."

They followed Lila to a hallway off the bar where a middle-aged woman sat behind a small table.

"Los dos," Lila told her.

The old woman studied Charlie and Raul and then handed Lila a room key and two condoms. She snapped her fingers at Charlie and held out her hand. "One hundred dollar," she said. "American."

Charlie peeled off five twenties and followed Lila and Raul into the shabby room. It contained a sagging bed, a nightstand and table lamp, and a ceiling fan that wobbled overhead. Nothing else. She shut and locked the door behind her and then looked at them, wondering what came next. Charlie walked around the room, looking for peepholes, microphones, and most importantly, alternative exits. He opened the small window in the bathroom and stood on the toilet to look out. He saw nothing outside the window but some trash bins and the Laguna de Tampamachoco. Clear exit, he decided, if he could somehow squeeze his six-foot-plus body through the window opening.

"What now?" asked Raul.

"We wait a few minutes. However long it would take for us to uh, conduct our business."

Raul inadvertently glanced at Lila and blushed. *What would Rosie make of this?* He tried not to imagine. "Right, but what then?"

Charlie held up a finger and spoke to Lila. She confirmed that it was not unusual for a client to ask if he could buy a girl, permanently, but she added that Z-17 rarely complied, especially if the girl was young, healthy, and pretty.

"Like you," added Charlie. "Well, it won't hurt to ask for a meeting with the boss man. So who does the asking, me or you?"

"Mejor yo," she said, pointing to herself.

When they figured enough time had passed, Charlie nodded at Lila and she stood up to leave. He placed his hand on her arm and told her that if Z-17 agreed to talk to them, then her part would be done. He pulled out his wallet to give her more money, but she stopped him and looked at Raul.

"Fue muy amable tu hijo. Es un buen tipo." Your son was very nice. A good guy.

"Gracias," said Raul. He already knew how special his son was, but it was nice to hear her say it all the same, even if it came from a prostitute.

A few minutes after she left, two of the narco bodyguards entered the room. One pointed a gun at them while the other frisked them for weapons. Charlie hoped like hell Z-17's soldier would miss the skinny knife hidden in his boot. He did. The man with the gun gestured for them to follow him. They were led up some stairs into a little office where Z-17 sat behind a metal desk smoking a cigarette.

He smiled sardonically at the pair in front of him. *"Siéntate, viejo,"* he said to Charlie, gesturing for "the old man" to sit down. And then to Raul, *"Tu también, pocho."* A moment later he motioned for his bodyguards to depart. The old man and the skinny, worried-looking younger fellow with him didn't seem like much of a threat.

The room was sparsely furnished, with a ragged couch against one wall, a fancy stereo set and big screen TV on the other, and a velvet painting of a naked Aztec princess hanging over the couch. Charlie noticed an open window behind the desk, allowing a breeze from the lagoon to cool the room. A creaky ceiling fan spun overhead.

They sat in the two chairs across the desk from Z-17. When he asked them what the hell they wanted and why they were bothering him, Charlie gave him a big goofy smile and tried to explain to *"the señor"* that both he and his nephew had fallen in love with Lila and wanted to see if he would consider selling her to them. He said he had American money and was willing to pay top dollar. He had to speak loudly over the music blaring below them.

Z-17 laughed and asked Charlie in English if he could even get it up at his age.

"With her I can."

"What about this asshole?" he asked, pointing to Raul. "Is he a faggot?"

"Not with her he isn't," said Charlie. Everyone laughed except Raul.

There was a knock on the door and one of the guards stuck his head in and told Z-17 that a fist fight on the dance floor was getting out of control. The boss told the two men to take care of it, for fuck's sake.

In the interim, while the man was distracted, Charlie's eyes cut to Raul. They had that slightly crazed look that Raul had seen before. *Oh, boy. Here we go.*

"You speak damn good English," Charlie told the narco. "Better'n my Spanish, that's for sure."

Through a cloud of exhaled smoke, the narco narrowed his eyes at them. "How much money you got on you, *viejo?*"

"Enough." Charlie stood up, slowly reached into his back pocket for his wallet and handed him a wad of money. While Z-17 counted out the bills, Charlie asked him for a cigarette. He absently pushed the pack towards Charlie, and when he did, Charlie reached over, grabbed the man's head with both hands, and slammed it hard onto the table. He heard Z-17's nose break with a liquid crunch.

"Grab him from behind!" he said to Raul, and then he smashed the narco's head onto the desk again.

Raul ran behind the chair, his heart pounding, and pulled the man's arms back while Charlie unbuckled his own belt and tossed it to Raul.

"Strap him to the chair," he said. "And find his guns. There's probably one on him and another one in the desk."

Raul ran his hands down the narco's chest. "Got it," he said, holding up a Glock.

"Check the desk."

Raul found two more semi-automatic pistols in the side drawers.

Z-17 lifted his dazed head, his eyes crossed and a knot beginning to form on his forehead. A river of blood streamed from his nose. Charlie pulled a bandana out of his back pocket and stuffed it into the man's mouth. When the narco regained his senses, he thrashed around in rage, trying to free himself. He finally stopped struggling and glared at them with hatred so savage and predatory that it almost unnerved Charlie.

"Here's what it is, Z," said Charlie, bluffing through his fear. He switched to fluent Spanish. "We're looking for something you stole from us." He snapped his fingers for Raul to produce Augie's picture and then held it in front of the man's face. "This boy. This boy is *his* son and *my* nephew. You drugged him, kidnapped him, and from what we've heard, sold him to a commercial fishing boat." Charlie grabbed the guy's chin. "And we want him back."

Raul realized he was almost hyperventilating, stunned by how quickly it all had happened. Here was one of the most dangerous men on the Mexican Gulf Coast, and Charlie was threatening *him*.

Charlie told Raul to put the gun to the back of the man's head. "I'm going to take out Mr. Z-17s bandana so he can talk to us. If he yells and his bodyguard comes in, shoot them both, got it? Z first, then the bodyguard second."

"Okay" said Raul, trying to keep his hand from shaking.

What you need to know, Z," Charlie continued, "is that we will do anything to get this kid back. Anything. We will kill you and risk getting killed ourselves to find out where he is. Do you understand?"

The man continued to glare at him.

Charlie switched back to English. "I'm going to assume you do, and when I take this rag out of your mouth, you are going to tell me where he is. Now don't yell, *comprende?*"

Charlie removed the rag and the man yelled, so Charlie slammed his head into the table again and reinserted the rag. They listened for footsteps, but the thumping mariachi polka playing downstairs was all that they could hear.

"Not cool, Z. Give me the gun, nephew." He looked at Raul and reconsidered. "Wait, I have a better idea." Charlie retrieved the fillet knife from his boot and held it to the narco's throat. "I like knives. Less noise, hurts more, kills just as good," he said. "Let's try this again."

Charlie pulled out the rag and the man launched into a sputtering stream of expletives . . . but quietly.

"Good. You got that out of your system. Now let's talk about our boy," Charlie said in English. He put the knife point to Z-17's throat and began applying pressure.

"There are many boys," the narco answered in English.

"This one is an American, the one in the picture. Do you want me to show you the photo again?"

"I don' know where he is."

"I don't believe you."

"I tell you, I don' know. I sell him to a boat—"

"What was the name of the boat?" Charlie interrupted.

"The *Mañana,* but the captain, he say he sell him to another boat . . . ." Charlie pushed the knife point in and the narco winced. "To the *El Dorado.* The other boat, it is called *El Dorado.*"

"So he's on the *El Dorado?*"

"I don' know."

"You don't know? Or you won't say?" At the tip of the knife, a small trickle of blood began to thread down the man's throat where the point had pierced the skin.

"No one has heard from this boat."

The office door opened, and Raul raised the gun. Lila slipped in quietly and closed the door behind her.

"What are you doing here?" Raul asked her in Spanish.

"*Voy con ustedes,*" she answered.

"You can't go with us."

"*Ustedes no entienden. El va a matarnos.*" You don't understand. He is going to kill us.

Charlie looked at Z-17. "Is that right, Z? Are you going to kill us?"

The narco looked at Charlie, sizing him up. He smiled crookedly. "Yes, 'cause you don' have the balls to kill me first . . . *viejo.*"

Charlie smiled back, but he knew the man was right. Z-17 had called their bluff. Neither he nor Raul were cold-blooded killers.

"Well . . . if you already know you're going to kill us, you might as well tell us what happened to our boy."

Z-17 laughed, feeling in control again. "Okay, I tell you . . . . I don' know. They say those fucking pirates attack the fishing boat," he smiled again, "and if that happen, your boy is dead anyway . . . *pendejo.*"

"How do you know this?" asked Charlie.

The narco snorted. "I know everything, *cabrón.*" The blood from his busted nose had run into his mouth and, when he smiled, his teeth were ghoulishly red. And I know I will have fun killing you two fuckers." He turned his head toward the girl. "You, too, *puta.*"

Charlie stuffed the rag back into the narco's mouth and looked at Raul. "I think that's all we're gonna get out of this guy." He went to the window blinds and cut a section of cord "Let's tie him up good and get the hell out of here."

While Raul held the gun on him, Charlie used the sash cord to lash Z-17 firmly to the chair. When they finished, the two Sweetwater men began walking for the door, but Lila stopped them and shook her head. "*No.*" She pointed to the window. "*Mejor la ventana.*"

They went to the window and looked down. They were on the second floor, but they realized that if they hung from the sill, the drop was manageable. Raul dropped first. Before Charlie followed, Lila grabbed his arm.

"*Dame el cuchillo,*" she said. Give me the knife.

Charlie looked at her and handed her the fillet knife, and then he climbed over the window sill and dropped, hard. "Son-of-a-bitch!" he said under his breath.

"What about Lila?" asked Raul.

They looked up and saw her climbing through the window. When she jumped, Raul caught her.

They walked quickly around to the parking lot on the other side of the club, climbed into the truck, and drove off toward the hotel. Charlie looked at Lila. *"¿Donde esta el cuchillo?"* he asked. "Where's the knife?"

She whispered, *"Está en el corazón del demonio."*

"What did she say?" asked Raul.

"She said she left it in the devil's heart."

"Christ Almighty," Raul muttered, crossing himself and pushing the accelerator.

At the hotel, Raul quickly retrieved his bag and threw it in the back of the rental car while Charlie collected Augie's belongings from the hotel room and did likewise.

"What about Lila?" asked Charlie. "We can't leave her here."

"I know."

Charlie watched as Raul handed Lila a thick wad of money, the keys to Augie's truck, and Father Canul's calling card.

"The Padre will help you," Raul told her in Spanish. "Drive to Matamoros tonight, right now, as fast as you can. Go directly to his church. The address is on the card. Do you know how to drive?"

She nodded.

He gave her brief directions for getting out of town and then a quick embrace. *"Vaya con Dios,* Lila."

They watched her drive away. "She is sixteen years old," said Raul. "The same age as Yolanda."

"I know."

"So where do we go now, Tío? The narcos will be looking for us."

"They'll expect us to head north for the border. So, let's go south, to Villa Rica. We'll be safe at Roy Lee's place . . . at least for tonight. We go right by the Holiday Inn on the way out of town. You can pick up your car and then follow me." He looked over at his nephew. "Are you okay?"

Raul inhaled deeply. "I think so. My hands won't quit shaking."

"I know what you mean."

They got into the rental car and Charlie slowly exited the hotel courtyard, looking carefully up and down the road before he continued.

"We still don't know where Augie is," said Raul.

"No, but we know more than we did an hour ago. The good news is that he's alive."

"Why do you think that?"

"I just do." Charlie raised his still-shaking hand to adjust the rear-view mirror, and then he turned onto the Boulevard de Independencia. "I have to."

Raul thought about that. "What's all that stuff Z said about pirates? Do you think he was just messing with us?"

"Could be. I don't know. We'll find him, Raul. We'll find Augie. We're getting closer."

———

CHAPTER 28

Augie was astonished when he turned the lever to the cabin door and it opened. He and the other captives had been crowded into the small sleeping quarters all night and part of the day, and no one had thought to check the door to see if it was locked. Augie had tried the door out of boredom and because he'd had his fill of the paranoid bullshit he'd been hearing for the last several hours.

The men had been speculating about El Mal de Ojo and his supposedly evil powers—repeating sketchy third-hand stories, embellishing their own stories, and just flat making shit up. The only thing he'd heard that he agreed with was that the boat they were on was most likely heading for Cuba.

His fellow captives had convinced themselves that the pirate captain was a Santería priest, undoubtedly skilled in black magic, probably in league with Satan, and possibly a practitioner of human sacrifice. One guy, an Aztec kid from Hidalgo, suggested he might be a zombie, or more accurately, a half-zombie, part of him dead and part of him alive. Whatever the pirate captain was, and whatever his plans for them might be, the men had gradually managed to scare themselves silly and, by the next day, were absolutely convinced they were done for.

They had excluded Augie from their discussions because they *knew* he was done for, already as good as dead. Mal de Ojo had cursed him with his evil eye. So Augie had passed the time lying in a bunk, listening to the ravings of his mates, and trying to think of ways he might escape.

None of the men followed him outside, even though he left the door ajar for them. Out in the open, a couple of the pirate crewmen glanced his way but seemed not to care. After waiting indecisively at the rail a few minutes, Augie decided to risk entering the galley for a drink of water; he'd only had a few handfuls since yesterday. He opened the door and saw two men sitting at the mess table playing dominoes. They glanced at him as he crossed the threshold, but soon returned to their game. Augie cautiously walked to the faucet and drank, and then he filled to the brim a dented tin pitcher he found in the ceiling-hung cabinet. As he left the galley, one of the pirates handed him a sack of stale *bolillos*. He took the water and the bread to the bunkroom and shared it with the men.

Augie ate and then went outside to relieve himself over the rail. Emboldened by his freedom, he set out to explore the supply ship. Strangely, the pirates paid him no mind, acting almost as if he were a guest passenger or one of the crew. Augie wondered if perhaps that's what he was—a crewman, a new recruit. Maybe the interview process had simply been to choose men to work on Mal de Ojo's boats. And if that were the case, Augie wondered, what was his status? A paid crewman free to leave once the boat docked in port? A fellow pirate? *Boy*, he thought, *the family would love hearing about that: 'Dear Mom, Dad, and Sis—It's been a good month for pillage and plunder. Our bloodthirsty captain, Mal de Ojo, is very pleased. We buried some treasure on a beach in Quintana Roo and I will try to send you some doubloons and souvenir T-shirts after we raid Isla Mujeres later this week. Love to all, Augie.'*

But deep down, Augie knew he was neither guest, nor crewman, nor fellow pirate—he was still just a captive. That night he stood at the bow and searched the sea, scanning the horizon for light: light from ships, light from oil platforms, light from land—*any* light that might give him a glimmer of hope. But he saw nothing but blackness and about a billion stars. He figured they allowed him to roam free on the boat because there was nowhere to escape to. The night was so dark he was unable even to determine the exact line of the horizon. He put his forehead on the bow rail and closed his eyes. He had never felt so lost or alone.

He turned and looked up at the pilothouse. In the glow of the instrument panel he saw the silhouette of the captain standing at the helm. He could make out the pale outline of his head and torso. *Is he looking back at me?* he wondered. *Fixing his dead satanic zombie evil eye on me? Well, fuck you Mal de Ojo, and fuck the captains of the* Mañana *and the* El Dorado, *fuck El Gordo and El Martillo, and fuck the devious whore who lured me into this. Fuck all y'all.*

When he returned to his cabin—his unlocked prison cell—he found that all the bunks were full, so he climbed to the deck atop the cabins and curled up inside a life raft. He slept fitfully for a few hours and then bolted awake from a vivid dream. In the dream, his Uncle Charlie had been shouting at him from his old shrimp boat, *The Johnny Roger,* which he'd named for his long-deceased brother. *What the hell did he want?* Augie wondered groggily. He sat up and rubbed his eyes, waiting for his head to clear. When he looked around, he spotted a light in the far distance, so he climbed stiffly out of the raft and went to the starboard rail to check it out.

After a few minutes, he decided the light was fixed. Was it coming from an offshore rig or was it on land? A street light in a small town perhaps? The mast light on an anchored sailboat? He looked around to get his bearings. Behind him, portside, he noticed stars beginning to fade along the horizon. Dawn would be coming soon. The artificial light to the west must be coming from Mexico. His best guess was that the supply ship was rounding the tip of the Yucatan Peninsula and entering the Caribbean.

Augie stared at the light, trying to calculate the distance, wondering if he could swim that far, wondering if he could swim at all given his cracked ribs and his swollen nose. He stretched and lifted his arms, fighting through the pain, and rotated his torso trying to loosen his stiff muscles. In another twenty minutes it would be light enough to see and light enough for the pirates to see him diving in. In another hour Mexico would be behind them, and his chance for escape would be gone.

He knew a strong current flowed through the Yucatan Channel. Which direction did it flow? Would it help him reach the shore or sweep him out to sea? He searched the deck for a life preserver but couldn't find one. He considered stealing the life raft but determined it would be too heavy and too cumbersome to wrestle into the water without drawing attention. If he swam for the light, he'd have nothing to hang onto if he began to tire.

All these thoughts were running through Augie's head when he smelled cigar smoke and was startled to see a man standing at the rail not ten feet away from him.

"You might make it," said the man. "But I wouldn't bet on it."

He spoke perfect English, and Augie looked at him carefully—El Mal de Ojo. His arms rested casually on the rail, and he seemed to be studying the distant light along with Augie.

"That's the lighthouse of El Cuyo," he said. "It's a small village on the Yucatan coast. The tarpon fishing is good there, but these days there are too many *yumas* for my taste."

Augie was quiet, caught off-guard by the captain's English and by his genial manner.

"Your friend said you are a strong swimmer," he continued. "But the shore is twenty miles away and the current is strong . . . . I'm not sure anyone could make it, especially with broken ribs."

"Where are you taking me?" Augie finally managed to ask.

"To Cienfuegos."

"I don't know where that is."

"It's in Cuba."

Augie turned and saw that the captain was watching him. Even in the dark he could see the dead eye shining dully in its socket.

"What happens to me when we get there?"

"I don't know, yet. I might put you to work, I might let you go . . . or I might sacrifice you to my Santería god, Eleguá." An uneven smile appeared on his face.

"You're just trying to scare me."

The captain laughed—a strange laugh that seemed to come from somewhere deep inside his chest—and then he turned to go. "It's up to you, Texas. You can try and swim for it, or you can trust me. Either way, I don't care."

———

CHAPTER 29

Charlie and Raul both thought the three-hour drive to Villa Rica was the longest of their lives. They had tensed up at every set of head-lights they saw, and they dared not stop for water, gas, or a bathroom. They drove straight to Roy Lee's compound and found that the cabaña Charlie had stayed in before was empty, so they hid the cars in a shed and crawled into their beds, wrung out as a pair of dishrags.

When they awoke, they learned that Roy Lee had taken his guests deep-sea fishing on his yacht, *The Miss Inclined*. The groundskeeper said they wouldn't be back until late afternoon. Neither Charlie nor Raul talked much during the day, each of them worrying about Augie and mentally replaying their run-in with Z-17. Raul, especially, could scarcely believe it had happened or that they had survived. He and his uncle were accomplices in the murder of a high-ranking Zeta lieutenant, and the drug lord that Z-17 worked for had no doubt heard about it by now and sent his assassins to find them. He wondered if they would be safe anywhere in Mexico.

Regarding Augie, Charlie had said he believed he was alive, a notion which Raul found comforting even without concrete evidence to support it. But sometimes a feeling was enough to hang on to.

Raul remembered Father Canul's admonition when they parted in Matamoros. *Remain hopeful.*

As though in answer to his prayers, Father Canul called that afternoon.

"Mr. Sweetwater?"

Raul thought he recognized the voice, but it was cutting out. He walked outside the cabaña to get better cell phone reception. "Yes?" he answered tentatively.

"Mr. Sweetwater? This is Padre Canul of the *Templo de la Familia Sagrada.* I am calling to report that the package you sent to me has arrived safely."

The package, the package. Father Canul. It took Raul a moment to figure it out. *Lila. She made it to Matamoros.* "That's good, Father."

"Yes. All is well, for now. We plan to send her across soon, send her to some people on the other side."

"Thank you. She isn't safe in Mexico."

"I agree. Where she is going she will be well cared for. By the way, I have your vehicle. When you are ready to retrieve it perhaps we can meet in Brownsville? I will deliver your truck, and you can buy me lunch. I know a superb steakhouse just ten minutes from the courthouse."

Raul could almost see the Padre smiling as he talked. Despite his heartbreaking work, he always found something to look forward to. "I would very much like that, Father."

There was a pause on the line, and Raul thought the conversation was over.

"There is something else," Canul began. "It is the other reason I am calling you. A man just passed through here on his way to Texas. He recognized the picture of your son on the bulletin board."

Raul stopped pacing and froze in place. "He's seen Augie? Is he alive?"

"He was alive when this man saw him."

"When did he see him, Father?"

"Only yesterday. This man—Luis is his name—he said he worked with your son on a sardine boat out in the Gulf. Apparently, this boat was receiving supplies from another boat when both vessels were captured. Luis was put on a skiff with some other fishermen and put to sea. Soon after, they were picked up by a Pemex crew boat and taken to an offshore platform where a helicopter was able to fly them to Tampico. Luis took the first bus to Matamoros and briefly stopped by my church to pick up supplies for his journey north."

"But what about Augie? Was he with the rescued men?" Raul realized that he was almost shouting into the phone. Charlie came outside to see why.

"Luis said that your son remained on the supply boat," said the priest.

"You said the boats were captured. What do you mean?" There was another pause.

"Father?"

"Do you remember the Guatemalan fellows we talked to when you were here?"

"The captives who were forced onto the fishing boats? The two brothers?"

"Yes. You will remember they spoke of a pirate."

"The Evil Eye, or something like that."

"They called him Mal de Ojo. Luis said this is the pirate who captured the boats. He also took hostages. I am afraid your son was one of them."

"Padre, I don't understand. Why did these . . . pirates release some men and not others? Is Luis still there? Let me speak to him"

"I'm sorry. He was in quite a hurry to leave. The important thing is that your son is alive."

"What else did he say about this Mal de Ojo, Padre?" Raul wanted to get some sense of the man who had kidnapped his son.

"He was quite scared of him. That much I could tell. He said the man was a *brujo*, who could cast spells and also inflict curses with his evil eye."

"A *brujo*, Father?"

"I told you these country people were very superstitious."

"Yes, I remember."

"However, he did say something that concerned me."

"What is that?"

Another hesitation on the other end of the line, which Raul didn't like.

"He said this Mal de Ojo killed the two boat captains in front of everyone . . . and that he seemed to take pleasure in it."

Raul closed his eyes and cursed under his breath. "Any idea where they went, Padre? Or where I should look?"

"I asked Luis that, but unfortunately, he said he had no idea . . . . However, he did say the pirates sounded to him like Cubans. Mr. Sweetwater, there is something I want to say."

"Yes, Father?"

"In my line of work, I have seen many terrible things, cruel things. But it is important that we not surrender to our fears or our despair. I would not want you to do that, Mr. Sweetwater."

Raul heard the priest, but his mind was already elsewhere, refocusing, searching for answers. He hung up with the Padre. Charlie stood in front of him, waiting. "Tell me."

"Augie is alive."

———

CHAPTER 30

Charlie and Raul were waiting on the dock when Roy Lee's yacht returned that evening. As soon as Sasha walked across the gangplank, Charlie met her and pulled her aside. Raul couldn't hear what they were saying, but he could guess. Charlie had told him that Sasha knew Mal de Ojo personally, she knew where he lived, and she would by God take them to him if he had to carry her to Cuba in a duffle bag. Judging by the way they were arguing, Sasha didn't seem a hundred percent onboard with the plan.

Raul studied her from the dock. Yet another woman from Charlie's past—how many were there? She stood almost as tall as Charlie. Her strong features and dark hair and eyes reminded him of the Greek actress Irene Pappas. Charlie had told him that she inherited her poise and beauty from her mother, but she got her *cojones* from her dad. After hearing about her success as a maritime repo-man, he learned that she'd often used these attributes—the beauty and the balls—to distract pirates, thieves, and corrupt port officials while she or her team stole back the ships that had been stolen from her clients.

Roy Lee's other guests, most of them the worse for sun and alcohol, wearily disembarked from the yacht and headed to their cabins, glancing over their shoulders and wondering what in the world Charlie and Sasha were going on about. Raul decided it was time to intervene.

"She says she won't help us," said Charlie when Raul walked up.

Sasha sighed and shook her head. "I didn't say that!" She looked sympathetically at Raul. "I am so sorry about your son. I want to help you get him back, I really do."

"Then why the hell won't you—"

"Shut up, Charlie. Let her finish."

"Thank you, Raul," she said. "I never said I wouldn't help. We're simply arguing about how. Your uncle wants to go in like Rambo, with guns blazing. That's a stupid idea and wrong."

"I never said I wanted to go in with guns blazing."

"You said that when you found the man who kidnapped Augie, you would take care of him yourself. That's the kind of macho shit that will get us all killed."

"We're talking about Mal de Ojo, right?" asked Raul. "Is it true you know where he lives, Sasha?"

"Yes, but—"

"Then what's the problem?"

She took a deep breath. "I don't want anybody to get hurt . . . and to be honest, I'm not sure I believe Augie *was* kidnapped, not this last time, anyway."

Raul cocked his head, feeling his temper rise. "Why not?"

"Because Ivan is not like that. He doesn't hurt innocent people."

Charlie was shaking his head. "Ivan? You're on a first name basis with this murderous sonofabitch?"

"He's not the ogre you think he is, Charlie. He's a lot like you if you want to know the truth. Reckless, stubborn, and about half crazy, but he's not a . . . murderous sonofabitch."

"What about the two captains he killed?"

"I doubt they were innocent. They must have done something terrible."

"Naw, I don't buy it. You've slept with him. Your judgment is clouded."

"I've slept with you, too, Charlie."

Raul looked at both of them, beginning to understand the subtext.

"Sasha," Raul said as calmly as he could. "How do you think we should get Augie back? You said you would help us . . . . How?"

She paused before she answered. "Let me talk to him."

Raul held out his cell phone. "Talk to him."

Sasha shook her head. He doesn't use a cell phone. He insists on living off the grid."

"So we'll go there, to him."

She nodded tentatively. "We can go to Cuba together, to Cienfuegos, and I promise we will get your son back, but you . . . ." She turned and looked pointedly at Charlie. "But you have to promise you'll let me talk to Ivan, alone."

Raul nodded. "That sounds reasonable."

"I want to hear you promise."

"I promise," said Raul.

Both of them waited for Charlie to respond. He narrowed his eyes at Sasha. "Fine, but if I find out Augie has been harmed, all bets are off."

Sasha insisted that they shake hands on their agreement. It seemed a little silly to all of them, but it did help to lighten the mood.

"So, what now?" she asked. "Commercial flights are going to take awhile. Even though Cuba's less than a thousand miles away, we'll probably have to make three plane changes before we finally get to Cienfuegos. It might be day after tomorrow before we arrive."

"I've got a better idea," said Charlie. "Raul, let me borrow your cell phone."

CHAPTER 31

Swim for it, or trust Mal de Ojo? Augie wrestled with the question all day and most of the night. His ribs still hurt like hell, but he could move a little better now, and the pirate crew had provided enough food and water for him to regain some strength. Several times he had made up his mind to jump ship and swim for it, but swim for where? The Yucatan was far behind them, and he had seen nothing but blue water all day. Twice, container ships had passed by, but in the far distance and moving very quickly. He knew that by now Cuba must be somewhere to the east of him, but how far?

Augie hadn't seen the captain since they'd talked the night before, but he could smell his cigar smoke whenever he was downwind of the pilothouse. Did the bastard ever sleep? He kept thinking back to what Mal de Ojo said would happen to him when they reached Cuba: he would either be put to work, set free, or sacrificed to some pagan god whose name he couldn't remember. Regarding the first option, did "work" mean joining the captain's pirate crew? Or would he remain with them as a sea slave? Or was it some other kind of work?

Augie hoped for—but didn't expect—Door No. 2. It hardly seemed likely that the pirate captain would haul him and his fellows all the way to Cuba just to kick them loose. He'd already resolved to run for it the moment the supply boat touched the dock, if he could. Then somehow, he'd find help.

The third option troubled Augie more than he wanted to admit. Even though he suspected Mal de Ojo was just messing with his head, why did he have to bring up Santería? The men hunkered in the bunkroom below him sure as hell believed in it. They were convinced Augie was marked for death. Each time he entered their cabin, he could feel their anxiety. Since they didn't want him anywhere near them, he began avoiding them altogether. But gradually their fear began to transfer to him. Why was he the only captive allowed to walk free on the ship? He hadn't seen them leave their cabin once. Were they too scared, or had they tried to leave and been forced to return? If so, why did he have special status?

A seed of doubt began grow in him that maybe there was something to the Santería sacrifice thing. Ironically, the fear had been planted there originally by his mom. In a misguided effort to keep her son from going to South Padre for Spring Break, she told him the appalling true tale of the American college kid (a *University of Texas* college kid she added for effect) who crossed the river into Matamoros to party with his friends and was kidnapped by a devil-worshiping cult that cut out his heart, lungs, brain, and genitals. "They found his decapitated body in a shallow grave behind the Santería altar," she had concluded ominously.

Nice story, Mom. Thanks a lot.

So Augie waited uneasily on the supply ship as it motored toward Cuba, avoiding the other captives, steering clear of the pirates, and keeping to himself. The next morning, when it was light enough to see, Augie spotted some land off the port bow. When he asked one of the Cuban pirates about it, he was told it was Playa Sirena, an island off of Isla de la Juventud. *"Llegamos a Cienfuegos en cinco horas,"* he said.

"Playa Sirena," Augie repeated to himself. "Cienfuegos in five hours."

When the crewman wandered off, Augie remained at the rail, studying the distant shoreline for signs of habitation—a water tower, a billboard, a harbor—but the land was too far away, just a low dark line on the horizon. Augie calculated the island was at least six miles away. *Surely I can swim six miles. Do I trust the captain, or do I trust myself?*

But by the time he had talked himself into going for it, the shoreline had disappeared. He rubbed his eyes, hoping it was a trick of the morning light, but now he saw nothing but water on all sides of the boat. He sat down wearily on the edge of the life raft and hung his head, cursing himself for hesitating. He didn't move for an hour. The courage he had worked up had drained away, and he felt utterly defeated. For the first time since the misery began, he believed he would never see his family again.

A crewman had been working nearby, but he disappeared below, leaving Augie alone on the deck. He lifted his head and gazed out listlessly at the morning sky. It was almost dead calm, the only sound the constant droning of the diesels and the splashing of water pushed aside by the moving vessel. A few wispy clouds reflected on the surface of the glassy sea, but otherwise, the water seemed indistinguishable from the sky. Augie felt adrift, as if he was traveling through a featureless void. *Purgatory,* he thought. This must be what purgatory is like. An intermediate state, where nothing happens, where there is only the waiting for what comes next.

Out of the corner of his eye, to starboard, Augie noticed an anomaly on the horizon, something vertical, jutting up—a bright, red-and-white-striped column standing erect and incongruous on a tiny tongue of land, less than a mile away it seemed. *Less than a mile away.* He stood up and looked again, wondering if he was hallucinating. But there it stood—a material lighthouse, solid, functional, well-tended, which meant people had been there recently and might even be there now. He could easily swim that far, right? The question surfaced in his mind again: *Trust Mal de Ojo or trust myself?*

Without a second thought, Augie climbed over the rail and jumped.

———

CHAPTER 32

Alberto had been eager to help. He promised Charlie he would provide his jet to fly them to Cienfuegos; his pilot would pick them up at Roy Lee's private airstrip. At the appointed time, Raul and Charlie saw the Beechcraft approaching.

"Are you sure your runway is long enough to handle a jet?" Raul asked Roy Lee.

"Oh, shit yeah. Couple of years ago an Aero Mexico 727 had to make an emergency stop here. Piece of cake. Only four people got hurt."

Raul's eyes cut to Roy Lee and then returned to the jet until it landed and taxied to a standstill. When the door opened, Alberto stuck out his big head and waved. While the pilot stowed bags, Alberto lumbered over and gave Charlie and Raul *abrazos*.

"I want to come with you. I hope that is alright."

Raul nodded. "Of course it is. Thanks for taking us to Cienfuegos, Alberto. Charlie said you know people there?"

"Yes, and they know we are coming. I still have quite a few connections in Cuba, believe it or not—remnants of my student days when I was an impassioned socialist."

"Before you sold out and became an impassioned capitalist," added Charlie.

Alberto shrugged. "What can I say? I like to own stuff."

"Alberto," Charlie continued, "You already know Roy Lee. And this is Sasha Vasiliki. She's in the, uh, boat brokerage business, and she's also going to help us once we get to Cuba."

Alberto shook her hand and then addressed Charlie. "*Bueno*, I see everyone packed light, so I think there will be enough room on the plane. Are we ready?"

As they followed Alberto across the runway, Raul walked next to Charlie. "Enough room? There's four of us, plus the pilot. I thought the plane seated six."

They boarded and were surprised to see Petra and Pablo, the Alexanders' bodyguard, already inside. When Sasha climbed in, Petra sat up straight. "Why is she here?" she asked.

Everyone felt the tension in the air, and when Charlie made introductions the two women greeted each other coolly. Charlie took a seat across from Petra at the back of the plane, with Alberto and Raul sitting opposite each other across the aisle. Sasha and Pablo sat in the two forward-facing seats at the front.

As the jet taxied to the end of the runway, Petra leaned forward and pulled Charlie toward her so that their heads almost touched.

"Why is she here?" she asked again, sotto voce.

"She can help us find Augie."

"She cannot be trusted."

Charlie tilted his head. "Why do you say that? Do you know her?"

"I know about her. Did she tell you she knows Mal de Ojo?"

Charlie nodded. "Yes."

"Did she tell you *how* she knows him and what her connection to him is?"

"Why don't *you* tell me?"

"The man is a criminal. He steals other people's boats, and she sells them for him on the open market. The way I see it, she is as bad as that barbaric pirate."

Charlie was taken aback by her rancor, but he wasn't dissuaded. "Petra, I don't care. I'll team up with El Chapo if it'll help us find Augie."

"You know she is sleeping with him, too, don't you?"

Charlie pulled back, surprised she knew about that, surprised she knew *anything* about Sasha or the pirate. "I don't care," he lied. "Petra, if you don't mind me asking, why did you decide to come on this trip?"

"I am here for you and Raul, of course. You should know that."

He patted her on the knee. "Don't worry, okay? Everything will be fine."

She snorted. "*Espero que si*, Charlie. I truly, honestly hope so."

The jet took off and arced in a wide circle before heading out to sea. Charlie stared down at the small bay bordering Villa Rica. On that same bay Hernán Cortés, faced with the staggering might of the Aztec empire, famously burned his boats so that his men had to either march forth and conquer, or else die. Charlie felt an unsettling connection to that long past event, although he couldn't say why. All he knew for sure was that he was another step closer to finding his nephew. He didn't care how many boats and bridges he had to burn to get there.

The trip across the Gulf, which in a fishing vessel would have taken more than two days, took less than two hours by air. When they landed, they were quickly escorted through Cuban customs. The Mexican cell service worked fine in Cuba, but Raul's phone was useless. He borrowed Alberto's to touch base with the Rockport office and to ask Judy to call Rosie. "Tell her I'll be out of reach for a little while. Don't tell her where I am." If his wife knew he and Charlie were in Cuba, she would bust a gasket.

Alberto called his local contacts and told Raul and Charlie that a friend of his in Havana—a buddy of Fidel's, no less—had released Augie's picture to national, provincial, and municipal police organizations, as well as to the port authorities.

"Of course, my friend insisted that the boy could not have been taken by Cuban pirates because piracy and kidnapping are illegal in Cuba and therefore do not exist. But we came to an understanding after I promised him a case of Johnnie Walker Blue."

Outside the airport there was a moment of confusion about what to do next: stay together as a group or divide into teams? They decided to split up. Alberto, Petra, and Pablo would use the car Fidel's *compadre* had provided for them. They would talk to the local cops and government officials, while Charlie, Raul, and Petra would take a cab and check out the harbors. Charlie didn't expect that Mal de Ojo would be obliging enough to fly a Jolly Roger flag from the mast of his boats, but he could hope.

Raul hailed a taxi—a bluish 1953 Bel-Air Coupe, or at least that's what it started out as. Now maybe half the vehicle was original, while the rest had been created from a dozen other automobiles and retooled Russian parts. It was a lovely Frankenstein of a car.

It took a few minutes to explain to the *taxista* that they wanted him to drive them to every dock and harbor in the city where commercial fishing boats were berthed. The driver took that to mean that they were interested in visiting bars and restaurants with a nice view of the boats. No, they wanted to see the vessels themselves. He replied that if they wanted to *rent* a boat, his cousin ran a charter service and could give them a very good price. No, they were looking for a certain boat. Finally, Sasha just told him to drive; she would tell him where to go.

"I forgot that you've done business here before," said Charlie when they were underway. "So how does it work, exactly? He steals the boats, you miraculously locate them and then return them to their rightful owners, receiving a nice commission in return, which the two of you split? That's Petra's take on your set-up."

"I don't trust that woman," she said at the mention of Petra's name. "To answer your question, I usually sell the boat to the highest bidder and then receive my standard commission."

"You never return the boat to the original owner?"

"Rarely. Most of the vessels Ivan seizes belong to some pretty bad people."

Charlie and Raul both looked at her dubiously. "What qualifies as 'bad people'?" Raul asked.

"Well, for starters, outlaw captains who buy kidnapped victims from slavers and then force them to work against their will."

The taxi driver pulled up to a pier where several dozen handmade fishing skiffs were bobbing in a small laguna. *"Botes de pesca,"* he said proudly, thinking that tourists usually loved seeing colorful fishing boats like these.

Sasha shook her head impatiently. *"Muelle de la Pacas, atrás del Paseo el Prado,"* she demanded, directing him to the port's main commercial dock.

"How does he know which boats are using slaves?" asked Raul.

"I don't know how he knows; he just does."

It sounded like a rationalization to Charlie. He suspected she still had a thing for this pirate and needed to believe he was some kind of nautical Robin Hood so she could feel good about screwing him. In Charlie's eyes, Mal de Ojo was in it strictly for the money, just like every pirate since the beginning of boats.

They rode in silence through the streets of Cienfuegos, barely noticing the beautiful architecture and wide boulevards. The cab driver couldn't understand it. He was proud of his town. Why were these Americans just sitting in the back seat acting like pouty children? *Look around you,* he wanted to say. *Look at the antique cars, the bright-colored buildings, the pretty girls on the street, strolling, talking, shopping. Listen to the guajira music drifting out of the bars and cafes—this is old Cuba, this is authentic Cuba, just like in the movies. How could they not appreciate it?*

On the way to the commercial docks, he couldn't help himself. He slowed almost to a stop in front of the city's magnificent yacht club, a neoclassical jewel perched on the bay. And to show that he was sticking to the agenda, he pointed to the expensive yachts and sailboats moored in the slips.

"*Mira,*" he announced. "*Mas barcos.*"

"*Muelle de la Pacas,*" Sasha repeated tersely.

The taxi driver sped off in a huff. The *Pacas* industrial port was the ugliest part of town. But if that's where these *yumas* wanted to go, then fine, he'd take them there and charge them double the fare.

"Sasha," Raul began. "Earlier you said Mal de Ojo contacted you whenever he had a boat to sell. How did he contact you?"

"He would buy a burner phone and send me texts."

"Does he live here? Have you been to his home?" Charlie asked her.

Sasha looked at him, trying to decide if the questions were pertinent to finding the boy, or if Charlie was just being a jealous ass again. She noticed Raul waiting for an answer, too.

"No. I have a general idea where he lives, but I've never been there."

"Then why are we here in Cienfuegos?" asked Raul.

"This is where he docks his boats. It's where we've always transacted our business. I think he lives a couple of hours from here, somewhere near or on the Bahia de Cochinos, but I've never been there."

"You don't know the name of his hideout?"

"It's not a hideout, Charlie. He's not hiding from anybody. Basically, it's just a small fishing village with a few nice beaches. The truth of the matter is that Ivan's really just a common fisherman when you come down to it. It's what he's done his whole life. This other business was fairly recent. He wasn't looking for it. I think it found him."

"And when it found him he grabbed the opportunity with both hands, didn't he?"

Sasha scowled. "And where would Augie be now if Ivan hadn't seized the boat he was on? Huh? Tell me that."

Charlie looked away. "He better be alive, that's all I've got to say."

"Enough!" said Raul. "Remember why we're here." The commercial docks were coming into view. "We're looking for fishing boats named *El Dorado* or *Mañana*, and any other vessel that Sasha might recognize. After that, let's start asking around. Somebody is bound to know this pirate or fisherman or whatever he is, or at least may have seen him."

Their search around the docks proved fruitless. There were plenty of fishing boats, but none that they were looking for. The people they talked to seemed friendly, but they said they didn't know and hadn't seen a bearded, one-eyed boat captain.

"He's careful, isn't he?" said Raul.

Sasha nodded. "Very. He always arranged things ahead of time. By the time I arrived, everything was ready to go. I simply took pictures of the vessel, assessed its value, and began contacting potential buyers. The transactions were always quick and smooth."

"I wonder how many port officials he had to pay off for it to go so smooth?" asked Raul.

Sasha shrugged. "He didn't say, and I didn't ask."

"Do you have any pictures of him?" asked Charlie. "Or maybe of the two of you together?"

Charlie knew he was being a dick, and he wasn't sure why it bothered him so much that Sasha was Mal de Ojo's boat broker and sometime lover. Charlie had never been more than her sometime lover himself, and they had both been happy with the arrangement. Maybe it was the respect he'd had for Yannis and Inga, Sasha's parents. While it was true they had known some colorful and less-than-honest people in their careers, they never once compromised their integrity; they never crossed the line. It troubled Charlie that Sasha might have crossed the line with this pirate, or that she might have erased it altogether.

Sasha ignored Charlie's question. Her memories of Ivan were private, goddammit. When they had met as lovers, it was usually at a secluded mountain inn at a natural park a couple of hours east of Cienfuegos. There they hiked, swam in the rivers and waterfalls, fucked, ate, drank, fucked some more. When they were together there, they were able to shut out the world entirely. They never felt the need to talk about their pasts or their futures. They simply enjoyed being with each other.

When Charlie asked again, she snapped at him. "There are no pictures."

They left the docks and asked the taxi driver to drop them off at the Plaza José Martí. Even though they tipped him well, he was glad to be rid of them.

—

They sat quietly in the gazebo at the center of the plaza, waiting for the rest of the group and wondering what else they could do to find Augie. Charlie announced that he was going for a walk. He was frustrated, mostly with himself, and wanted a little solitary time. He bought a map at a little kiosk and then found a café with a clear line of sight to the gazebo.

While he sipped his espresso, he studied the map. There were only two villages on the Bahia de Cochinos—Playa Girón at the mouth of the bay, and Playa Larga at the other end. He wondered which one the pirate would choose to live in. He tried to remember where he'd heard the names before, and it finally came to him: they were the two principal landing sites for the disastrous Bay of Pigs invasion in 1961, one of the biggest military clusterfucks of all time. The CIA-sponsored rebels had been massacred by Fidel's forces, their boats sunk, and twelve hundred of them captured. Charlie pictured the sites as bombed-out towns with concrete bunkers and rusted landing crafts half-buried in the sand. He decided to ask his waiter about it.

"Oh, no, *señor*," he answered in English. "They are both very nice."

"Which of the villages would *you* live in?"

"Oh, Playa Larga for certain. The village is smaller than Girón, but the water is nicer and it has more trees. Also better fishing, prettier girls, and better cafes. Are you planning to live here in Cuba, *señor*?"

"No, just visiting."

Charlie glanced up at the plaza and noticed that Alberto and Petra had returned. Pablo wasn't with them, and he guessed they had sent him on an errand of some kind. Considering Cuba's high number of taxis and low volume of crime, they had little need for a bodyguard or a driver while they were there.

Charlie left some money on the table and began walking across the square to rejoin his group. Even from a distance, he could tell that something very bad had happened. Raul was slumped over the rail of the gazebo, sobbing uncontrollably. Alberto and Petra stood beside him trying to offer comfort.

When Alberto saw Charlie running toward them, he broke away and met him before he reached the gazebo. He had a stricken look on his face.

"What the hell happened, Alberto?"

"The police called. Charlie, they found a body. The description matches Augie's."

Charlie stopped and simply stared at Alberto. He felt faint, wounded, as though blood was draining from his body. "Where?" he managed to ask.

Alberto gripped Charlie's shoulders with both hands to steady his friend. On the Isla de la Juventud. Some fishermen found the body washed up on the southern shore."

"Are they sure it's Augie?"

"They said they are sure." Alberto wrapped his big arms around him.

Charlie broke away. "I need to talk to Raul."

Alberto cleared his throat. "They want a relative to identify the body, Charlie. There is an airport on the island, in the town of Nueva Gerona. We can go there in the jet today, this afternoon. The authorities will take us to the hospital morgue where they are holding . . . Augie."

Raul stood up when Charlie came over. The two men embraced.

"How will I tell Rosie?" asked Raul, his voice shaking. "This will destroy her."

Charlie wiped his eyes and then placed his hands on Raul's arms. "Alberto can fly us to the place where they have him. One of us needs to identify the body. Do you think you're up to it?"

Raul nodded. "Yes." He continued nodding, as if to convince himself. "I can do it . . . . I *need* to do it. I have to see him one last time."

Charlie nodded back. "I understand." He paused a moment and cleared his throat. "Raul, I won't be going with you. I've got something *I* need to do, too."

Raul searched his uncle's eyes and saw the fury there. Charlie didn't want closure; he wanted revenge. Raul didn't know how to think about that. At the moment, he didn't feel hate in his heart, or anger, or revenge. He felt only emptiness and a deep, almost debilitating remorse.

"You do whatever you have to do, Charlie. I have to go to my son."

Charlie walked away from the gazebo and sat down on one of the park benches. He closed his eyes and raised his face to the late afternoon sun. A humid breeze cooled his sweat, and he heard kids playing. He felt a presence next to him and opened his eyes.

Petra put her hand over his. "I am so sorry, Charlie."

He nodded, and they sat together in silence.

"Charlie," she asked gently. "What are you going to do about this?"

At first Charlie thought she was referring to identifying the body on Isla de la Juventud, but when he looked at her and saw her eyes, he knew it was something else.

"I think I know where he lives," he said. He didn't have to spell out who.

"Then it should not be too difficult for you to find him."

"It's a small town called Playa Larga . . . on the Bay of Pigs."

Petra was silent, but she squeezed his hand.

"I will need to leave the country quickly," Charlie continued.

"I understand. I will talk to Alberto. After we go to Juventud, we will fly back here and wait for you. The jet will be ready to leave as soon as you return."

Charlie took a deep breath and nodded. "Okay. Thanks, Petra."

She released his hand and got up to leave. As Petra walked away, Charlie saw Sasha watching him. She stood apart from the others and seemed to be questioning Charlie with her eyes. When she saw the desire for vengeance written on his face, her expression changed, reflecting the fear, horror, and sadness she felt. She blinked back tears, turned, and walked away. Charlie let her go.

Alberto and Raul went to the avenue to flag down a taxi while Petra stepped away and called Pablo on her phone. Soon the three of them, Raul, Alberto, and Petra, were speeding away toward the airport, leaving Charlie on the park bench alone with his rage.

———

CHAPTER 33

They rode in silence during the brief hundred-and-fifty-mile flight to Nueva Gerona. In that short time, the water shoaled from green to deep blue to the familiar Caribbean coastal palate of cream and azure. Under other circumstances, Raul would have enjoyed the view, but since they'd left the plaza he had been overcome by a profound physical and emotional numbness. He had briefly considered calling Rosie but didn't want to break the news to her until he saw the body, so he simply waited in a sort of suspended animation.

Alberto had arranged for a car to meet them at the airport, and it was waiting on the runway when they landed. As they drove to the hospital, Alberto tried to make small talk to pull Raul out of the dazed state he seemed to be in, but to no avail. They pulled up the Hospital General Héroes de la Revolución and saw a clean, two-story white stucco building. Blooming hibiscus and bougainvillea lined the entrance.

"A surprisingly fine facility for such a small town," Alberto remarked, trying to break the mournful silence.

"It serves the entire municipality," the driver said in English. "And it has excellent doctors."

Alberto looked at the driver. "If there is one thing Cuba has in abundance, it is excellent doctors."

The driver smiled appreciatively. "Thank you, sir. We do our best."

"You are a doctor?" asked Alberto.

He smiled. "The state, in its wisdom, offers us wonderful medical school training and then pays us almost nothing to practice. Thus, heart surgeons become fishermen, pediatricians repair TVs, and neurologists drive taxis."

The trio entered the hospital, and Alberto spoke with an attendant at the admissions desk who instructed them to wait in the lounge; a doctor would escort them to the morgue. A few minutes later, a slender woman wearing a name tag that said Dr. Barragán appeared. Alberto walked over to greet her.

"You arrived so quickly," she said. "You are the American?"

"No, I am Alberto Alexander, a friend of the family. That is my wife, Petra, and that," he glanced over at Raul, "is the father of the boy."

Raul looked up listlessly, his eyes glazed over, his face slack. It was the type of emotional vapor-lock the doctor had seen too often on the faces of grieving family members.

"May I talk to you in private, Mr. Alexander?"

Out of earshot of the others, Dr. Barragán explained that the body had washed up on the island's southern shore earlier that day.

"Fishermen found it floating in with the tide. We sent an ambulance to retrieve the body and then ran the fingerprints in our national database. When no match turned up, we checked the missing persons *avisos* and noticed Mr. Sweetwater's image right away. We immediately notified the police. But we can never be 100% sure until someone close to the deceased identifies the body."

"Yes, I understand," said Alberto.

"Is the father prepared to do this? Or will it need to be you?"

"Raul can do it."

"Seeing a drowning victim can be quite a shock, Mr. Alexander, especially when there has been additional trauma to the body."

"What kind of trauma?"

"It appears the victim encountered a large group of the, um, *caravela portuguesa*, the Portuguese jellyfish. There are many marks," she moved her hand over her face and torso, "many . . . *picaduras*."

"I understand. But it is important that the father see the body of his son. He is ready."

She looked dubiously at Raul and nodded. "Okay. I will take you to see the boy."

Alberto called to Raul. Petra stood up with him.

"Are you sure you can do this?" the doctor asked him.

Raul looked at her as if he were noticing her for the first time. "*Sí, vamanos.*"

They walked through the hospital, and Dr. Barragán escorted them through several doors. When they reached the small morgue, they saw a gurney in the middle of the room and a body covered with a white sheet.

Raul took a deep breath and walked alone to the gurney. He slowly lifted a corner of the sheet and quickly dropped it. They watched him lift the sheet again and this time leave the face uncovered. As he continued to stand there, his back to the others, they wondered if he was overcome. Alberto took a step forward to help him, but then Raul spun around to face them, his eyes shining.

"It's not him. It's not Augie."

——————

CHAPTER 34

Augie was having doubts. He'd been sitting on the rocky island all day and hadn't seen a single boat. The lighthouse was locked up tight, and the structures he'd seen from the water—structures he had hoped might be residences—were only roofless concrete shells. The island was approximately two hundred yards long by thirty yards wide. He'd walked the length of it three times already and there was nothing more to see.

A lone palm tree had somehow taken root in the rocks, but it provided scant shade from the tropical sun. The island was dominated by the lighthouse, which resembled a red-striped rocket. It towered above everything in sight. Augie estimated the tower would be visible to boats up to fifteen or twenty miles away, but where the hell were they? Only later did it dawn on him that the purpose of the lighthouse was to keep boats *away* from the rocky island, not draw them to it. Hence, the doubts. Had he merely traded one prison for another?

Augie sat under the palm tree and watched a lone seagull watch him back. He supposed the bird was hoping for something to eat, but it eventually gave up and flew away, which was lucky for the bird, because Augie had been trying to figure out a way to catch the sonofabitch and eat him.

Augie was hungry, tired, sunburned, and his ribs hurt like hell every time he moved. When he dove into the sea during his escape, the pain had taken his breath away, and he nearly blacked out because of it. But with his adrenalin pumping, he swam as fast as he could to put distance between him and Mal de Ojo. Strangely, no one jumped in after him, and the boat never slowed or deviated from its path, although he could have sworn he saw the pirate captain watching him from the bridge.

A favorable current allowed him to make the one-mile swim to the island without too much trouble. Despite his injuries, he kept telling himself he could make it as long as he kept his head and didn't panic. He had swum much farther distances before.

Augie sighed and threw a rock into the water. "What now, Juan Antonio Augustus Sweetwater?" he said aloud. He'd been talking to himself a lot the last few hours, and he knew he was on the verge of losing it. A couple of times, he felt compelled to get up and put his hands on the lighthouse just to make sure he hadn't hallucinated the colossal object. Mostly, he sat and waited—for a boat, a plane, a rocket, a little prince on an asteroid—waited for something to rescue him from the terrible nightmare he'd been living the past ten days.

Late in the day, he fell asleep and dreamed about his family. They had all gathered in the backyard of his house in Fulton. His dad was barbecuing ribs over an open fire. His mom was setting the picnic table, and Yolanda was helping. Near the fire, Charlie drank beer and told a yarn about his crazy uncles, Rupert and Noble and Flavius, and some crazy shit they got into on Ransom Island. Augie heard his mother calling to him. Why was she speaking in Spanish? Couldn't she see he was listening to Charlie's story? But the calling continued.

Augie opened his eyes and saw the sun was low on the horizon, and then he realized he was still hearing the voices, real voices, calling to him from below. He stood up quickly and saw a small, steel-hulled fishing boat idling safely away from the rocks. One of the fisherman called to him again.

"*Bue-nas tar-des, señor,*" he shouted. "*¿Necesitas ayuda?*"

Augie began laughing. Hell, yeah he needed help. "*¡Sí . . . por favor!*" he yelled back. "*Sí, sí, sí!*"

He continued to laugh and even danced a little jig under the palm tree. The fishermen looked at each other. Was this one touched in the head? *Loco? Bobo? Borracho?* Whatever his problem, they decided the decent thing to do would be take him to land and turn him over to somebody who could take care of him. The poor kid obviously needed help.

The boat, which reminded Augie of the *African Queen,* had five fishermen aboard. They had been diving for lobsters in the area and were heading back to Cayo Largo to sell their catch to a small resort there. He was welcome to go with them.

Augie could hardly believe his luck. He swam out to the boat, and they helped him climb aboard. When they were underway, they shared a couple of their empanadas with him, which he devoured quickly, washing them down with lemon-lime soda. As the boat chugged toward Cayo Largo, he sat under the canopy and enjoyed the ride, grinning the entire time. It was dark when the lobster boat reached the pier on the cay. Augie gave an emotional *abrazo* to each of the fishermen and then turned his attention to the welcoming lights of the Playa Paraíso Resort.

Now, he thought as he loped towards the resort clubhouse, *where the hell can I find a telephone?*

—

CHAPTER 35

Charlie couldn't understand why the taxi driver wanted to charge double to take him to Playa Larga. He would pay the extra money, sure, but "because of the crabs?" Although he had no idea what the *taxista* was talking about, they settled on a price and left Cienfuegos for Playa Larga, dropping down and following the coastline for most of the way.

The shock over Augie's death had dulled some, but Charlie's resolve had only sharpened. The way he saw it, that fucking pirate had either pushed his nephew off the boat or killed him and thrown him overboard. Either way, Augie was dead, and Mal de Ojo would answer for it.

The first town they came to was Playa Girón. At the entrance to the town, Charlie saw an old army tank resting on a platform and a series of concrete bunkers facing the beach. Signs along the highway reminded travelers that a great victory had been won there against the imperialists, and that heroes had died so the people could live. *¡Viva Fidel y Viva la Revolución!*

After they left Playa Girón, the sun set and the brief tropic twilight departed. Charlie sat back in the seat and closed his eyes, trying to clear his head and prepare for his own impending battle. But about ten kilometers outside of Playa Larga, his concentration was interrupted by an extremely loud crunching sound, as if the taxi was driving over lightbulbs or shards of glass. He was certain all four tires must have blown, but the car didn't lurch and the driver didn't pull over.

"What in Christ's name is that?"

"*Son los cangrejos, señor,*"

The crabs?

The driver pointed ahead and Charlie saw a vast, dense river of *cangrejos*—crabs, tens of thousands of them flowing over the road. They covered both lanes as far as the car's headlights allowed him to see. Yellow ones, red ones, black ones—a clacking, crunching mass of them pouring out of the pine and mango forest and scuttling toward the sea. The terrible crunching continued as the car drove over and through the *cangrejos*.

"*Es su migración anual,*" said the driver. "*Ojalá que no tengamos un pinchazo.*" It's the annual migration. I hope we don't get a flat.

Charlie said he understood and agreed with the driver. He sure as hell didn't want to get out of the car and help change a flat tire. It was like something out of a Fifties science-fiction movie. Watching the army of crabs, he had the fleeting, unbidden notion that they had been summoned there to protect the village of Playa Larga from harm. Didn't the Padre tell Raul the pirate was a brujo of some kind? He closed his eyes and tried to shut out the distraction.

They finally got through the crab migration, leaving behind a smashed wake of shell and guts, and Charlie heard the smooth hum of rubber on asphalt again. Up ahead, a small hand-painted sign welcomed them to Playa Larga.

The village sat right on the water, and there seemed to be only one paved street running through it. The street was lined with low-rise concrete block houses, some bed and breakfast hotels, and a few colorful restaurants. Intermittent streetlamps cast yellow cones of light along the road. Between the buildings, he could see small wooden fishing boats tied up in the cove. The taxi proceeded slowly, stuck behind a horse-drawn cart and some vendors on three-wheeled bicycles. Within a very short time, the car reached the other end of town.

The cab driver twisted around to face Charlie, a "What now?" look on his face.

Charlie paid the driver, throwing in some extra bills for the possibility of a flat tire on the way back, and then began walking through town, deciding where to begin his search for Mal de Ojo. In a town this tiny, he figured it wouldn't take long to track him down. The place was even smaller than Fulton. Two restaurants stood out along the street: one called Chuchi el Pescador, and the other, a little further down, Chuchi el Gordo. Charlie chose Chuchi the "fisherman's" restaurant first. He would visit "fat" Chuchi's place after that.

Trying not to betray a sense of urgency, Charlie told a waiter he was looking for Ivan, an older gentleman with only one good eye.

"Ah, Ivan el tuerto?" asked the waiter, using the Spanish name for a one-eyed man.

"Sí," Charlie answered, his pulse quickening. "Es él."

"No lo he visto. Quizás su cuñado, Chuchi el Gordo, sabe donde está." I haven't seen him. Maybe his brother-in-law, Chuchi el Gordo, knows where he is.

Chuchi el Gordo's restaurant was a lively two-story establishment with tables both upstairs and down. Charlie asked for Chuchi, and a waiter sent him upstairs where a young mozo pointed him out. Chuchi el Gordo stood behind the bar cleaning a glass with a dish towel. Despite his advanced age, he appeared remarkably robust. And jovial. His teeth almost glowed in the dark when he smiled. Charlie sat down at the bar and ordered a seven-year-old Havana Club rum on the rocks.

"Siete con hielo," said Chuchi, smiling broadly as he grabbed the bottle of dark rum. They struck up a conversation, and Charlie explained that he was planning to do some fishing around Playa Larga and wondered if he might recommend a good place to stay. Chuchi said he'd come to the right place; the fishing around Playa Larga was perhaps the best in the world, "especially the rios and aguas tranquilas," he added. He also told him that he happened to have a couple of guest rooms attached to his restaurant and would be happy to rent him one. Charlie said he just might take him up on that.

Gradually, Charlie led up to a fabricated story about having met Ivan in Cienfuegos—in fact, Ivan was the one who suggested he come to Playa Larga in the first place, and it was he who recommended El Gordo's restaurant. This seemed to delight Chuchi. Charlie said he'd love to thank Ivan personally and asked if he might be coming by the restaurant later that evening. Chuchi said he didn't know; his brother-in-law was a fisherman and often at sea, but he did know where he lived. Charlie asked for directions, saying he might drop by and say hello sometime. Chuchi smiled and eyed him closely, then he described the house and street where Ivan El Tuerto lived. Charlie thanked him and continued to make small talk for a few minutes until Chuchi excused himself to wait on other customers and talk to some of his staff.

Not wanting to seem too eager, Charlie sipped his drink and tried to appear outwardly calm. But inside he boiled with anger and anticipation. He finished his drink, left money on the bar, and quietly left the restaurant. Soon he was back on the street, heading for Mal de Ojo's house.

———

CHAPTER 36

After the revelation at the hospital, it had all happened so fast: the phone call, the quick flight to Cayo Largo de Sur, the reunion. Only hours before, Raul had been in a freefall, tumbling into a dark chasm, when suddenly the hand of God plucked him out of his descent and set him on firm ground again.

The dead body in the morgue certainly resembled Augie—he could easily see why someone would think so—but Raul knew his own son. Afterwards he'd felt guilty about feeling so happy at the hospital's mistake. Another family would be mourning the death of their son. But it wouldn't be his family. Not today.

And then Alberto's phone rang.

Raul could tell by the elation and surprise in Alberto's voice that it was good news. Smiling, he handed the phone to Raul. Rosie was almost incoherent she was talking so fast, her words interspersed with catches that sounded like she was crying and laughing both at once. But Raul heard the most important parts: Augie was alive, he was safe, he was nearby, he was waiting for his dad to pick him up.

Their good fortune continued when Alberto learned there was a runway on Cayo Largo del Sur that could handle his jet, and that the resort from which Augie had called was less than two miles from the airfield. It took longer for the plane to taxi the Nuevo Gerona runway than it did to make the eighty-five mile trip to the island.

The reunion that Raul had imagined all week took place in the marbled foyer of the Sol Cayo Largo Hotel. Although he was initially distressed by Augie's appearance—the tattered clothing, the swollen nose and black eye, a crisscross of bruises on his arms and neck—he couldn't contain his joy. A barrage of questions tumbled out of Raul's mouth, but Augie insisted they would have time to go into that later. Right now, he wanted more than anything else, more than anything in the entire world, a tall piña colada—he had been dreaming about one for days.

In the bar, Augie asked about Charlie.

Raul's eyes widened. In the excitement, he had completely forgotten about him.

"Where is he?" asked Augie, noting his dad's reaction.

Alberto seemed anxious, too. He asked Raul if Charlie had his phone on him.

Raul shook his head. "Even if he did, it wouldn't work in Cuba."

"He's here?" asked Augie, but no one answered him.

"Wait, I know," said Alberto. "We can call Pablo. I'll send Pablo after him."

Petra stood up quickly. "Let me talk to him, *amor*. I know where Charlie was going."

"Tell him to hurry, Petra," said Raul.

She nodded and walked away from the others to make the call.

"Where is *Charlie?*" Augie asked again, louder.

Raul looked at his son. "He went after Mal de Ojo."

Augie's face turned white. "Oh, no."

———

CHAPTER 37

The house wasn't what Charlie expected. It was on a dirt street a few blocks from the restaurant and appeared just as Gordo described it—a turquoise-painted bungalow with a red tile roof and a blooming bougainvillea by the gate. Besides appearing tidier than the other houses on the block, it didn't really stand out. A short, wrought-iron fence enclosed the small yard, two rocking chairs rested on a covered porch, the front door was painted navy blue. To the side, laundry swung gently from a clothesline.

Charlie walked by the house twice to make sure he had the right place, but this had to be it. There was no security at all: no brick walls with broken glass embedded on top, no locked gates, no bright lights, not even a barking dog. The house seemed deliberately disarming, even open and inviting. Sasha had mentioned that the outlaw pirate was hiding in plain sight, but the quaintness of the place surprised him.

Charlie moved under the cover of a mamey tree across the street and continued to study the house. The curtains and front door were open, and he could see and hear people inside. While he watched and waited, two women strolled by arm in arm. A man rode by on a rusty bicycle followed by a milkman on a horse-drawn cart. Everything seemed peaceful and quiet. Some children came out of the house, followed by a young woman who appeared to be their mother. Because of the way the kids were dressed—the boy in a white button-down shirt and the two girls in dresses—Charlie got the impression they were on their way to church. A matronly woman walked out last and called over the little boy so she could smooth his hair and adjust the collar on his shirt.

Behind the screen door, a man (or the silhouette of a man as there was no porchlight), watched the family prepare to leave. The mother and her children waved goodbye, opened the gate, and began walking down the street. Before the older woman followed after them, she leaned across the threshold and gave the man a brief kiss.

Watching the scene, Charlie felt his resolve wavering. Could that really be him? Could that be the dreaded and notorious Mal de Ojo, his house, his family? Was this the home of a murderous pirate and kidnapper? Not that he was expecting the skull and crossbones to be flying outside the door, but the picture was so different from the one he had imagined. It was like finding out the Godfather really *was* just an olive oil salesman.

There was only one way to know for sure. Charlie waited until the family had disappeared around the corner, and then he cautiously approached the house. He peered through a side window into an empty living room and then crept around to the back. Through an open window at the back of the house, he saw an old man standing at a kitchen counter pouring himself a glass of rum. His back was to him, but when he turned, Charlie saw the side of his face—the dead side, the side with the clouded, unseeing eye.

He was taller than Charlie expected, at least as tall as he was, and older, too. Despite his lean build and wiry arms, he didn't seem physically imposing. When the time came, Charlie figured he could overpower him, and after that . . . . After that, *what?* Now that he was there, he wondered if he had it in him to kill the man. An ex-con friend of his once told him that you had to have *sangre fría* to commit murder. He was right. He also told Charlie he didn't know a damn thing about killing. He was right about that, too.

Then Charlie's thoughts returned to Augie, and he felt his blood rise again. He would give this pirate a chance to plead his case, but if he concluded that he had anything to do with his nephew's death . . . . The truth was he didn't know what would happen. He supposed he would do what he always did and follow his gut. He took a deep breath, quietly opened the back door screen, and entered the house.

Inside the kitchen, Charlie saw the glass of rum still resting on the counter, and he saw Mal de Ojo's back unhurriedly receding down the narrow corridor to the living room. The pirate sat down in a leather armchair, his back still turned. He produced a cigar, rolled it between his fingers, and then picked up a punch cutter from the side table and clipped the end. Charlie crept to the counter and extracted a paring knife from the knife block. He slipped it into his waistband and walked softly through the arched pass-through into the front room. When he was close enough to tap the pirate on the head, he hesitated.

"You are the American who is looking for me?"

Charlie jerked. Looking up at the front window, he saw the pirate watching him in the window's reflection.

"I poured a rum for you," the man continued in a deep, smoky voice. "I left it on the kitchen counter."

Charlie remained motionless, somewhat stunned. The Cuban pirate spoke perfect English, and what's more, he seemed to have been expecting him. It was confusing and effectively disarming. Charlie returned for the rum and then lowered himself into a matching leather armchair directly across from his adversary.

"You're Mal de Ojo?"

"I prefer Ivan."

"I think I'll call you by the other name."

They each took a sip of rum and studied each other. Charlie noticed the pirate had turned off the lamp while he was getting the rum, so from his perspective, the man's face was in shadow, backlit by the kitchen light down the hall. He also noticed a slight slurring in his speech, as if he had been drinking all day.

"How did you know I was coming?"

The old man shrugged. "It's a small town. My brother-in-law sent word." A match flamed as he lit the end of his cigar. He drew in a few puffs. "Does this have to do with the American boy? The one I picked up in the Gulf?"

"That American boy is dead."

After a pause the pirate responded. "I am sorry to hear that."

"Did you kill him?" Charlie asked, shifting in his chair and feeling the haft of the knife against his back.

"Kill him? No, I didn't kill him. He jumped overboard and swam for land. I watched him do it."

"Well, he didn't make it." When the pirate didn't answer, Charlie pressed on. "You didn't *push* him overboard? Or drown him like you did the two boat captains?"

"No. It was his decision. He jumped on his own. I would have let him go once we reached Cienfuegos. I even told him so."

"Why should I believe you?"

The pirate looked down at his drink and swirled the rum in the glass. The cigar smoke drifted upwards and floated above his head. "The island he swam for was not too far away. I was told he was a strong swimmer. I thought that he would make it." After a pause, he looked up at Charlie. "Did someone hire you to look for the boy?"

"The boy is my nephew."

He nodded thoughtfully, almost sympathetically. "How did you find me?"

"We have a mutual friend. A business associate. You know her . . . intimately."

A muted laugh rumbled from the pirate's chest. "Sasha. Well, it serves me right. My wife would tell me that God is punishing me for my infidelity."

"Does God know you are a murderer as well? Does your wife?"

"I would like to keep my family out of this."

"Is that so? Well, I would like to have my family back. Whole and alive." Charlie felt the pirate watching him, sizing him up. "Maybe God sent me to punish you for taking my nephew."

"I don't believe that. And I don't believe in God."

"No? Then what *do* you believe in?" Charlie's looked around him— the unassuming living room, the modest house. "It doesn't appear you're in it for the money. Are you some kind of crusader?" Charlie really wanted to know. The man was an enigma to him. "Or do you just get your kicks from kidnapping and murdering people?"

"You don't know anything about me, Americano. I may not believe in God or money but I *do* believe in justice and retribution. I didn't kill your nephew. I *rescued* him. I picked up his SOS, and I liberated him . . . him and the other poor bastards who were being worked to death on those fucking slave boats. The two boat captains . . . they deserved to die. They're not the first slavers I've killed, nor will they be the last."

Charlie sat still, surprised by the pirate's response. Could it be true that he *rescued* Augie? Sasha had insisted that the Ivan she knew was not an ogre, his merciless reputation notwithstanding.

"The boatload of sailors they found floating in the Gulf, the ones you released . . . if you rescued them, why are they so scared of you? They say you're a monster. A witch doctor who can kill a man with his evil eye."

Ivan snorted. "Blackbeard tied lit fuses to the ends of his dreadlocks so he'd appear demonic. He created an image to scare his enemies. When you go fighting monsters, it's best to appear monstrous yourself. Mal de Ojo serves my purpose."

"You seem to have a lot of enemies."

"It may appear that way to some, but I only target certain boats—slave boats. If enough of their captains are killed and enough of their boats are taken, the corporations that own them—one in particular, as it turns out—will put an end to the practice. For them, profit is all that matters."

The two men continued to watch each other warily through the smoke. Finally, Ivan spoke. "Are you absolutely sure your nephew is dead?"

"They found a body."

"You've seen it?"

"A family member went to make the identification."

"Where did they find it . . . the body?"

"Isla de la Juventud."

"There are many islands and cays around Juventud. They found him on the big island?"

Charlie thought back to what Alberto had said. "Yes. On the southern shore."

The pirate leaned back in his chair and seemed to relax somewhat. "I watched your nephew jump ship and swim toward the last bit of land on the Juventud archipelago—it's a little island with a lighthouse. The island is called Cayo Guano del Este, and it's almost a hundred miles east of Isla de la Juventud."

Charlie felt like he'd been tossed a life preserver. Was he telling the truth? Not only did he *want* to believe him, but the story felt genuine. "How far away was the island when he jumped?"

"Less than a mile."

A mile was nothing for Augie. He once swam across Aransas Bay—Fulton to Saint Jo Island, more than five miles—just to win a bet. What if the body they found belonged to someone else? Charlie wanted so badly to believe it.

The pirate put out his cigar and stood up. "My rum is gone," he said. "Let's go to the kitchen for a refill." He held out his hand for Charlie's glass.

Charlie tossed back the last of the rum, handed him the empty glass, and followed him into the kitchen.

Ivan splashed more rum into the glasses and, when he turned around, Charlie was able to see him clearly for the first time. There was something eerily familiar about him, although he couldn't say precisely what. The old man clearly had lived an arduous life. His long hair and grey-streaked beard partially covered a face that was lined and weathered. He had sinewy arms and hands that were scarred and rough. A couple of fingers were misshapen. But the principal corruption was his face—one half hung slack, as if he'd suffered a stroke . . . and of course there was the dead eye. Charlie noticed a long scar spanning the top of his head, transforming the part in his hair into a jagged line, which made him wonder if Ivan's paralysis had been the result of a head injury. That would explain the slurred speech.

"You want to believe me," said the pirate, watching him closely, "but you still have doubts."

"Until there's proof that he's alive, why should I believe you?"

Ivan shrugged. "Fair point."

"Do you have a phone?" asked Charlie. "We can clear this up right now."

He shook his head. "Sorry, I don't. But even if you do find out he drowned, I'm telling you I didn't hurt him. I actually liked the kid."

At that moment, Charlie knew he couldn't kill this man, even if it turned out Augie was dead. The possibility—the potential—for vengeance had passed. This man wasn't like Z-17. He wasn't a remorseless, wanton killer. But what was he, exactly? Charlie wondered.

Ivan seemed to sense the change, too, and the tension between them palpably eased. They continued to watch each other, but with curiosity rather than wariness. Charlie took the knife out from under his shirt and laid it carefully on the kitchen counter, a gesture the old man noted but did not remark upon.

Sipping his rum, Charlie decided to raise an issue that had been bothering him since he'd arrived.

"Why is your English so good? You have an American accent."

"I lived there once."

"Where?"

"It doesn't matter. It was a long time ago."

"You're an American citizen?"

He shook his head. "I have a Cuban wife, a Cuban daughter, and three Cuban grandchildren. This country is my home."

"That was your family I saw leaving the house?"

"Yes, they were going to church. I expect they'll be home soon. So tell me, Americano, where are *you* from?"

"It's a little town on the Texas coast . . . not much bigger than Playa Larga."

"The name of the town?"

"Fulton."

The man stroked his beard, studying Charlie with acute interest. "Fulton, huh? Your nephew, he's also from there?"

"Yes."

"What is his name?"

"His name is Augie . . . Augustus."

"His last name?"

Charlie hesitated, trying to think if there was any reason not to give his name. He decided there wasn't. "It's Sweetwater."

The pirate's good eye blinked rapidly, as if he were working something out in his head. He knocked back the swig of rum in his glass and turned to pour more.

"I knew some Sweetwaters once," he said, his back to Charlie. "Shrimpers and bar owners mostly. They were half-crazy, but they lived big up there on the Texas coast."

Charlie eyed him suspiciously, wondering if the man really was a *brujo* and had penetrated his mind. "How the hell would you know that? I've lived there almost all my life. I don't remember you."

The pirate set down the glass and placed both hands on the counter, as if to steady himself. "You don't?" He turned around and looked at Charlie with such intensity that Charlie was momentarily disoriented. Was he missing something?

A breeze blew through the house, and Charlie felt cool air on the back of his neck.

"Would you remember your own brother if you saw him?"

Charlie sucked in a breath, feeling dizzy, almost nauseous.

"My brother is dead."

"You believe he died in the Gulf, don't you? Bashed on the head," he tapped the scar with his finger, "and then thrown into the sea."

Charlie stumbled backwards and fell into a kitchen chair, his head spinning.

"Well, that *is* what happened, except the part about me dying."

"Johnny? . . . It's . . . . It's impossible."

But he was beginning to see it now: the prominent Sweetwater nose, the full lips and generous mouth. But it was the one good eye, especially, that he recognized—it contained that same spark he remembered from before, as though his brother still viewed the world with the same wonder and wry amusement.

A lopsided smile creased Johnny's face. "Spooky, huh?"

Charlie dropped his rum glass and rubbed his eye sockets with the heels of his hands. Johnny picked up the glass, filled it, and handed it back to his brother.

"Let me tell you a story, Charlie."

Charlie listened as Johnny Sweetwater began with that warm October day in 1979 when both their lives careened off course. The first part Charlie already knew and had pictured in his head many times. His brother had come to the aid of a burning, foundering shrimp boat in the Gulf—a boat run by a criminal Vietnamese brigand he had been feuding with. And for his troubles, Johnny was attacked, thrown overboard, and left to die.

What Charlie never imagined, never even considered, was that a Cuban shrimp boat fishing illegally in American waters had also answered the burning boat's distress call. The Cubans arrived soon after the Vietnamese left, and they found an abandoned American shrimp boat drifting in the Gulf, and nearby, a half-drowned, most-ly-dead man floating in the water.

After giving him CPR, they detected a faint pulse, but no one aboard thought the man would live. The crew even placed bets—the odds were a hundred to one against him. But one of the crewmen was a trained doctor—a Cuban doctor could make more money shrimping than working for the *Ministerio de Salud Pública*—and he was able to stabilize the unconscious shrimper and keep him alive until they returned to Cienfuegos.

The hospital in Cienfuegos was surprisingly good, even back in those days, with top-notch Russian-trained surgeons. They removed part of the skull to reduce the swelling inside the cranium and then added a steel plate over his temporal lobe. But some of the damage was irreparable: partial paralysis and near total amnesia. The shrimper had come back from the dead, but when he awoke from his coma, he could no longer remember who he was.

Then there was the question about what to do with him. He was in no condition to travel back to the U.S., but the hospital needed to make room for new patients. The owner and captain of the shrimp boat, a good man, volunteered to take in the injured shrimper until he recovered enough to return home, wherever that might be.

"So the boat captain took the shrimper into his own home," Johnny continued, "and the captain's own daughter helped nurse him back to health. It was three months before he learned to walk again, a full year before he could speak his first words. Gradually, the nurse fell in love with her patient, and along the way, the patient fell in love with his nurse."

Charlie noticed that Johnny had switched to Spanish, perhaps unconsciously. It was as if the story no longer belonged to him, but now belonged to Ivan.

"The woman I saw outside?" Charlie asked in Spanish.

He nodded. "Her name is Béatriz. We've been together for thirty-seven years. Near the end of the second year, Béatriz became pregnant, and we married. We had a beautiful daughter who grew up, married, and had beautiful kids of her own. If you saw my wife leaving the house, then you also saw my daughter and my grandchildren."

Charlie put his elbows on his knees and hung his head. Looking at the floor, he tried to process what he had just heard. His mind was unable to grasp the entirety of the story all at once, but slowly it sank in.

"Do you remember why it happened?" he asked, his head still bowed, "Do you remember who attacked you and left you for dead?"

Johnny shook his head. "No."

Charlie considered telling him—telling him that he had been avenged, and that the man responsible had been killed—but he didn't. The details seemed unimportant now.

"I only recognized you when we came in here, into the light," Johnny continued, switching back to English. "At first I thought my brain was playing tricks on me. It's never been the same since the accident. But when you said your name . . . ."

Charlie looked up. "You never once wanted to return? You left a family in Texas, too, you know. You had a life there."

"Yes, but I didn't remember it, not for a long time anyway, and then only slowly, incrementally . . . and incompletely. It was as if I were remembering a dream I once had as a child. It didn't seem real to me. It doesn't seem real now. Besides, by then I had a new life. A new family. Here."

Charlie rotated his rum glass in his hand. "You still could, you know . . . come back . . . reconnect, fill in the missing pieces." Even as he said it, he wondered if it were possible, or if it were even principled. He could only imagine the emotional chaos it would unloose. Yet part of him wanted it to happen anyway, *expected* it to happen.

Johnny didn't answer, and Charlie couldn't read his thoughts. He wondered if his brother was even considering the possibility. The hesitation bothered him, and he realized that his initial shock and disbelief was slowly moving toward anger, or something close to it. Losing his brother, or thinking he had, had been the single most painful event in his life, an open wound that never fully healed. How could his brother not acknowledge this? How could he not want to repair the damage? Didn't he feel it, too?

"So tell me, brother . . . when did you finally remember . . . us? When did you remember you and me?"

Silence.

"Johnny? When did you—"

"I remembered you first, Charlie." His voice grew heavy with emotion. "It was several years after I was attacked. It was weird. At first you were simply this familiar face in my dreams. In the dreams we were kids, young and happy . . . happy to be together. We had adventures together." A sad smile appeared on his face. "I loved these dreams. Then slowly I began to realize the dreams were real and that the memories of you and of us were real."

Charlie noticed Johnny had begun to tear up.

"And after you," he continued. "I remembered Mom, Dad, my uncles, Ransom Island—the oldest connections came back first. The later ones came back fuzzy or not all."

"Do you remember your son? Raul?"

Johnny's face showed surprise, and then he shook his head sadly. "No." He looked at Charlie. "The boy, Augie . . . is *his* son?"

"And your grandson."

Johnny slumped to the floor, his back sliding down the cabinet.

"I never knew. It's . . . it's as if I died and came back as someone else."

"You did."

The two brothers sat there in the kitchen, grappling with the sudden upending of their worlds. Both of them felt emptied out.

They were still too stunned to grasp the significance of what had just happened. The shock was still too raw, too painful. They couldn't begin to imagine what would happen next.

Half a glass of rum later, Charlie broke the spell. "And somewhere along the line you decided to become a pirate. What the *fuck?*"

Johnny half smiled. "When I was well enough, I began working on the shrimp boat with my . . ." he searched for the right word, "with my Cuban father. I became a full-time commercial fisherman, a bonafide member of the Communist proletariat." Johnny effortlessly switched back to Spanish as if to emphasize his point. "My father and I worked on the boat together for many years, and when he died I continued to shrimp. But a few years ago, I began hearing stories about captains kidnapping men and forcing them to work on their boats. I didn't believe it at first, but then I met some of the survivors." He looked up and concluded in English, "I had found my cause."

"You never could abide a bully."

"No, I guess I couldn't."

"So you steal the boats, and Sasha sells them. What do you do with the money?"

"I pay off Cuban authorities so they'll ignore my little war, buy passage back home or to the U.S. for the men who have been held as slaves for months and sometimes even years." He waved his arm around the little kitchen. "As you see, I don't keep much of it." He looked at Charlie. "I confess I've saved some for my grandkids, but the rest goes to expenses. My crew isn't cheap with the profit sharing and all. Communism doesn't really work, you know."

"Pirates always split their loot."

"It's part of our code," he said deadpan. He cocked his head at Charlie. "And what about you?"

"Me? Retired. I fish, mostly."

Johnny nodded and the two brothers looked at each, both of them wondering how different things might have been if they had been in each other's lives all those missing years.

"Are you happy, brother man?" Charlie asked.

Johnny nodded pensively. "Yeah. I suppose so. You?"

"Yeah . . . happy enough."

Johnny heard someone outside and stood up.

"Your family?"

Johnny walked to the window and looked out. "I don't know who it was. A neighbor maybe." He took a deep breath. "Charlie, when my family does return, it might be better—"

Charlie stood up, too. "No, I understand. I should leave. It would be a lot to unload on them all at once."

"I've never told them anything about my . . . other life."

"Will you?"

He opened his hands, palms up. "What purpose would it serve?"

Charlie nodded and realized he agreed. What purpose would it serve to mention it to *anyone?* It would break Raul's heart to know his father didn't remember him, and he would never forgive him for not coming back. Everyone else who mattered—everyone his brother would remember or would remember him—was dead.

Johnny opened a kitchen drawer and found a pen and paper. He wrote down a phone number and handed it to Charlie.

"This is the phone number of my *cuñado's* restaurant, Chuchi el Gordo. If you haven't found your nephew by tomorrow noon, call and leave your name and a meeting time. I will meet you at the harbor in Cienfuegos and we'll take one of my boats to Cayo Guano to look for Augie together. And if you find him before then . . . well, leave that message, too."

Charlie placed the slip of paper in his pocket. They stepped outside, and Charlie inhaled the fragrant tropical air. "I like Playa Larga. What are the chances I might come back?"

"The chances are good. In fact, I would like it very much. We're getting old, you and I. Let's take advantage of the years we have left."

"You can tell your family I'm your crazy American friend."

"And I won't be lying."

They heard the front gate opening and voices—the family returning from church. The brothers embraced and then let each other go, but only until they met again.

CHAPTER 38

Alberto and Petra had planned to serve dinner on their expansive deck overlooking Key Allegro's Little Bay, but it was a typical April day on the coast—in other words, blowing a gale—which compelled them to move the party indoors. The occasion was to celebrate Augie's homecoming, and the invitation had been extended to Charlie, Raul, and Raul's family. But Raul had RSVP'd that he and his family couldn't come; they would be attending a special Mass across the bay at the Stella Maris Chapel that night.

They'd been to Mass a lot lately, Charlie noticed. Raul said it had to do with Rosie making good on promises she'd made to the Almighty if her prayers for Augie's return were answered. Which they were. But Charlie did accept the Alexanders' invitation. He had something he wanted to talk about with Alberto and Petra. It would be better if Raul and his family weren't there to hear it.

For that reason, only three sets of china, crystal, and silver had been laid out on the Alexanders' dining table. Charlie stood at the living room window sipping Alberto's expensive scotch and looking down at the choppy, white-capped bay. Not a single boat was on the water that evening. It was even too windy for canal-hopping, a venerable Key Allegro cocktail-hour tradition.

"Charlie?" Alberto shouted from the kitchen. "Remember those cows you saw when you were on my *hacienda*?"

"I remember."

"Well, that's where these steaks came from, my friend; farm to table. I want you to know that I had to smuggle them into the country. The customs form said all meat products have to be unopened and commercially labeled, so I had one of our captains hide them in his boat freezer until he docked in Corpus. What Customs doesn't know won't hurt them, right?"

"Wouldn't it have been easier to fly them up in your jet?"

"It would have if we had come in our jet. Our pilot is bringing one of Petra's clients up tomorrow to look at a property she found for him— some big-shot with the government. Anyway, we had to fly commercial."

Charlie went to the kitchen to watch Alberto grill the steaks.

"I think they are ready," he said, poking the ribeyes with his finger. "I'll go find Petra. Have a seat, Charlie. Make yourself at home."

Charlie was restless and walked outside instead. The bright-colored koi windsocks Petra liked to fly from their deck extended so stiffly in the wind they looked like they were made of papier-mâché. The evening was cool and overcast, reflecting Charlie's mood. He stood at the rail and thought about how he would handle what he had to do next.

He had been busy since he returned from Mexico. After Augie's happy reunion with his family, Charlie turned his attention to some loose ends and questions he'd filed away during their eleven-day ordeal. The more he pulled on the loose ends, the worse it looked. Judy Dang had helped him a lot. She was good at digging up hard-to-find information, good at looking into dark corners.

When Charlie went back inside, the food was laid out on the table, and Alberto walked out of their wine closet with a bottle of wine in each hand. Petra breezed in and apologized for being so rude.

"Business must be good," said Charlie.

She waved her hand as if to indicate it wasn't important.

Alberto laughed. "If she keeps at it, Mexicans will own half the Texas Gulf Coast."

"Well, no more calls, I promise," said Petra. "I turned off my phone so we won't be molested."

Alberto pulled out a chair for his wife. "She's a liar," he mouthed behind her back.

Sure enough, they heard her phone buzzing on the counter just seconds later. Alberto gave Charlie a knowing glance, but Petra acted as if she didn't hear it. During dinner she asked about Augie and said she was delighted to hear that he had recovered so quickly.

Charlie sipped the wine and picked at his meal.

"You don't like my steak, Charlie?"

"No, it's great, Alberto. I'm savoring it."

"Well, you better finish it. Otherwise Petra will feed it to her damn cat."

"Alberto!" Petra said teasingly. "You will hurt Consuela's feelings."

At the sound of her name, Consuela suddenly appeared, and Charlie and Alberto watched the fat Persian jump onto Petra's lap. The cat's diamond-studded collar looked as expensive as the gold Cartier necklace around Petra's throat. She cut a piece of Alberto's prime beef and placed it gently in the cat's mouth.

Alberto huffed. "That cat eats better than most people. I don't know why it can't be satisfied with Purina like other cats."

"Because Consuela is not like other cats," said Petra. "Are you, Consuela?"

"Did you know that something like eighty percent of the seafood your boats haul out of the Gulf is turned into pet food?" Charlie inquired mildly.

"Hmm, I didn't know that." Alberto looked at his wife. "Did you know that, *cariño?*"

"No, I suppose I didn't."

"In fact," Charlie continued. "Purina is one of your biggest customers."

Alberto poured more wine into Charlie's glass and then into his. Petra put her hand over hers. "No thank you, dear."

"I have to confess that I don't pay much attention to the inner workings of our seafood business," said Alberto. "Petra's family handles most of the day-to-day stuff. Occasionally, I see the reports. We seem to be doing well, though."

"Extremely well," said Charlie. He looked at Alberto. His friend really didn't have a clue. He almost felt bad pressing forward. Almost. "To be honest, over the past month I've observed some interesting things about your business."

Petra sighed. "Again with the business? I thought we agreed not to talk about it over dinner."

"What things?" asked Alberto.

"Well, for instance, how well your processing plants are doing when all the other plants are closing their doors or barely getting by. Or how your fishing fleet has quadrupled in size while others are shrinking. I kept asking myself, why? Part of the answer is because of the forage fish."

Alberto laughed. "I'm not even sure I know what a forage fish is."

"*Sardinas,*" Charlie answered. "Menhaden and all the other little fishies you pick up when you drag a trawl net or a seine through the ocean. We shrimpers call it bycatch, and usually we just rake it overboard, but that's mostly what you're selling to the pet food companies—thousands of tons of it."

"It seems like our competitors would be doing the same if it's so profitable."

"It does, doesn't it? But it's an expensive proposition to catch, sort, and store that many fish—much too expensive for most fishermen. It's backbreaking, around-the-clock work, and very dangerous. Most captains simply can't find men to crew the boats, even in Mexico."

"I suppose we must be doing something right, then," said Alberto.

"Oh, it's not *right,* but it sure is profitable."

"I don't follow you, Charlie."

Petra put the cat on the floor and stood up. "Alberto, *mí amor,* could you help me clear the plates so we can serve dessert?"

"Sit down, Petra," Charlie ordered. "You will both find this next part very interesting." Alberto cocked his head at the abrupt change in Charlie's tone.

"Don't you think we have talked enough about the subject?" she said. "I find it so boring."

"This won't be boring, I promise."

Petra sat and fixed Charlie with an icy stare

"What's going on, Charlie?" Alberto asked.

"Alberto, where do think your captains find the men to work on your fishing boats?"

"I suppose they hire them at the docks, like everyone else."

Charlie leaned across the table. "That's the thing . . . they don't. Some maybe, but most they don't 'hire' at all."

Alberto looked confused. "I don't understand."

"They are abducted, Alberto. Kidnapped. Shanghaied. *Secuestrado.* Either tricked onto the boats and then never allowed to leave, or simply drugged, abducted, and then forced to work for no pay. You save a fortune on wages. And if they die or don't work out, you just throw them overboard."

"Is this your idea of a joke, Charlie?" Alberto's face was pale. Petra's was crimson.

Charlie sat back in his chair, his expression grim. "I'm not joking, Alberto."

"Our company would *never* do that. We don't *kidnap* people. *Christ.*"

"No, you're right. Your company doesn't handle the kidnapping part directly. You outsource it . . . have others do it for you. You contract the narcos to do it."

"The *narcos!*"

"Your captains communicate with their cartel contacts in, say, Tuxpan or Tampico, and the narcos fill the order. After the delivery, your captains or their *jefés* pay them a finder's fee."

Alberto looked at Charlie, aghast.

"Why are you doing this?" asked Petra, her voice heated. "You have your boy back. Your company is making good money selling to our company. We should all be happy."

"What about all those poor bastards being worked to death on your boats, Petra?"

"It is not as bad as you say."

"Augie might beg to differ. So might the kid he was chained up with for two days. Only that kid was tossed overboard like garbage . . . even though he was still alive. Did you think I wouldn't check the registrations of the boats Augie was held on? The *Mañana,* the *El Dorado,* the *Pegaso?* Those are *your* boats."

Alberto shook his head emphatically. "Our captains don't snatch men from ports and make them slaves, Charlie. Or throw them overboard. Our company doesn't work with the cartels."

"They do, Alberto, and you and your wife do. And not just in the fishing industry. All those properties you are buying and selling. Who do you think they are for?"

"They are for personal friends."

"Right. Friends like Diputado Abrigo . . . *politicos.* Dirty politicos who need a place outside the country to hide the money they take from the narcos . . . because large bank accounts in Mexico draw unwanted attention, don't they? For them and for you, too . . . and for your company. So you use your corporate holdings like International Supply in Brownsville to funnel profits from your Mexico-based operations. And you wash your friends' bribe money by helping them convert it into Texas real estate, probably under a shell company that your wife set up.

Charlie turned to Petra. "My theory is that you didn't go searching for people like Z-17, the Zeta lieutenant who drugged Augie and delivered him to the captain of the *Mañana*, but someone like Diputado Abrigo probably put you on to them. Maybe he told you he knew people who could help you with your labor shortage problem. And once you let the narcos inside your tent, you can't ever get them out, can you, Petra?"

"Charlie," Alberto's voice was shaking. "Do you have any proof for these insane accusations?"

"You have eighty-seven vessels in your fishing fleet, Alberto. Nineteen of them were taken by pirates, according to Lloyd's of London. I checked with your competitors and *none* of their boats have been taken. None. Zero. Mal de Ojo only targeted boats that used slaves. Your boats."

Petra looked at her husband. "He heard this from that crazy Cuban pirate, Alberto. They are all lies. What else would you expect from a murderer and a criminal?"

"That's not the only place I got my information, Petra."

"Oh, yes, there is also Sasha, the pirate's whore."

"Most of the information I learned from your own people when I visited your operations. I just didn't put two and two together until later."

"I don't understand you, Charlie," she continued. "That pirate kidnapped your nephew. You should have killed him in Cuba when you had the chance."

"That pirate *rescued* my nephew . . . from one of *your* boats."

"*¡Pura mierda!*" Petra shook her head forcefully. "Mal de Ojo is a *brujo*. He has poisoned your mind. I should have known you were too weak to stand up to him . . . that you were too much of a coward to kill him."

"You *were* worried about that, weren't you, Petra? And you were also worried I would find out the truth if I talked to him . . . so worried that you had Pablo follow me to Playa Larga. You ordered him to kill Mal de Ojo if I didn't."

"You're wrong, Charlie," Alberto interjected. He sounded almost desperate. "She sent Pablo to find you, to tell you that Augie was safe. I saw her make the call myself."

Charlie looked at Alberto. "Pablo was already in Playa Larga. He followed me there on her orders and then shadowed me until I found where the pirate lived."

"Pablo was already there? Then why didn't he tell you about Augie? And that we'd found him and he was safe?"

"Pablo didn't know any of that. Petra didn't tell him. She simply told him to finish the job . . . to kill the man who was hurting your business." Charlie shrugged. "But when I confronted Mal de Ojo, Pablo was there, hiding outside the house, listening to us talk. It turns out he believed the pirate's story, too. Pablo and I talked about it on the way back to Cienfuegos. He even gave me a ride in the government car you had been given to drive."

Alberto's head moved side to side, slowly, almost involuntarily, and then it gradually begin to nod up and down, as though he finally understood. "I wondered why you acted so surprised to see your nephew when we met up later that night . . . like you didn't know he'd be there."

"I didn't know. Last I heard, his body had been found in Juventud."

"This is madness," Petra said with growing panic. "Charlie, do have any idea what you are doing to us? You will ruin everything."

Alberto looked at his wife with sadness and disbelief. "Petra? Is it true? Is *any* of it true?"

"That fucking pirate was costing us millions of dollars! He had to be stopped."

Alberto's face fell as he listened.

"I did it for us, *querido*," she said in a quiet, solicitous voice. "We were running out of money. Your fortune was almost gone." She reached over and put her hand on his. "You have never had a head for business, my love, so we had to do something . . . *I* had to do something, so we could have the life we wanted."

Alberto pulled his hand away. "Kidnapping? Slavery? Narcos and corrupt politicians?"

"I didn't know the boy would be caught up in this. That was an accident."

"What about the *other* boys?"

"They were nobody, *corazón*, mostly refugees from Central America, they—"

"They were *nobody? My God*, I don't even know you anymore."

He held his head in his hands and moaned, and then he turned to Charlie, his eyes on fire. "I will make this right, Charlie. I will fix it. You have my word." He stood up and began pacing, speaking aloud, but mostly to himself. "We will stop enslaving workers. We will cease doing business with the narcos and with men like Abrigo, We will—"

"We will lose everything, Alberto," Petra interrupted. "Think about what you are saying. We will be left with nothing!"

He stopped pacing and looked at her sadly. "Then let nothing be enough."

"You will lose me, too."

"I already have, Petra."

She stormed out of the room, leaving Charlie and Alberto alone.

Charlie slid back his chair and stood up to go. "I'm sorry, Alberto, but you needed to know."

___

CHAPTER 39

Charlie's new boat skimmed the surface of the bay as gracefully as a tern. Standing behind the console, his loose shirt flapping in the wind, he admired the craft's clean, classic lines. It had a wide beam, a stable foredeck, and hardly any deadrise—the perfect fishing boat for the area's grass flats, skinny bayous, and shallow back lakes. And on calm, smooth days like today, it was an absolute blast on the open water. Ragnar the Younger had christened the boat *Ægir*.

When Charlie returned from his south-of-the-border odyssey, he was surprised to find the boat he'd been dicking around with for the better part of a year already completed. A kind of makeshift nest of cardboard and blankets in the corner of the shed led Charlie to believe Ragnar had worked and slept there while he was gone, if he had slept at all. The shop floor was littered with crushed cans of Red Bull, Big Red, and Old Milwaukee, as well as sundry fast food wrappers and empty Frito bags.

Ragnar and the mutt showed up minutes after Charlie returned from Mexico.

"You did this?" Charlie asked him, pointing to the boat.

"You got a problem with it?"

"No, it's beautiful. I didn't know you knew anything about boat building."

"I been watching you for almost twelve months, haven't I? I got tired of waitin' for you to finish."

Charlie ran his hand over the smooth mahogany hull and admired the shiny bronze fittings. The work was flawless, and all the hardware had been expertly installed, which meant Ragnar had broken into his house to retrieve and open the UPS boxes that contained them. Charlie was almost afraid to go upstairs. For all he knew, Ragnar had founded a Viking settlement up there.

"What the hell does *Ægir* mean?" The name was hand-painted across the transom.

"Don't change it. It's already done. Took me a long time."

"I didn't say I was gonna change it. I just asked what it meant."

"Look it up."

Charlie pulled out his new cell phone and looked it up. Wikipedia said *Ægir* was a Norse sea god who liked to brew and drink ale and throw big-ass parties. The name worked for him.

The next day, Charlie bought a 40-hp outboard to give the boat some giddy-up, and he and Ragnar trailered it to the water. They put it in the bay, but Ragnar refused to get in himself.

"I ain't gettin' in."

"Why not?"

"'Cause I can't swim."

"What the hell kind of Viking can't swim?"

When Charlie saw Ragnar's red-eyed glare, he dropped the subject.

The boat ran like a dream. Charlie was so impressed, he made a deal with Ragnar the Younger—a partnership of sorts. Charlie would supply all the necessary materials and tools for Ragnar to set up shop in his storage unit. If Ragnar built the boats, Charlie would sell them and they'd split the money fifty-fifty. They sealed the agreement with a forearm handshake (Viking tradition) and a cold beer (Sweetwater tradition).

Charlie crossed under the Redfish Bay Causeway just as the sun's edge peeked over Stedman Reef. He slowed when he approached Ransom Island. Raul and Augie hadn't arrived yet, so he beached the boat and got out to look around. Regrettably, there wasn't much to see anymore: vestiges of shellcrete foundations, broken docks, and crumbling water cisterns. The island was slowly returning to its natural state.

He walked down the sandy beach to where the bait house had once been. Rotting pilings marked the outlines of the former docks and piers. When they were young, Charlie and Johnny helped outfit the fishing skiffs that launched from the dock and took guests to honey holes in Aransas Bay. They worked, slept, fished, and happily whiled away their time in and around the bait house. Now only a weedy footprint of the foundation remained.

Dew soaked Charlie's shoes as he followed a grass-lined path inland to the site of the legendary honky-tonk/bar-and-grill that had been the heart, soul, and headquarters of the Sweetwater clan for six full decades. In its later years, Shady's served as a last stand against the gaudy, cookie-cutter developments that were overtaking the coast—the Sweetwaters' own private Alamo.

So much had happened at Shady's: epic dances, great music, hurricane parties, barroom brawls, and an endless parade of anglers, oddballs, raconteurs, and more or less heroic figures that only the Texas Gulf Coast produced in such abundance.

All of the Ransom Island originals were dead now: Rupert Sweetwater, his brothers Noble, Flavius, and Dubber. Zachariah Yates, Barefoot Nelson, Miz Leona, Juan Estrada—they were gone, too. Vita (Rupert's last, best, and longest-lasting wife) returned to Baton Rouge a couple of years after Rupert died, telling Charlie that she wanted to end her life in the place where it began. With no one there to keep it up, Shady's closed its doors and began to fall apart. After Hurricane Ike swept the island clean in 2008, nothing remained but ruins and stories. Lots and lots of stories. Johnny was right—the Sweetwaters had lived big on the Texas coast.

When Charlie returned to the *Ægir*, he saw that Raul and Augie had beached their boat alongside and were already waist deep in the bay.

"Hey, Tío!" Augie yelled. "You better get busy if you wanna keep up."

He held up a stringer with two nice-size speckled trout. Charlie could see his grandnephew's white-tooth smile beaming across the grass flats. While Charlie dug around in his boat to retrieve his fishing tackle, Raul and Augie hooked up again. He heard their reels whirring as the fish ran on them. Raul laughed, and Augie actually whooped with joy.

Charlie grinned as he tied a lure onto his leader. Augie was going to be fine; there seemed to be no lasting damage from his terrible ordeal. *The kid's a survivor*, thought Charlie, *just like his dad and just like the granddad he'll never know.*

Others hadn't fared so well. Alberto had ignored Petra's pleas and made good on his promise to shut down their seafood business, thrusting them into a nasty bankruptcy and divorce fight that threated to ruin everyone involved. Diputado Abrigo, Charlie was pleased to learn, was under investigation by his own agency for conspiring with the Zetas.

Charlie hadn't seen or heard from Sasha Vasiliki since Cuba. She had simply disappeared after he'd last seen her at the square in Cienfuegos. When he returned to Texas, he sent her flowers and a note that read: "You were right. I was wrong. Our mutual friend is unharmed. If you ever want to talk about it, you know where I live." Charlie knew that without her, they never would have found Augie—something he would never forget and could never repay.

And Raul . . . Raul had devoted considerable time to working with his own parish to establish a fund to help Father Canul's work. They had already raised over a hundred thousand dollars, including a substantial donation from someone who simply wanted to remain anonymous.

As Charlie pulled on his reef boots, he glanced up at a 737 that caught the morning light. He had read in the paper that commercial flights would be opening up between Cuba and the USA in the fall. Maybe he'd make a trip to Playa Larga in October and meet Johnny's family, where he would no doubt be introduced as Ivan's "crazy American friend." Maybe he'd take a couple of fishing rods.

Fleetingly, he thought of the sadness he'd felt in Octobers past when he'd made his annual pilgrimage to the spot in the Gulf where he believed Johnny had died. But those memories were nudged aside by the happy realization that he had been given a great gift. Charlie had his brother back.

——

THE VERY END

ABOUT THE AUTHOR

Miles Arceneaux; three guys, who for thirty years managed to collaborate on five books without killing each other. Texas-based writers Brent Douglass, John T. Davis, and James R. Dennis began their writing adventure at a Rockport-Fulton Labor Day party in 1987 when someone casually suggested they write a mystery novel together. Twenty-five years later, they published the popular mystery novel *Thin Slice of Life* (2012), followed by *La Salle's Ghost* (2013), *Ransom Island* (2014), and *North Beach* (2015). *Hidden Sea* is the fifth in this series of salty Gulf Coast mystery-thrillers.

CPSIA information can be obtained
at www.ICGtesting.com
Printed in the USA
LVOW07s0850221117
556876LV00005B/3/P